Method of Revenge

A SPENCER & REID MYSTERY
BOOK TWO

CARA DEVLIN

First Cup Press

Copyright © 2025 by Cara Devlin

All rights reserved.

No part of this book may be reproduced in any form or by any electronic or mechanical means, including information storage and retrieval systems, without written permission from the author, except for the use of brief quotations in a book review.

Any references to historical events, real people, or real places are used fictitiously. Names and characters are products of the author's imagination.

Edited by Jennifer Wargula

ISBN paperback: 979-8-992305715

Chapter One

London
March 1884

Screams of wild laughter filled the dance hall, piercing Leonora Spencer's ears and grating on her nerves. She winced and knew she'd made a mistake.

The nightlife at Striker's Wharf had always been lively, but Leo didn't recall it ever being this boisterous. As the other patrons raised their voices above the fast tempo of the piano, trumpet, and clarinet, all she could dwell on was how quiet the Spring Street Morgue would have been at this time of night. Leo worked there as an assistant to her uncle, a city coroner, and in fact, an evening in the morgue's office appealed vastly more to her than the popular dance club on the Lambeth wharves.

However, as it wasn't at all ordinary for a young woman to work at a morgue, let alone prefer the company of dead bodies to living ones, she kept the disquieting thought to herself.

Next to her at their table, Nivedita Brooks swayed in rhythm with the music, her eyes turned toward the busy dance floor with longing.

"Go," Leo urged her friend. "I can see it's torturous for you to sit here with me when there's a polka playing."

Dita cut her rapt attention away from the dozens of dancers. "It isn't torture to sit with you," she said, appearing offended. "Besides, I can't possibly take to the floor by myself. I'd need a partner."

Leo gave her arm a gentle shove. "I'm quite certain a number of gentlemen would appear as if out of the ether if you were to take one step toward that dance floor."

Thanks to a handful of favorable articles in *The Illustrated London News*, the club was packed with a surfeit of men, many of them from the upper classes. In fact, the surge in popularity was so noticeable, Leo had started to think Eddie Bloom, the proprietor at Striker's Wharf, must have held some power over the paper's editorial choices. As the head of a criminal gang operating out of this area, his influence over the newspaper wouldn't have been out of the realm of possibility.

Despite Mr. Bloom's questionable business practices and the establishment's mixed clientele, this was one of Dita's favorite places to go for music and dancing, and she had decided it was high time Leo threw off the mundane nightly routine she'd been keeping for the last several weeks.

Habits were easy and comfortable, and Leo had fallen into the practice of returning to her home on Duke Street from the morgue, preparing supper for her aging uncle and aunt, and then trundling off to bed with a book. The singular interruption to her schedule had been an evening she'd spent out at a chophouse with a Scotland Yard constable—though she had yet to tell Dita about it. Her friend would have made too much of it, and Leo wasn't even certain she'd enjoyed herself enough to accept a second invitation...*if* the constable ever extended one.

"You could have your pick of dance partners," she told Dita now as she glanced at the tables surrounding theirs. "The gentlemen at the table behind you have been looking your way since we arrived."

The three men had been taking furtive glances at Dita for the last quarter hour. She was pretty when she wore her blue wool Metropolitan Police matron uniform to her shifts at Scotland Yard, but she was downright stunning when she put up her dark hair and wore one of her brightly hued dresses for an evening out. Sunset-orange silks and deep pink taffetas looked radiant against her darker skin, compliments of her late mother, who'd hailed from Calcutta, India.

Leo, however, with her dark hair and pale, ivory skin, preferred more somber shades. Tonight, she'd consented to wear the deep sapphire-blue satin dress Dita had selected from Leo's limited wardrobe, the skirt fashionably gored, if unfashionably long-sleeved. She was certain none of the men at the neighboring table would be casting out their nets toward her. And in truth, she didn't care for any of them to attempt it.

Dita covered Leo's hand with her own. "Forget dancing. This is your first night out in ages, and I'm not leaving you to sit alone at our table."

"That never stopped you before," she replied with a

good-natured grin. Dita would usually bring her steady beau, Police Constable John Lloyd, with them to Striker's. They would spend half of the time on the dance floor, while Leo remained at the table. Dancing was not her forte, nor was she interested enough in it to improve her skills.

"Perhaps not, but you weren't in mourning before," Dita reminded her.

Leo sighed. "I'm not in official mourning. I wasn't family."

Not exactly, anyway.

It had been two months since Detective Chief Superintendent Gregory Reid had succumbed to a prolonged illness. The Inspector, as Leo had always called him, had taken his last breath one night at the end of January while sleeping. It was just one week after the tumultuous case that concluded with his good friend, Police Commissioner Nathaniel Vickers, being accused of murder.

It had been Leo and Detective Inspector Jasper Reid, the Inspector's adopted son, who had exposed the police commissioner's desperate plot to thwart a blackmail operation that had threatened to reveal compromising intimate photographs of his seventeen-year-old daughter, Elsie. The illicit photographs would have ruined both father and daughter publicly and personally, and Sir Nathaniel had decided there was no line he would not cross to prevent that from happening—including lowering himself to murder. He'd even planned to have Jasper and Leo killed once they discovered the truth of his involvement in a series of murders connected to her uncle's morgue.

The only consolation for Jasper and her had been that

Gregory Reid was already unconscious when his longtime friend had been found out. He'd been completely unaware of his friend's decision to end his own life rather than face the humiliation and consequences of his crimes.

"He thought of you as family," Dita said, then sneaked a coy glimpse toward the table of men behind her.

Leo shook her head, amused. Her friend simply could not resist flirting. Dita was correct though; the Inspector had thought of Leo as family.

For a short while when she'd been nine years old, he'd taken her in and cared for her after the murder of her family. The Metropolitan Police had been tracking down Leo's maternal aunt, Flora, who'd been living on the island of Crete at the time with her husband, Claude Feldman. While awaiting their arrival back in London, Leo had stayed with Gregory Reid, who at that time had ranked as Detective Inspector. His home on Charles Street was an affluent address, a residence any other police inspector would never have been able to afford. However, Gregory had married a viscount's daughter, and the home had been bestowed upon them at their marriage.

When Gregory's wife, Emmaline, and their two young children died in a horrific accident while ice skating on Regent's Pond, he'd been distraught. A year later, he'd still been in mourning for them when he'd rescued Leo from the attic of the Red Lion Street home in which her family had been brutally slain. He'd treated her with all the tenderness and care of a father, and even after her aunt and uncle had arrived to claim her, he'd stayed a prominent figure in Leo's life.

She still felt the swift plunge of her stomach when

remembering that early Sunday morning in late January. Heavy knocking on the front door had roused her from sleep just past seven o'clock. Throwing on her dressing gown and hurrying downstairs, she'd had the inkling in the back of her mind that it would be news of the Inspector's demise. She'd been correct.

There was Jasper, standing on the threshold, his hat crushed in his hands. Even now, months later, her memory drew up the vivid image of the anguish cutting through his green eyes. Grief had seized her too, crumpling her up inside like old newsprint bound for a stove, and it hadn't relinquished her yet. The detailed memory of that moment would never leave her.

All people could remember things, of course, but Leo's mind was particularly—and unusually—sharp. It stamped images into her mind as photographic memories for her to draw up and inspect, time and again. They never faded or became hazy. Significant moments, like the one of Jasper telling her the Inspector had died, seared most deeply into her mind and stayed readily available for easy viewing. Other details—from what everyone was wearing at the butcher's last week while she was standing in line, to the contents of every postmortem report she'd ever typed at her uncle's morgue, to the names and faces of every officer at Scotland Yard—were stored away permanently, and vividly too.

Once, Dita had likened her memory to magic, but Leo thought it more like a well-organized inventory room: Registers upon registers of memories that she could locate, draw down from an endless number of shelves, and look at again with clarity. However, just as her work at a city morgue tended to make others eye her strangely, so did having a perfect memory. So, she mostly kept that ability to herself.

Dita leaned over the table, set at the edge of the dance floor, and clinked her glass of wine against Leo's. "For tonight, at least, let's not discuss anything remotely miserable. We're here to have fun."

Leo sipped her drink obligingly, but her rebellious mind thought of the cherry liqueur that she and the Inspector had shared a love for. The last bottle of Grants Morella cherry brandy she'd brought him was likely still half full in his study. Or rather Jasper's study now.

Though he wasn't the Inspector's legal heir, Jasper had been listed as the main recipient of Gregory Reid's estate in his last will and testament. The home granted to the Honorable Emmaline Cowper's new husband when they'd married had come from her grandmother, not her father. So, when Emmaline died tragically, the embittered viscount had been able to rescind his daughter's dowry but not the home.

Leo had always suspected maintaining the residence at 23 Charles Street had cost the Inspector most of his working wages, and now, Jasper had been given the home to keep up. Or sell. She wasn't certain what he would do with it.

At the will reading, Gregory Reid's solicitor, Mr. Wilhelm Stockton, had given Jasper a bundle of papers detailing his inheritance, which included the home and some modest savings. For her part, Leo had been bequeathed an exquisite pair of drop pearl earrings and a matching necklace. The set had belonged to the Inspector's mother, and she'd given them to him with the wish that he might someday pass them along to his daughter.

While preparing for her evening out with Dita, tears had pricked Leo's eyes when she'd opened the worn, blue velvet case and put on the pieces.

"Thank you," Leo said to her friend, touching the string of pearls at her throat. "For bringing me out tonight. I did need it." The cackling blare of a woman's laughter as she danced close to their table nearly shredded her eardrum. "Though a quiet restaurant might have done just as well."

Dita pursed her lips. "Careful, Leo, you're beginning to sound just as starchy as Inspector Reid," she said, referring to Jasper, who deplored not only Eddie Bloom and his club, but the fact that Leo frequented Striker's Wharf from time to time. Jasper's disposition had always leaned toward surly and ill-tempered, though ever since his promotion to the Criminal Investigation Department at Scotland Yard, he'd become even more austere and grumpy.

It had been weeks since she'd last seen him. With the Inspector gone, she had no reason to go to Charles Street anymore; she most certainly couldn't call on Jasper there alone. He was a bachelor, and she was unmarried. It didn't matter if the Inspector had tried to bring them together as brother and sister, or at best, distant cousins. The fact of the matter was they were not related, and without the Inspector in their lives, she wasn't sure what they were to each other at all.

Oddly enough, as fractious as Jasper usually was toward her, their time spent solving the case in January had not been wholly disagreeable. And when he'd arrived at her home on Duke Street last month on the anniversary of her family's murders with an offering to accompany her to their graves at All Saints Cemetery, just as the Inspector had always done, she'd been touched by his thoughtfulness.

In fact, she was beginning to think that the tight, unrelenting coil in the pit of her stomach stemmed from not having seen Jasper since then. It was a thought she found unacceptable. She did not want to miss Jasper when he probably was not missing her in return.

"Let's not speak of Inspector Reid or anything else too serious tonight," she told Dita as she tapped her glass against her friends again. "Here is to a pleasant evening out without a care in the world."

A scream, one of alarm rather than of gaiety, preceded a loud clatter at Leo's back. She swiveled in her seat to see a woman who'd been seated at the next table, convulsing on the floor, her chair overturned. Other patrons quickly closed in around her. And yet, Leo observed one person swiftly moving away. A black-cloaked figure hurried past the encroaching crowd and began to slip from Leo's view.

"Is she choking?" Dita asked as she left their table amidst shouts for help.

Leo kept her eyes on the retreating figure. The hood of the cloak was raised, obscuring the person underneath, but there was a distinct feminine grace to the person's movements.

"I'll be right back," she told Dita.

"Where are you going?" she called as Leo skirted around the influx of people, who were craning their necks for a better view of the commotion. "Leonora!"

She carried on, however, reluctant to let the cloaked figure out of her sight. Instinct told her that this person had something to do with what had happened back at the table, whatever it may be. As Leo had no medical training for the living—her only experience being the handling of dead bodies—she knew she would not be of any use to the afflicted woman. None of the other bystanders seemed to have noticed the retreating cloaked figure. Pursuing the person across the club, Leo got a better look as the crowd thinned out: it was almost certainly a woman. The cloak, embroidered with robin's-egg blue threading, rippled as she rushed in the direction of the club's front doors, revealing a lighter green skirt hem. Leo tried to hasten her pace but was caught behind a wall of shoulders suddenly moving into her path.

"Excuse me." The polka music came to a halt, and her next impatient, "Excuse me!" rang out loudly.

The men moved aside, albeit grudgingly, and Leo darted through the gap. The woman in the hooded cloak was gone. Leo passed the doorman and ran outside, straight into a damp fog rolling off the Thames. The wharf linked to Belvedere Street, but in this brume, she could barely see five feet in front of her. To go any further would be to disappear into the fog alone, and that would be foolhardy.

Leo turned back to the doorman. "Did you see a woman come through here just now? Wearing a dark cloak?"

He frowned, a deep crease furrowing his forehead down to the bridge of his nose. "Sure. She went that way." He nodded to the right, toward the street.

"What did she look like?" Leo asked. "Did you recognize her?"

"Didn't see a thing of her. Had her head covered. Why?" He looked back inside. "What's going on in there?"

The music had not resumed, and the noise of a panicked crowd began to overtake the club.

"A woman is hurt," she told the doorman as she made her way back inside.

The gawking crowd had erected a blockade as she moved toward her table. Employing her elbows, she physically parted arms and shoulders to force her way through the group of bystanders.

By the time she saw Dita again, standing over the woman on the floor, a few minutes had passed. A grim pall enveloped the circle of patrons surrounding the immobile form. A pool of bloody vomit lay on the floor next to the woman, and blood leaked from her eyes, nose, and lips. Her eyes stared blankly, seeing nothing.

She was dead.

"What is it? What is happening?" a man's loud voice shouted from outside the circle.

With another burst of commotion, he shoved people aside and lurched forward. He was tall, dark-haired, and handsome. Leo recalled seeing him and the dead woman at the neighboring table when she and Dita had taken their seats earlier. The couple had been seated close together, leaning toward each other to talk and be heard above the music.

The man's eyes clapped onto the woman with a grimace of horror.

"Gabriela?" He took in the blank stare of her eyes just as Leo had. "No! Gabriela!" The man threw himself to the floor and gathered her into his arms as he grated out a bellow of grief. Leo's heart clenched, and gooseflesh tightened her skin.

"Someone, call for the police!" a woman in the crowd cried out.

A loud murmur rustled through the room, and several distressed onlookers fled at the mention of the police being summoned. Another man pushed his way into the center of the circle. Eddie Bloom removed his hat, a dark purple bowler to match his suit, and stared at the scene. "I won't have bobbies in my place."

Mr. Bloom signaled to a few of his waitstaff and pulled them aside, away from the commotion and the man cradling the woman's limp figure. Leo wriggled free of Dita's hand, which had been gripping her elbow, and followed the club owner through the crowd. She caught up to him as he began giving instructions to his waiters to clear the club.

"Mr. Bloom," Leo interrupted. "A woman is dead. You must summon the police."

He cocked his head. "This is my establishment, Miss Spencer. I give the orders here, not you."

Leo jerked back an inch. *He knew her by name?* Though she wondered how, right then, it wasn't her main concern.

"From the vomitus on the floor and the leaking blood, which is evidence of ruptured capillaries, it looks to have been an acute poisoning. If you refuse to call for the police, they will think you have something to hide, Mr. Bloom."

The waiters gaped at Leo's defiance, and Eddie Bloom hitched his chin to peer down his nose at her. Holding the pause a moment longer, he then snapped his fingers toward one of his uniformed waiters. "Go find a sodding constable," he barked.

Chapter Two

The bell above the lobby door inside the Spring Street Morgue pealed. Jasper's head throbbed in protest. It had been in a tender state for days, thanks to several late nights at Scotland Yard—and probably more drams of whisky than were strictly necessary. A Jane Doe case had been lingering on his desk for nearly a month, and it had a hold on him.

The young woman had been found in an alley, her skull crushed, and according to Claude Feldman, the city coroner, she had been with child. The murder had precious few leads to begin with, and now, they'd all dried up.

Detective Chief Inspector Coughlan at the C.I.D. had quit pressing him for updates on the investigation last week, commanding Jasper to instead give his full attention to other cases. But he hadn't been able to let the Jane Doe case go. The last several nights, he'd stayed late to pore through the interviews he'd had with the pair of vagrants who'd found her, the details of catalogued items that had arrived at the morgue with her body, and her postmortem report, searching for some clue he'd missed.

Standing at nearly six feet, Jasper was tall enough to raise his arm and close his fist around the lobby bell, silencing the lingering chime. He did not want to be here. Nor did he want this new case. The chief had cornered him first thing that morning, assigning him the suspicious death at Eddie Bloom's nightclub. "It's high-profile and needs to be handled swiftly and with care," Coughlan had instructed Jasper. Lowering his voice, he'd warned, "And discretion, Reid. Utter discretion."

When he'd explained who the victim was, Jasper understood his chief's concern, even as his temples started to pulse with new pain.

The door to the postmortem room opened, and for a bewildering moment, Jasper believed he'd mistakenly stepped into the wrong morgue. An unfamiliar man had entered the lobby. He wore the same type of examination coat and apron Claude always did with a pair of tall rubber boots into which his trouser legs were tucked. He was young, with a small, rodent-like face and disinterested eyes.

"May I help you, sir?" he asked, though with an inflection that hinted it was the last thing he wished to do.

Jasper blinked in confusion. "Who are you?"

"Ah, Inspector Reid." Claude came into the lobby behind the other man. "I don't think you've had the pleasure of meeting our Mr. Higgins. He's come to us as an apprentice from the medical college, placed here by his professor, who happens to be a friend of Chief Coroner Giles." The older man's overly jovial tone and raised silver brows hinted that this was not, in any way, a pleasure.

"Mr. Higgins, may I introduce Detective Inspector Reid of Scotland Yard. You will likely be seeing more of him while you're with us."

The young man continued to look peeved, eyeing Jasper's extended hand a beat too long before grasping it in a listless shake.

"Come in, Inspector," Claude said.

The city coroner was a kind man, pushing seventy, and unsurprisingly, he was a bit eccentric. One would have to be when one's work involved the dissection and examination of corpses. The term eccentric applied to Claude's niece too, considering Leo had, on occasion, assisted her uncle with opening incisions and closing sutures on the bodies when his hands shook uncontrollably—something the two of them had been trying to conceal from the deputy and chief coroners. Having an apprentice observing him at the morgue would not be a welcome thing.

"You must be here for the young woman who was brought in last evening," Claude said as they entered the postmortem room.

"Yes, Gabriela Carter." Jasper couldn't mask his lack of enthusiasm. Anything having to do with the Carter family —the front-runners of the East Rips, a criminal gang out of London's East End—put him in a foul mood.

Gabriela had been the new wife of Andrew Carter, the youngest of Patrick Carter's many sons. Patrick had formed the East Rips a few decades ago and had led it until his death three years earlier. Now, the syndicate was headed by his eldest son, Sean.

Claude led them through the vast space that had once been a church vestry. The building, attached to St.

Matthew's Church, had an alcove lined with stained glass windows. When the sun shone through them, as it currently did, colorful light shed over several autopsy tables in the room, a number of which were occupied.

Jasper looked toward the open door to the back office, from where the clacking sounds of a typewriter's keys emanated. "I'll also need to speak to Leo."

The noise of the typewriter ceased. The sound of a chair sliding along the bare wooden floor followed, and a moment later, Leo Spencer appeared at the threshold.

Earlier, when Jasper's detective sergeant, Roy Lewis, had given him the Gabriela Carter report, sent over from L Division in Lambeth, the name *Leonora Spencer* had jumped out at him. Jasper stared at it for several moments, awestruck. She'd been one of the first witnesses questioned when constables arrived at Striker's Wharf. In fact, her recorded statement indicated that Mrs. Carter's death wasn't a fatal choking or an otherwise innocent occurrence. *Witness (slightly hysterical female) claims to see signs of arsenic poisoning in the victim.* The aside had amused Jasper, as he knew Leo had likely never had a hysterical moment in her life. She was measured, serious, and obstinate—the last of which was what had likely caused the constable to incorrectly label her as hysterical.

Leo entered the postmortem room, her bright hazel eyes hinging on him. She passed the other sheeted corpses without so much as a blink.

"Jasper," she said, her gaze direct and keen. "I'm glad you're here."

The warm greeting set him back on his heels and gave his mood an unexpected lift. It had been a few weeks since he'd last seen her—just after the Jane Doe's postmortem, on the anniversary of her family's deaths, to be precise. Since his father was no longer there to accompany her to the cemetery, Jasper had stepped in. They'd remained quiet for most of the journey there, then again while she laid flowers at the graves of her father and mother, older brother and younger sister. Pleasantries had been exchanged. She'd asked a few questions regarding his work at the Yard, none of which had dissipated a strange friction that lingered between them. One that had not been there before the Inspector's death.

This morning, Leo's sable hair, usually pinned into a low, plain knot at her nape, was twisted and pinned higher, with a curled tendril loose to frame her face. He tried to remember if she'd ever worn her hair like that before.

"The constable I spoke to last night was roundly dismissive of my observation," she went on without pause.

He stopped looking at the glossy, dark tendril of hair and focused on why he was at the morgue to begin with. "Your observation that Mrs. Carter was poisoned?"

He followed Claude to a table occupied by a sheeted figure, the new Mr. Higgins trailing behind them at an indifferent pace. The drape of the sheet, and the small, bare feet exposed at the base of the table, revealed that the corpse beneath was a slim, white female.

"Yes," Leo replied. "And that I'm almost certain I saw who did it."

He cut his eyes to her, a streak of alarm arcing through him like fire. The throbbing of his temples crushed with renewed vigor. "That wasn't in the report."

She crossed her arms. "Constable Fulton wasn't

willing to believe a woman could possibly possess helpful information to the investigation."

Many Metropolitan Police officers suffered from the same shortcomings when it came to their opinions of women, but that wasn't what kindled the concern in Jasper's chest just then.

"You *saw* who poisoned her?"

Leo nodded. "I believe so. And it was indeed a poisoning, as I told the constable," she answered just as Claude was turning down the sheet to reveal the victim's face, neck, and clavicle.

Gabriela Carter had been a pretty brunette with delicate features. A dainty nose, thin, dark eyebrows, and full lips, now ashen with the pallor of death. Jasper frowned, tucking away the usual pang of sorrow he felt when a young victim lay on one of these tables. The postmortem had been completed; the closing sutures were visible just below her collarbone.

"I ran the Marsh test as required for proof of arsenic in the system," Claude began. "It was conclusive that Mrs. Carter had consumed a large quantity of the poison shortly before her death. Evidence of foaming in her lungs supports the presence of pulmonary edema, and the capillary collapse my niece observed at the scene—the blood leakage from her nose, eyes, and lips—is in line with a precipitous drop in blood pressure. Both findings are commonly seen with acute arsenic poisoning."

Jasper nodded at the coroner's explanation, already familiar with some of the signs of arsenic toxicity. One of his first inquests as a detective constable at E Division had been the case of a woman who had sprinkled the tasteless, odorless poison into her mother-in-law's porridge every morning for three weeks. The old woman had rapidly fallen ill and died, and if not for a thorough postmortem, the daughter-in-law might have gotten away with murder.

"She would have consumed the poison roughly fifteen to twenty minutes before she began exhibiting distress," Leo added.

Jasper had read Constable Fulton's report, so he'd come to the morgue armed with some of the facts. But there were still plenty of questions left to answer.

"I'd like to know what you saw, starting from the beginning," he said to Leo.

Claude covered the corpse's face again, and the trembling of his hands was visible in the split second before he released the sheet. The coroner glanced at Jasper briefly to see if he'd noticed, then over his shoulder at the apprentice. Mr. Higgins was leaning against an empty table, chewing on a fingernail absentmindedly. He wasn't taking an interest in the conversation or anything else, for that matter.

In the lobby, the bell above the door chimed again. Claude seemed happy to leave them to greet the new arrival. Mr. Higgins lingered aimlessly where he was. Leo gestured toward the back office, and once she and Jasper entered the room, she closed the door behind them.

"That man is a nuisance," she whispered. "He's been here a week and hasn't done a lick of work."

"I also imagine he's keeping you from lending Claude a hand from time to time."

Leo crossed her arms and glared, and Jasper wished he'd kept his mouth shut. It was a sore subject. She shouldn't have been helping her uncle in such a manner, and yet, Jasper could understand why she did. He waited for her to make some cutting remark, but instead, she lifted her chin, her eyes drifting slowly over him. Her brows pinched together.

"Is that a new suit?"

Jasper looked down at his clothing, surprised by the question. "Relatively new. Why?"

She shrugged. "I haven't seen it before."

He ran his palm down a panel of the brown tweed frock coat. "Do you not like it?"

"It's perfectly fine." She broke her stiffened posture and headed for the desk where she typed inquest reports for Claude. "I just haven't seen you in a brown suit before."

He had no choice but to trust her memory. Leo's mind was a steel trap, her ability to recall every detail uncanny. If she said she hadn't seen him in brown previously, then it was so.

He'd purchased the suit secondhand a few weeks ago. The inheritance from his father had been modest, and Jasper hadn't wanted to spend a penny of it, especially after discussing the land tax for the Mayfair address with Mr. Stockton. He had no idea how he was going to afford it and was even more perplexed that his father had managed to do so.

"Two hundred pounds per annum?" Jasper had repeated after the solicitor had gone over the estate details. "That is impossible. My father couldn't have afforded such an amount."

It would have equaled the whole of Gregory Reid's annual wages, most likely. And yet, Mr. Stockton said it was paid every year without fail.

"You needn't choose what to do about the house just yet," the solicitor had remarked with a pitying tone. "You have until next autumn, at the earliest, to make a decision."

There would be no choice, Jasper had wanted to tell him. The home might have been his, but the government taxed land and property owners, and if he didn't cobble together two hundred pounds, he'd be in arrears.

"My suit isn't important, Leo. Can we get back to Mrs. Carter?" he said, taking out his notebook and pencil.

She narrowed her eyes on him but didn't argue. "Very well. Mrs. Carter and her husband were seated directly behind us at the club. They were already at their table when Dita and I arrived at Striker's."

He bit back the urge to chastise her again for patronizing Eddie Bloom's establishment. Ever since he'd seen her there in January, he'd wondered if she still frequented it. The place was owned and operated by the head of a small syndicate situated around the Lambeth wharves. In comparison to the East Rips, Bloom was small-scale, but he was still dangerous. Unfortunately, Jasper had no control over what Leo did or where she went. If he tried to warn her to stay away from Bloom's club, she'd likely only want to go there more often.

"Who else were you with last night?"

The time before, she'd been with Miss Brooks and her beau, Constable Lloyd, as well as Constable Drake. PC Drake had taken great pains to avoid Jasper at Scotland Yard since then, even once turning down a hallway that led nowhere and then needing to backtrack. All to Jasper's amusement.

"It was just Nivedita Brooks and me. She thought I could use a night out."

"Why was that?"

Leo broke eye contact and fiddled with a few papers on the desk. "It's been a difficult few months."

Guilt lanced through him. She'd loved the Inspector too. Losing him would have affected her deeply as well.

"I'm sorry." He lowered his notebook. "I should have called to check on you more often."

She shook her head and crossed her arms over her chest. "It's all right. You're busy. And I know that Jane Doe last month perturbed you. Have you discovered anything more about her?"

Changing the topic to the Jane Doe case had been purposeful; she clearly didn't want to discuss anything personal with him. That would be easier, he agreed, especially since he wasn't sure what the rules were surrounding Leonora Spencer, now that the Inspector was gone.

"Nothing. I've had to close the case."

She nodded, and another silent moment passed before she resumed her recounting of events. "I heard a commotion behind our table. Mrs. Carter had fallen from her chair onto the floor. She was convulsing, and as people closed in around her, I noticed a woman in a black, hooded cloak, embroidered with light blue thread, moving swiftly in the opposite direction. So, I followed her."

Jasper's pencil tip skidded off the paper. "You did what?"

"I followed her," she repeated, more slowly this time as if he was hard of hearing.

"You followed a potential murderer?"

"I wasn't in any danger."

"She could have seen you." His blood began to simmer in his veins. When Leo rolled her eyes, it neared a boil.

"I don't believe she did. Whoever it was disappeared into the fog on the wharf. A fog I knew better than to enter alone, I'll have you know. I'm not entirely reckless."

"Thank God for small mercies," he muttered, not put at ease in the least. "You are certain it was a woman?"

"Yes. Later, Dita told me she'd seen the cloaked woman sitting in conversation with Mrs. Carter shortly before she fell from the chair and began convulsing. My back was to the Carters' table, so I didn't see anything until after the commotion began."

Jasper tapped his pencil against the paper. "None of this information was in the constable's report."

"I don't know why you're surprised by that. As I've said, the constable dismissed both me and Dita as hysterical females. It wasn't until his superior officer arrived and announced they were sending the case to the C.I.D. that the constable even bothered to write down my comments at all."

L Division had likely realized the East Rips connection to their victim and wanted it off their hands. *Lucky bastards.*

"What else can you recall?"

Leo peeled the paper in the typewriter from the platen and extended it toward him. "I've typed it all for you."

Of course she had. He took the paper; it was filled to the margins with details. "Perhaps you could summarize?"

She sighed as though annoyed, but he knew she was happy to do so. "Since I thought it might be a poisoning, I noted what was on the Carters' table. There were three glasses. I kept an eye on them while the police were summoned, thinking they could be collected for testing. But the club became rather chaotic when the officers arrived, and unfortunately when I looked again, the table had been cleared."

Likely by an unthinking waiter, Jasper guessed. Then again, it might have been intentional.

"Anything else?"

"I think the most important thing to note is that Mr. Carter wasn't at the table when his wife fell ill. He didn't reappear until after I returned from following the woman in the hooded cloak. At least three minutes had passed by then."

"Did he happen to say where he'd been?" Jasper asked.

She shook her head. "And I didn't ask."

"I'm glad you didn't. I don't want you speaking to a Carter or anyone connected to the East Rips. They're criminal scum."

She pressed her lips against a reply that he could practically hear in his mind: that she would speak to whomever she pleased.

Jasper would have to question Andrew Carter himself. He ignored the reflexive cramp in his gut. Andrew wouldn't recognize him; he was nearly certain of it. Jasper hadn't been part of that East End world since the Inspector took him in sixteen years ago. Still, he'd rather have been assigned to any other death inquiry than one having to do with a Carter.

"There is also the matter of a photograph I found in Mrs. Carter's handbag," Leo added. "I've catalogued all her personal effects for the inquest report and sent the box over to your office. However, the photograph stood out as a bit...strange."

Intrigued, he waited for her to explain.

"It was some death photography," she said. "Of two young children."

The topic of death photography reminded him of the case in January. One of Sir Nathaniel's victims had been yet another Carter family member, this one William, the black sheep among Patrick Carter's five sons. William had been employed at a funeral service, and one of his duties had been the staging of the recently deceased, positioned to look as though they were alive. These pictures were popular keepsakes, the last photographs captured of loved ones before burial.

"Could the children have been her own?" he asked.

"No, Uncle Claude confirmed she'd never borne a child."

"Then, they're probably a relative's children."

"But to carry it with her in her handbag?" Leo shook her head and grimaced. Her views on death photography matched his own: that it was a maudlin, morbid trend. "The edges of the photograph had been cut, removing the photographer's stamp," she added.

Most reputable photographers would foil stamp the corner of their work. Without the signature mark, there would be no way to track down the studio from which it had come.

"I'll see what I can find out about it when I talk to the husband," Jasper replied.

"Are you going to see Mr. Carter now?"

He was keen to put off the trip, if only by a few hours.

"No, I'm going first to Bloom's club. I need to interview him and his staff."

"I'll come with you," Leo said, eagerly. He held up a hand.

"That isn't necessary."

"I know him somewhat. And Mr. Bloom doesn't like you, if you recall." She needn't have reminded him. He hadn't forgotten Eddie Bloom's cold reception at Striker's Wharf in January.

"A lot of people don't like me," he remarked. "I'll be fine. Tell Claude he can release the body to the victim's family."

He started for the back door, where a dirt lane ran behind the morgue, dividing the old vestry from the church's burial ground and gardens. This door was where the bodies were delivered to the morgue, providing greater privacy.

"You should also question Dita," Leo called after him. "She had a better view of the Carters' table and might remember more today than she did last night, what with all the commotion."

Jasper faced her again. "I don't need you to tell me how to do my job, Leo."

She flinched. *Hell.* He hadn't meant the statement to bite as sharply as it had.

Leo turned and sat back down at her desk. "Very well. I'll have the report to you by the end of today."

He exhaled and softened his voice. "I shouldn't have barked at you. I apologize."

"No need." She fed a piece of paper into the typewriter and avoided looking at him.

"Thank you for your statement," he said, folding the typed sheet she'd given him and sliding it into his pocket.

He opened the back door to leave but was detained once more.

"Would it be a bother if I stopped by the house later this evening?" Leo asked.

Jasper pulled up short, lingering in the threshold. He didn't know what to think about the catch in his pulse.

"No bother at all. Why?"

"I'd like to collect the file the Inspector wanted me to have."

Jasper nodded, his pulse returning to normal. "Of course."

He'd noticed it was still in the desk drawer in his father's study. The thick file held everything Gregory Reid had ever collected regarding the investigation into the murders of Leo's parents, brother, and sister. Jasper had hoped she would leave it alone. That damn file would just drag up old demons.

Something he suspected this case was going to do too.

Chapter Three

Just before noon, Leo finished the postmortem report on Gabriela Carter, enclosed the papers in a manila folder, and started on foot for Scotland Yard. The walk there took only a few minutes, and as Jasper had said he'd be out interviewing Eddie Bloom and the victim's husband, she was willing to bet he wouldn't be in his office when she delivered the report. After his acerbic attitude earlier that morning, she intended to avoid him.

Jasper had always been prickly, but that morning, he'd flared from hot to cold with more alacrity than usual. He was grieving, of course. Losing the Inspector, who had been his father in every way but in blood, must have set him adrift. She grieved the loss of the Inspector too, but Jasper's absence had also left her feeling a bit wayward. A part of her had been, dare she say it, *happy* to see him that morning. A sentiment he hadn't reciprocated.

Just outside the Yard, Leo stopped at a vendor's cart, entering a sweet-smelling cloud of baked sugar and currants. She purchased two still-warm Chelsea buns and continued toward police headquarters, where Dita would be on duty as a matron.

Dita had been out of sorts after seeing Gabriela Carter's dead body on the dance hall floor. She'd always marveled at Leo's ability to work with the dead. Corpses, even the idea of them, made Dita feel ill. Her distaste was so acute, she had never set foot in the Spring Street Morgue. Not even into the lobby. However, with the benefit of a night's sleep between herself and the event, it was possible Dita would recall more details about the Carters' table. It had been in her direct line of sight, after all, and she had been actively watching the crowd.

Since Jasper might not bother to ask Dita about what she'd seen last evening, Leo would.

Holding the packet of buns in her hands, she greeted the front desk receiver at the Yard, Constable Woodhouse. The constable never gave her a difficult time and always allowed Leo to carry on into the building freely. So, when he held up his palm to indicate that she should hold, Leo was startled enough to trip to a stop.

"Who are you here to see, Miss Spencer?"

Her lips parted in surprise. She couldn't recall the last time he'd asked her that. "I'm here to see Miss Brooks on the matron's floor and to deliver a report to Inspector Reid. Why do you ask?"

He cleared his throat, looking bashful. "Just protocol, miss." He tipped the brim of his hat, and she took it as a sign that she should carry on. She did, though strangely disconcerted.

Constable Woodhouse had never been one to treat Leo with disdain or suspicion, unlike many others tended to do at the Yard. She was well known there, thanks in part to her family's infamous murder, but also due to the late Inspector's affection for her, and his support when she eventually expressed an interest in working alongside her uncle at the morgue. Because Gregory Reid was so beloved, and because he'd been the former Police Commissioner's closest friend, no one complained about the odd arrangement. Now, however, both the Inspector and Sir Nathaniel were gone, and she wasn't sure for how much longer her uncle would be able to keep his position.

Leo took the first flight of stairs, her destination the uppermost floor. There, several former bedrooms, in what had once been a royal residence, were now used as holding chambers for women and children brought in under arrest or for questioning. She and Dita would take tea there rather than go across the street to the Rising Sun public house where many of the officers gathered. Most of them were still skeptical that matrons were needed on the force at all. The eight women currently employed by the Met as citizen volunteers were all related in some way to a police officer; Dita's father, Sergeant Byron Brooks, was a longtime, upstanding officer in the Carriages Department.

Despite those family connections, the officers weren't comfortable around the matrons. In Leo's experience, most felt the same discomfort when around her too. Things had been even worse for her since the events that had unraveled with the former police commissioner. There were many at the Met who would have preferred to let Sir Nathaniel get away with his misdeeds rather than face another cycle of bad press in London's newspapers. But Leo refused to let her unpopularity at Scotland Yard prevent her from going about her business.

She was coming off the first flight of narrow stairs into a busy corridor of offices and turning for the next flight when she heard her name called through the commotion.

"Miss Spencer?"

A strange cinch and swirl of her stomach accompanied the voice. She took her foot from the bottommost step and turned to find a young, uniformed officer smiling at her.

"Constable Murray," she said, feeling distinctly timid. She hadn't stopped to consider that she might see him this morning.

For a few weeks now, she'd been providing detailed descriptions of John and Jane Does that came into the morgue for *The Police Gazette*, which Constable Murray edited and organized. The daily digest was distributed to the stations in every division, listing details of stolen goods and wanted criminals, the descriptions of both oftentimes accompanied by drawings. That way, officers in one part of London could keep an eye out for those wanted in connection to a crime committed in another area. The *Gazette* had been a constant presence in the Inspector's home. Leo used to enjoy reading older copies bound for Mrs. Zhao's kitchen stove, then questioning the Inspector about which cases had been solved.

When Constable Murray approached the morgue with the idea of running descriptions of unidentified bodies to help the divisions solve missing persons cases or murder investigations, she'd thought it would be a brilliant addition. The idea had come too late to help Jasper with his Jane Doe case, but Leo was excited by the prospect of helping to identify future unclaimed bodies. Ever since

January's investigation with Jasper, she'd longed to be useful in some way for other cases. Typing postmortems and inquest reports was serviceable, of course, but rather dull and monotonous.

After bringing several descriptions to the *Gazette* office at the Yard, she'd found Constable Elias Murray to be affable and good-natured in addition to somewhat handsome. Still, she'd been bowled over a little more than a week ago when he'd invited her to a chophouse one evening.

Leo stepped toward the officer now, awkwardly holding the paper-wrapped Chelsea buns in her hands. She and the constable pressed against the wall of the corridor so as not to cause a logjam in the crush of foot traffic.

"I don't have a description for you today," she said after another tongue-tied moment.

"That's quite all right. I just wanted to say hello." Heat infused his cheeks. With his pale Scottish complexion, complete with ginger hair and freckles, that was easily done.

"I see," she said, eager to be on her way to the matron's floor. The buns were losing their warmth. "Hello."

Constable Murray laughed, his cheeks still a bit flushed. "I enjoyed spending time with you last week. I wondered if you might like to dine out again soon."

She was not so startled this time. Only somewhat baffled and slightly wary. The officers here usually viewed her as an oddity. Indecent, even, since 'decent' ladies did not work in morgues.

"Oh. Again?" She cringed at her inept response.

He coughed, looking even more amused now. "Only if you'd like to, of course."

"I would," she said quickly. "Forgive me, I just wasn't sure if you would ask. The last time we shared a meal, I spoke more about autopsies than is deemed polite."

At this he belted out a laugh, and Leo jumped.

"I thought it was scintillating dinner conversation. Far more interesting than anything having to do with the weather or fashion or politics," he said, then dipped his head in a departing nod. "I'll call on you later this week."

She bid him a good day, relieved to retreat to the stairs and climb to the matron's floor. The odd jumble of her nerves kept her frowning as she joined Dita in the empty duty room.

"Oh, good, I'm famished," her friend said, reaching for one of the Chelsea buns. She pulled back at Leo's expression. "Gracious, you look like a thunder cloud. What has you so upset?"

She wiped the frown from her lips and decided it might be time to tell Dita about Constable Murray. Dita listened, rapt, as they ate their buns, her eyes growing round with delight.

"Why didn't you say anything before now?"

Leo shrugged. "I'm not sure anything will come of it."

Dita arched a brow. "Do you want it to?"

"I don't know, and it doesn't matter." She hadn't come here to discuss Elias Murray. "I'm more interested in hearing if you've been able to remember anything else about last night."

Dita sighed and bit into her bun. "Not really."

"What about Andrew Carter, the husband? He must

have left the table before Mrs. Carter began convulsing since he didn't return until after she was already dead—"

Dita held up her hand. "Leo, please, you know I can't stomach talking about dead bodies, especially while I eat."

She apologized and then sealed her lips. Dita's sensibilities were exactly what hers ought to have been, she supposed, but the topic of death and corpses had never fazed her, and she couldn't bring herself to pretend that they did.

They finished eating, Dita sending Leo annoyed glances as she chewed. Finally, she swallowed her last bite and sat back in the chair. "All right, you may start with your questions. Though I can't promise I won't still feel ill. It was an awful sight, seeing that poor woman dead on the floor. She's probably younger than we are, and it must have been so painful for her…"

Leo frowned. She hadn't considered Mrs. Carter's pain during her last minutes. Of course, they would have been excruciating. Why hadn't she thought of that? She squirmed in her seat, questioning her empathy—or lack of it.

"I want to help find out who poisoned her," Leo said, "so that they can be held accountable for what they did. You had the better view of their table while we were seated."

If only she'd been seated where Dita had been, she'd have the memories to explore in fine detail.

"But I had no reason to pay attention to a woman with her husband. I saw the wedding bands on their fingers and figured they were hitched," Dita said, shrugging.

She'd been far more interested in sneaking looks toward the table of gentlemen behind her. "I understand, but do try, Dita. It usually takes twenty or so minutes for arsenic to begin taking effect, so she must have ingested it right around the time we arrived."

Dita's thin, jet eyebrows furrowed as she visibly tried to remember. "If that is the case, then she was with her husband at that point. I noticed him when we arrived. Don't tell John," she added with a wink.

Dita had a shameless fondness for handsome men and openly admired them. However, the worst she would ever do was flirt and dance with them. It was PC John Lloyd with whom she was truly enamored.

"Do you recall when Mr. Carter left his wife's side?" she asked.

Dita shook her head. "No, but as I've already said, I do remember seeing the woman in the hooded cloak you spoke of. Having a hood drawn up indoors was odd, I thought. She obviously didn't want her face being seen. She and Mrs. Carter were seated alone at the table. I think it was right around the time you urged me to go dance the polka."

"They were talking?" Leo asked.

"Yes, and Mrs. Carter appeared quite serious." Dita lifted a shoulder. "But as I figured the woman in the cloak wanted her privacy, I tried to give it to her. I suppose that was the wrong decision."

"Not at all," Leo replied, "and what you've told me will be helpful."

"Should I tell Inspector Reid?"

Leo thought of Jasper's cutting remark to not tell him how to do his job earlier at the morgue. That hadn't been her intent, but it shouldn't have surprised her that he'd jumped to a different conclusion. He'd always been easy to provoke, even when she wasn't necessarily trying.

"Yes, and anything more you can recall. I'm sure he'll come speak to you today." She hoped he would, at least. Leo stood and smoothed her skirt. "I should get back to the morgue."

Dita stood as well, though she froze as soon as she was on her feet. "Wait, I do remember something else. It might not be anything important but..." She closed her eyes, as if trying to recall it more clearly. "I was distracted by the woman's hood when I noticed it, and it made me forget the very first thing I saw."

Leo waited, holding her breath.

"Mrs. Carter took something from the woman's hand and put it into her handbag," Dita finished.

"Do you know what it was?"

"No. She whisked it out of sight, and then the hood drawn up on her companion caught my attention, and I didn't think of it again."

Her handbag. Gabriela Carter's purse had been among her personal possessions when the body arrived at the morgue. As she did with every new arrival, Leo had thoroughly catalogued the contents. The black velvet brocade purse with a brass kiss lock had contained common things a woman of her status would carry: a paper tube of lip rouge, a hair comb, a lace-trimmed handkerchief embroidered with her initials in one corner, and a small round mirror.

The only item that had given Leo pause had been the folded photograph of the two young children, clearly deceased but staged to look as if they were still alive. The little boy and girl, both probably aged two or three years, had been propped up together on a wooden rocking horse. Eyes and lashes had been painted on their closed eyelids. She could see every detail of the picture in her mind and shivered again, as she'd done when she first found it.

It was the only thing in the purse that didn't belong. She had no evidence that the cloaked woman had given it to Mrs. Carter, but it seemed most likely. Two dead children. One dead young woman. How were they connected? Though Jasper would heartily disapprove, Leo was determined to find out.

When she arrived in the detective department to leave Gabriela Carter's postmortem report on Jasper's desk, she was met by Constable Horace Wiley. As he was so adept at reminding her, visitors to the department were to present themselves to him, and then he could decide who—if anyone—would see to them and their complaints. Unlike Constable Woodhouse, his strange behavior today notwithstanding, Constable Wiley never failed to uphold this rule. Or at least try to, because Leo had no intention of following it.

"Good afternoon, constable," she said as she tried to walk swiftly past his desk. He jumped from his chair to block her.

"State your business, Miss *LeoMorga*," he said, drawing out the puerile moniker he'd given her a few years back. She ignored it, as she always did in the hope that he would cease using it.

"I'm simply leaving this report on Inspector Reid's desk." She held up the manila folder containing her typed report and tried to edge around the constable's stout frame. But Wiley was built like an ice box and was just as cold in his demeanor toward her.

"You may leave the report with me," he said, extending his hand. Leo pulled it out of his reach.

"I would rather leave it on the Inspector's desk myself." She didn't trust Constable Wiley in the least. The man was an arrogant toad. On several occasions, when Gregory Reid had still been alive and at the Yard, she'd witnessed the constable turning away women who'd come to make valid complaints regarding abuse, missing children, and other violations of the worst sort. He often refused to allow them to speak to a detective, telling them they were wasting valuable police time with their "overactive imaginations."

"Shall I fetch the chief, then?" Wiley asked. His snide threat was enough to make her roll her eyes. Detective Chief Inspector Coughlan would likely give the constable a good dressing down for fetching him over such a trifling matter, and it was something she would enjoy seeing. However, it would still cast her in a poor light. Already, the chief had asked Jasper to limit Leo's presence at the Yard.

Reluctantly, she handed the slim folder to the constable. He plucked it away, grinning smugly. He then had the audacity to open it. "This about the Carter murder?"

"I'm quite sure you aren't authorized to look at that report."

He scoffed at her reprimand and continued to peer at the papers inside the folder. "Mr. Henderson was in this morning, wanting to know the cause of his daughter's death. He wasn't pleased at all that the coroner was taking so long."

Leo dismissed the jab at her uncle. "Henderson?"

The name sparked a memory. It took a few moments, but her mind brought it forward at last. A newspaper article. A gossip column.

"Gabriela Carter's maiden name was Henderson?" she asked.

Wiley scowled at her. "What about it?"

Leo smiled sweetly at him; she always enjoyed the moment they could part ways. "Thank you, constable. You've been most helpful."

He looked offended. "I have?"

"Yes, and please, do see a doctor about that blue tinge around your mouth," she called over her shoulder as she left the department. "I see it all the time at the morgue. A respiratory malfunction, if I recall. Extremely worrisome."

She resisted the temptation to look back, but she was almost certain Wiley would be seeking out a mirror in a panic to check his mouth. Jasper would have chastised her for teasing the man, but she put the unpalatable Constable Wiley to the back of her mind as she made her way from the Yard.

Leo needed to get to Fleet Street before the newspapers closed their offices for the day. There was an article she needed to find.

Chapter Four

The inside of Eddie Bloom's club on Striker's Wharf gave off a different atmosphere during the day than it did at night. Jasper and Detective Sergeant Roy Lewis entered the club after showing their warrant cards to the doorman, a meaty fellow with forearms the circumference of Jasper's thighs. Without the brume of cigar and cigarette smoke, the riotous hum of voices and music, and the gasoliers casting everything in a hazy golden glow, Striker's had a dejected, nearly forgotten quality to it.

Chairs had been flipped up and hung on the edges of the tables, but there were several men at the bar, Eddie Bloom among them. Bloom's boys ran rackets all along the Lambeth wharves, mostly in stolen goods, protection, and of course, women. They weren't as well known for violence as the East Rips were, but they were still criminals.

Bloom and his men turned their attention toward Jasper and Lewis as they approached the bar. Bloom raked them with an assessing gaze. Although there was no reason for the club owner to recognize him as anyone other than an irksome police inspector, a part of Jasper always tensed when meeting with someone from London's underbelly.

Before his death, Gregory Reid confessed that shortly after taking Jasper in off the streets, a woman came to him at Scotland Yard. She was looking for her young nephew, and when she'd shown the Inspector a daguerreotype, he'd recognized the street ruffian living under his own roof. After some consideration, he'd made a choice. One that had weighed heavily on him for the rest of his life. He'd transferred Jasper's old, ratty clothes, including the rosary his grandmother had given him, to the dead body of a boy roughly the same age that had been fished out of the Thames. The bloated remains had been impossible for Jasper's aunt, Myra, to identify, but she'd recognized the rosary. Myra had left Scotland Yard believing her nephew to be dead.

The Inspector explained that he'd known who Myra's husband was—*what* he was—and that he hadn't wanted to send Jasper back to him. He'd asked for Jasper's forgiveness, but there had been nothing to forgive. Jasper had left his previous life willingly, for damn good reasons—his uncle was only one of them—and Gregory Reid had simply helped him in his endeavor.

Honestly, the Inspector's confession lifted a weight of worry from his shoulders. After sixteen years spent wondering and worrying that someday, someone might pass him on the street and recognize him, he now knew there was nothing to fear. Everyone from his past believed he was dead.

And yet, there was still a strain of guilt Jasper felt

about his former life. The Inspector had not understood everything, as he'd thought he had. There were still secrets Jasper clung to. Secrets that could sink him, even now.

He showed his warrant card to Eddie Bloom. "Detective Inspector Reid, and Detective Sergeant Lewis."

"I remember you, copper." Bloom leaned an elbow on the bar as he sat on a tall stool. He looked entirely at ease as his sharp gaze evaluated Lewis in a brief sweep. "Suppose you're here about last evening's sorry event."

The lines around Bloom's eyes and the barest creases bracketing his mouth put him in his mid- to late forties, but his form was athletic and trim. Without a single gray strand in his boot-black hair, he could have passed for a man in his early thirties. The other men on the stools surrounding him wore cheap suits and unfriendly glowers. The bartender wiping down glasses behind the bar looked on with interest, his expression one of marked incredulity. As if to say, *Can you imagine the cheek of these two coppers coming in here?*

"The sorry event is now a murder investigation. We have some questions for you and your staff," Jasper replied, tucking his warrant card away. "Is the waiter who served the Carters here?"

Bloom jerked his chin, and the bartender took it as an order. He went through a door into a back room.

"It's a real shame," Bloom said, his tone ingenuine. "I heard they was newlyweds."

Jasper ignored the commentary. "What was a Carter doing at your club, Mr. Bloom?"

"You'd have to ask him," he replied blithely.

"I'm asking you."

Bloom pretended to laugh, but the sound broke apart quickly. "And I'm telling you, you'll have to ask him. I don't pry into my patrons' lives."

"Not even when they're a known member of the East Rips?" Lewis asked. Bloom didn't so much as glance toward the detective sergeant. Apparently, he didn't consider Lewis to be worth it.

"I don't have any barney with the East Rips, or with any other party, so long as they keep their business off my territory," he told Jasper instead. "I made that clear to Mr. Carter last night when he put questions to me and my staff."

It wasn't unexpected that Andrew Carter had already interrogated Bloom. In fact, he'd probably done a better job of it than the constables from L Division.

Jasper looked around the club. His eyes went directly to the table across the dance floor where he'd seen Leo and Miss Brooks in January with PC Drake and PC Lloyd. He wondered if that had been their table last night as well. The dance floor had a high polish to it, evidence that it had been swept and cleaned. Wherever Mrs. Carter had fallen and died, that area of the floor had been tidied. He cut his attention back to Bloom when the bartender returned, ushering in a nervous-looking young man.

"Harry, Scotland Yard has sent their finest to inquire about the poor lady from last night," Bloom said, his sarcasm thick. "Answer whatever questions they have."

The waiter, Harry, nodded, his Adam's apple bobbing nervously.

"You served the Carters' table last night?" Jasper asked. The waiter nodded again, his complexion pallid. He was either shaken up by the death or scared of Bloom. Probably both.

"What did she drink?" he asked next.

"A glass of wine, sir. Spanish claret."

"And her husband, what about him?"

Harry blinked but knew the information right off. "Whisky sour."

"You have a good memory," Jasper said.

The waiter huffed a shaky laugh. "Have to get the orders right, sir. Besides, it was a Carter. You pay attention when it's a Carter."

Bloom cleared his throat, and the waiter ducked his head.

"So then, just the two drinks?" Lewis asked.

Roy Lewis was a few years older than Jasper and had joined the force as a recruit shortly after he had. If he'd taken issue with Jasper's promotion to detective inspector while he remained a detective sergeant, he'd never let on about it. Still, Jasper was careful not to rub him the wrong way and didn't mind him cutting in with questions. Saying less and listening more was often more effective than dominating the conversation anyhow.

"That's right," Harry replied. "Although, there was a glass on the table when I took the Carters' orders. I'd cleared the table after the people before them left, so I didn't know what it was doing there. Figured someone set it down without thinking. I offered to take it away, but Mr. Carter told me to leave it."

"Could another waiter have delivered it to them before you got there?" Lewis asked.

"Not if he wanted to keep his job," Bloom answered. "One waiter to a table. My guests want to know who to signal for another drink. That table was Harry's and his alone."

Jasper changed tack. "You keep an eye on your assigned tables, I presume?" When the waiter nodded, he continued, "Who else did you see with the Carters last night?"

Jasper already knew from Leo that Andrew Carter had stepped away for a short while, and a woman in a dark, hooded cloak had joined Mrs. Carter. He wanted to check the veracity of Harry's answers. The young man proved to be reliable, explaining that the husband had left for a spell, and that shortly afterward, a woman in a cloak with the hood pulled up took the seat next to Mrs. Carter.

"Did you approach the table to take the woman's order?"

He grimaced. "No, I was serving another table, and before I had the chance, Mrs. Carter was…well, she was sick on the floor."

Lewis was rapidly jotting down the statement, his forehead creased in disappointment. So far, they hadn't learned much more than what Leo had provided in her statement.

"Did you see the woman in the cloak after that?" Lewis asked.

Harry shook his head.

"Who cleared the glasses from the table?" Jasper asked. "I know it wasn't the constables who arrived at the scene, as none of the glasses were taken in for testing. But we believe Mrs. Carter consumed a drink laced with arsenic. Their disappearance during all the commotion is suspicious."

Harry blushed guiltily, and Bloom held up his palms.

"Honest mistake, Inspector. The lad was only trying to do his job."

"I'm sure he was," Jasper replied, thinking it likely the waiter had rushed to follow Bloom's orders. The club owner was no innocent, and according to Leo's typed witness statement, which he'd read on the carriage ride across the river, she'd announced to Bloom that it looked like Mrs. Carter had been poisoned. Traces of arsenic found in a glass served at Striker's Wharf would be bad for business. The man's ability to think only of shielding himself from police scrutiny, even as a young woman lay dead on the floor of his club, was inexcusable.

"I'm going to need to speak to all your staff, Mr. Bloom. Even the ones not present last night. Names and addresses, if you will," Jasper said. Harry might have been the Carters' waiter, but that didn't mean someone else hadn't interfered.

"I'll be sure to get you that list right away, Inspector," he replied, his cynicism thick.

"See that you do by the end of the day. And how's your licensing, Bloom?" He would have taken great pleasure in being able to shut this place down, if only for a little while.

The proprietor sniffed and rubbed his thumb against his cheek. "All up-to-date and aboveboard."

"I'll be checking with the magistrate on that," Jasper said, though admittedly, to do so would be churlish. He just wished the trip to the wharves had turned up more leads. And now, he had to go visit the grieving husband, Andrew Carter.

"You do that, Inspector," Bloom said. Then, standing from his stool, he added, "And so's you know, you're welcome back here at my place any time. I know I said coppers bring down the mood that last time you were in, but so long as you don't arrest nobody, you'll be fine as peach fuzz. Bring along your pretty little thing too."

The *pretty little thing* that Bloom remembered was Miss Constance Hayes, the young woman Jasper had been courting since the autumn. Constance had brought Jasper to the club without knowing it was operated by a criminal. He'd met her through his friend, Oliver Hayes, a viscount Jasper had once arrested for drunk and disorderly, and whom he'd summarily clocked in the chin when the young lord tried to resist, claiming his status as a lord protected him from arrest. Once sober, Oliver's entitled attitude vanished, and he'd admired Jasper for his powerful right hook.

He didn't accept Bloom's offer, nor did Jasper reject it. It would be better to simply leave. Anyhow, he needed to get to Carter's address in Stepney. He thanked Bloom for his time, and he and Lewis turned for the door.

"You should bring along Miss Spencer too."

The muscles along his spine tensed, and Jasper stopped. "You are acquainted with Miss Spencer?"

That Eddie Bloom knew her by name irked him. The criminal seemed to recognize it.

"Sure. Seen her here from time to time. And when a lady works in a deadhouse, people are bound to whisper," he replied.

Jasper's temper spiked. "How do you know where she works?"

"Guv," Lewis said, attempting to redirect him toward the exit.

Bloom was baiting him, pure and simple. And yet, Jasper needed an answer.

"You mean to say you haven't seen it yet?" Bloom asked, all too pleased with himself. He snapped his fingers again. "Harry, get me that paper," he said, directing the waiter to the other end of the bar.

Jasper shifted his jaw in irritation as the waiter fetched it.

"Give it to the Inspector," Bloom instructed.

The waiter handed it over—*The Illustrated Police News*. Jasper had not yet seen this week's edition. As usual, there were numerous elaborate illustrations on the front page, all of them sensational and melodramatic. Police constables were shown placing a scantily dressed woman in handcuffs; a couple was drawn next to the small coffin of a child, the woman on her knees in anguish while the man bowed his head, his hat held to his heart; and a pair of thieves were shown smashing a shop window. The popular weekly paper was little more than shocking entertainment.

Jasper held it up. "What am I supposed to be looking at?"

"Page three," Bloom answered, his mouth curling into a smirk.

Grudgingly, Jasper flipped to that page—and saw it.

In the lower left-hand corner, a cameo-shaped illustration all but stopped his pulse. It was of a young woman in a gown of mourning black, standing in a deadhouse next to sheeted corpses. Her dark hair was down around her shoulders in a fashion she never wore, but the artist had captured most of Leonora Spencer's facial features well. The salacious headline underneath read: *Lady deadhouse worker knows all about murder!*

Jasper gripped the paper's edges, blood hammering in his ears as he scanned the first few lines of the short article. It seemed to be a profile on Leo, revealing that she worked in a deadhouse with her uncle, who'd taken her in after she'd been orphaned as a child. Her family had been brutally murdered *"right before her eyes,"* according to the author, while she was left alive *"for mysterious reasons."* And now, she worked with dead bodies, *"haunted by the Grim Reaper himself,"* while also being known to assist Scotland Yard in the solving of a murder or two.

Jasper searched for the name of the reporter, but the piece wasn't attributed to anyone. Who the bloody hell had written this? And how had the illustrator known so well what Leo looked like? He checked the date. It had been printed just yesterday.

"It seems Miss Spencer's making a name for herself," Bloom said. "Sad story about her family though. I'd nearly forgotten all about it."

Jasper slapped the paper onto the bar. "What do you know of it?"

"Only what everyone else who was around back then knows," he answered, unconcerned. "A terrible thing. But it's good to see she's grown up into a fine young woman. Safe and sound."

Jasper's pulse had steadily increased as Bloom was speaking. "This article is rubbish. Unless there is something more you want to say about Miss Spencer, I think we are done here."

Bloom only smiled, seemingly pleased to be working

his way under Jasper's skin. He'd wanted a reaction. Maybe a violent one. Any reason to sic his thugs on the two Scotland Yard officers. When Bloom spoke next, it took every ounce of Jasper's self-control not to give it to him.

"There is, in fact. I hear you and the lady are like family," he said. "I'm a gentleman. Old-fashioned like. Thought I'd check with you first before inviting her for a dance."

A tight grin stretched across Jasper's face. The bastard had no intention of asking Leo for a dance. He was just playing with him like a cat with a mouse.

Jasper sure as hell wasn't letting him have this round.

"Ask the lady yourself," he said as he gave his back to Bloom and walked toward the door. "She can reject you all on her own."

Chapter Five

Wistfulness and a touch of unease kept Leo from ascending the half-moon step fronting 23 Charles Street. The last time she'd been here, it had been to say goodbye.

The morning Jasper had arrived at her door on Duke Street to tell her the news of the Inspector's passing, Leo had quickly dressed and accompanied him back to the house. Once there, they'd entered the Inspector's bedroom to find Mrs. Zhao seated in a chair next to him, her cheeks wet and eyes shimmering. He had merely looked asleep, though Leo had noted his lividity right away; the cessation of blood flow had paled his skin. And when she'd taken his hand in hers, his cooled body temperature had been consistent with the time of death Jasper had reported on their mostly quiet ride over to Charles Street.

Leo had returned his hand to where it had been, folded over his chest, and had looked at the Inspector's body, seeing him not as he was then—thin and decimated by disease—but how he'd appeared when she first saw him. When he'd opened that steamer trunk in her family's Red Lion Street attic, and she'd first looked upon his face, she'd known, straightaway, that he was a kind man. That she could trust him. And when he lifted her into his strong arms and promised that no one was going to hurt her ever again, she'd known he'd meant it with all his heart.

Leo had seen countless dead bodies. But looking upon the Inspector's, she'd understood, perhaps for the first time ever, what one ought to have felt when looking at the dead: the absence of a life force within and a loss so profound that her insides felt as though they were being crushed by some invisible, giant fist.

Now, as her eyes went to the windows of the study on the first-floor, she felt the compression of her lungs again. Taking several deep breaths, she finally went to the door and brought down the worn brass lion's head knocker. After the sound of a lock bolt turning, Mrs. Zhao opened the door.

"Miss Leo, how good to see you. Come in, come in," she said with a happy grin.

The older woman had been the Inspector's housekeeper since just after his marriage to Emmaline Cowper. When Emmaline's grandmother had gifted her the house as a wedding present, it had not come with a staff. The couple had found it impossible to hire any servants who would lower their standards enough to wait on a common police inspector. Emmaline had tried to make do with just her longtime lady's maid, but when the Inspector had met the widowed Mrs. Zhao during an investigation, the two had found a good rapport. Aware that she was in need of work, he invited her to try her hand at being a house servant. Mrs. Zhao and Emmaline had immediately struck up the same good rapport. When her lady's maid soon complained that she could not work alongside a Chinese woman, Emmaline had told her she would not have to. She gave her lady's maid a letter of character and sent her on her way.

"I know I haven't been to see you in some time," Leo said as Mrs. Zhao collected her things to hang up. "How have you been?"

"Nothing is the same without Mr. Reid," the housekeeper replied softly. "I always thought he was a quiet man, but now, I realize what quiet truly is."

Jasper was certainly more subdued than the Inspector, and Leo imagined he wasn't at home half as much for Mrs. Zhao to dote on.

"Have you found more time to spend with your sister and her family?" Leo asked. The trip to Limehouse wasn't easy to undertake, and when she went, Mrs. Zhao tended to spend the night there.

"Yes, but I miss staying busy." She paused. "How is your aunt? Perhaps I could check on her from time to time?"

Claude had hired a new nurse, Mrs. Boardman, to look after Flora each day while he was at the morgue, but Leo found she couldn't bring herself to refuse Mrs. Zhao's offer.

"Please do. I think Aunt Flora would enjoy that."

She would prefer it to Leo's company, that much she knew. While Flora had always been reserved with her feelings toward her younger sister's child, it was only as her mind started to deteriorate that she'd begun to show open hostility toward Leo.

It seemed every time Flora now looked upon her niece, she was appalled, even terrified, to be in her presence. She would scream of murder and blood, and worse, she would lay the blame squarely on Leo's shoulders. Absurd, of course, since at the time she had been a little girl. But Leo had survived when no one else in her family had, and Flora was convinced there was a nefarious reason behind it.

Leo explained to Mrs. Zhao that she'd come to collect a folder from the Inspector's desk, one that he'd wished for her to have after he was gone. The housekeeper asked no questions; more than likely, she knew all about the file. She welcomed her to go about her business and offered to bring tea shortly.

Whether Mrs. Zhao kept a fire in the grate and paraffin lamps burning in the study out of habit or knew Jasper would come there first whenever he arrived home, Leo was grateful for the familiar comfort as she entered the room. Everything looked the same as when she had last been there. The desk in the corner, by the window; the leather Chesterfield perpendicular to the hearth and across from two leather club chairs; the low mahogany table in between them with the three daily newspapers the Inspector had long subscribed to, waiting for Jasper's perusal; shelves upon shelves of books against two walls; and just as she suspected, the bottle of Grants Morella she'd given the Inspector in January at the sideboard, among decanters of other spirits.

She went to it and poured a small amount into one of the cordial glasses. Though she knew it was absurd, she turned over a second glass, poured, and then tapped hers against it.

The desk—and its bottom right drawer—loomed large in the corner of the room. She sipped the liqueur on her way toward it, deciding to treat the folder inside as she would any dead body delivered to the morgue: with a fair amount of detachment. She brought out the folder, made of thick manila hemp and worn thin over the years by the Inspector's fingers, and placed it on the blotter. The Inspector had advised her to only open it when she was ready. Back in January, she'd thought she had been. Once opened, her gumption had lasted all of ten minutes. That night, and many more after it, nightmares followed. The same ones as in the past, though she hadn't experienced them since she was a child.

The police report, typed by Gregory Reid himself, had laid out the crime in stark detail. Reading it had summoned memories she'd worked hard to bury, including the vivid recollection of being carried down from the attic by the Inspector. *Close your eyes, now, little love,* he'd said to her, and she had…at first. Oh, how she wished she'd obeyed him. With her chin against the shoulder of his scratchy tweed coat, she'd opened one squeezed-shut eyelid. A blanket, partially covering her brother's body, had burned into her memory. Jacob's arm had been visible, the sleeve of his striped pajamas dotted with a spray of blood.

The Inspector's professional, if dispassionate, reporting had communicated that all four Spencers had been killed with blades. First, stabbed to subdue them. Then, their throats slit. Cleanly done for the most part.

Except for her father, who'd received multiple stab wounds—the killing one, to his heart.

In the folder, the edges of a few photographs had stuck out among the papers. Sixteen years ago, crimes scenes weren't often photographed, but the nearly wholesale slaughter of a family had warranted it. The first photograph she'd flipped to had been of poor quality, whitened at the edges from overexposure. It had been of her father, lying on his side on the sitting room carpet. If not for the dark blood stain on the front of his shirt, he might have looked as if he was sleeping. Black spots had filled Leo's vision as she'd stared at her slain father. Her head whirled, her lungs emptied of air, and she slammed the folder shut.

Two months later, she still wasn't ready to open the folder and try again. However, as she sat in the Inspector's leather swivel chair, which was wide enough for her to tuck her legs up underneath her, she was content to simply look at it.

Absentmindedly, she rubbed her thumb over the scars on her right palm. Tracing them soothed her sometimes when too many thoughts of that night began to creep in. Why that might be perplexed her somewhat, since she'd received the scars the same night as the murders. It should have made her pulse increase, rather than slow, to remember the darkened figure who'd entered the attic in search of her. The one she'd heard coming closer to her hiding spot, where she clutched a shard of porcelain, which had broken off her doll's leg when Jacob threw her to the floor earlier in the night. It was why she'd gone into the attic to begin with—to be angry and cry alone.

"Little girl? I know you're here," he'd whispered. Down-

stairs in her home, things had gone horribly silent. The cries and screams had ceased.

Knowing the piece of her doll's leg was sharp and that the shadowy figure would soon find her, Leo made a choice that still surprised her, even all these years later: She'd jumped out and slashed at him with the shard of delicate ceramic. The jagged edge had sunk into flesh, and he'd grunted in pain. But he hadn't struck back at her.

Instead, he'd told her to hide.

The ridged skin of the two parallel scars on her palm reminded her that she was alive. That the person who had been barely visible in the dim moonlight filtering through the small crescent window could have hurt her, just as she'd heard her family being hurt downstairs. But he hadn't.

She'd never told anyone about him. Not even the Inspector. For a long while, Leo half-wondered if he had been a figment of her imagination. But the scars were real. He had let her live…but why?

If she'd told anyone about him, they'd have demanded to know why one of the killers had saved her. Guilt over it had eaten away at her for so long, and the more time that went by, the more impossible it became to broach the subject.

Leo drained her cordial glass just as Mrs. Zhao arrived with a tea tray, and on the housekeeper's heels, entered the new master of the house. Already shed of his jacket and hat, Jasper appeared disheveled. He pulled up short when he saw her at the desk. She couldn't think why since he'd likely been informed by Mrs. Zhao that she was in the study. Then again, perhaps he didn't like seeing her in the chair. It was, after all, now his.

She stood up. "I'm sorry. I'm in your spot."

He waved his hand. "Stay, it's fine. I don't sit there."

Leo hesitated, now understanding his reaction. He'd been accustomed to seeing the Inspector in this chair. Not her.

"I'll have dinner ready in half an hour," Mrs. Zhao announced, splitting the tension. "Will you stay, Miss Leo?"

Her eyes clashed with Jasper's briefly, who seemed to grimace at the suggestion. Before, taking dinner with him would have been acceptable since the Inspector would have been there. But now, just the two of them, alone in the dining room, might be considered improper.

"Thank you, but I need to return home."

Mrs. Zhao left them to their tea, closing the door behind her. She clearly did not see leaving them alone in the study as anything unseemly. And Jasper, too, discarded propriety as he loosened the knot on his tie and approached the sideboard. He looked tired and cross as she followed his progress across the room, swiveling in the chair as she did.

"Your interviews didn't go well, I presume."

He took the stopper from a crystal decanter of whisky. "Carter wasn't in. I'll have to summon him to the Yard, which I'd wanted to avoid doing."

"And Mr. Bloom?"

Jasper poured, replaced the stopper, and took a deep sip, all before turning to spear her with a look. "I can't discuss the investigation."

She'd anticipated that response, just as he probably anticipated her pressing him for more information. Instead, she said, "Did you know that Gabriela was the daughter of Jack Henderson? Of Henderson & Son Manufacturing?"

He came away from the sideboard, taking another sip and tugging on his tie again. He opened a gap at his collar, exposing a golden triangle of skin at the base of his throat. "It was mentioned in the initial report from L Division. Why?"

She blinked and looked away from his neck. Her fingers, resting on the arms of the chair, tapped as she reconsidered her approach. "I've had a thought about Henderson & Son."

Indeed, after Constable Wiley had revealed Gabriela's maiden name, which churned up the memory of a gossip column she'd read last autumn, she'd gone directly to the Fleet Street offices of *The Times* and applied to the archives clerk to find the issue. She could already remember most of it, word for word, but Jasper would require more evidence than that.

"What thought?"

Leo stilled her fingers. "I'll tell you—if you tell me what you learned today from Mr. Bloom."

With a groan, Jasper sank down onto the Chesterfield and leaned his head against the back cushions. He closed his eyes and pinched the bridge of his nose. "I'm not bargaining with you, Leo. It's late. I'm tired."

She sighed and opened another one of the Inspector's desk drawers, pulling out the London City Directory he'd kept there. It was the most recent edition, from the previous year.

"Come now, Jasper, we worked well together in January," she said as she opened the thick directory.

He lifted his head. "Need I remind you that I was

reprimanded by the chief *and* the superintendent for your involvement? Another infraction, and I'll be sent back to E Division."

"No, you won't. You're Gregory Reid's son."

"I am not his son," he replied through gritted teeth. She didn't understand why he always fought the claim, especially when she knew Jasper had loved him as a devoted son would.

"As good as, and everyone knows it," she said, flipping the pages as she searched.

"Just like you're as good as my sister?"

Leo's fingers slipped from the directory's pages. It wasn't just the comment that struck her, but how he'd said it, scoffing as if the idea offended him. They'd been lumped together by many at the Yard as 'the Inspector's wards'; he'd taken them both under his wing and into his home around the same time. But she knew what it felt like to have a brother, and she'd never felt the familial connection to Jasper that she'd felt with Jacob.

She closed the city directory and took the case folder from the blotter. "You're right. It's late. I'll go."

Jasper stood from the Chesterfield and held out his arm to stop her. "I'm sorry, Leo. That was unfair. I don't…" He rubbed his eyes. "It's something Bloom said today. It got under my skin."

"Something about the case?"

He paused, seeming to falter over whether he should answer. He leaned down to fiddle with the newspapers Mrs. Zhao had fanned out for him on the table. Sliding them into a pile, he pushed them aside and stood tall again.

"Nothing about the case." Jasper raised his glass to his lips. "He wanted permission to ask you to dance."

Leo stared, utterly flummoxed. She hadn't known what she'd expected him to say, but it most assuredly hadn't been *that*. "Dance with me? But that is absurd; he isn't interested in me in the least."

Not to mention, he was a good decade or two her senior.

"I don't think he is either." Jasper's agreement was a slap of insult, even if it was Eddie Bloom they were speaking of.

She scowled. "Oh, well, thank you very much."

"That's not what I meant," he said. "Bloom wanted to needle me and knew to use you to do it."

"He did see us together in January." She arched her brow. "You were excessively protective that evening."

He frowned. "I was not. I was the only one being rational."

Leo shook her head. "You shouldn't let Mr. Bloom get to you. Besides, you ought to know I wouldn't step out with him or anyone like him. He's a criminal, after all."

Constable Elias Murray came to mind. She'd stepped out with him once and had all but agreed to do so again. But she bit back the information. There was no reason to share that with Jasper.

He tucked his chin and nodded before draining the rest of his drink. "There. I've told you something of my investigation today. Now, what is this thought you've had about Henderson & Son?"

"That wasn't about the investigation at all," she said, but as she was too impatient to reveal her discovery, she chose not to hold out.

She opened her handbag and retrieved the issue of *The Times* from the twenty-second of November of the previous year, just about four months ago. The clerk at the archives had told her she couldn't take it, but he'd conceded once she bribed him with a shilling and a hand pie from the costermonger across the street.

"In November, I read an announcement for the engagement of Miss Gabriela Henderson to a Mr. Lawrence Wilkes, a young man employed at Henderson & Son Manufacturing." Leo opened the paper to the society pages and handed it to Jasper. "And yet, she died four months later as the wife of Mr. Andrew Carter."

"What happened to Mr. Wilkes?" Jasper asked as he read the column, his honey-blond eyebrows furrowing in interest.

"That was my question." She went back to the London City Directory and continued her search. "I think we should find him and ask."

Jasper tossed the paper to the table, atop the other dailies. "We?"

"You know what I mean."

"Yes, unfortunately, I think I do." He came toward the desk. "You just happened to remember this announcement from November of last year?"

"Only when Constable Wiley mentioned Gabriela's maiden name. You know I can't help the way my memory works."

Jasper leaned against the desk, his arms crossed over his chest, as she continued to flip through pages in the directory. "Speaking of Wiley, is there any particular reason he asked me if I thought his mouth was turning blue?"

Leo bit her lower lip against a grin. "I've no idea. What an odd man."

He grunted. "Also, do I take it that you actually read the *society pages*?"

She peered sideways at him. "On occasion. Why are you turning up your nose? Doesn't your intended *type* them?"

Jasper pushed off the desk. "Constance and I are not engaged."

Leo kept her lips sealed against inquiring as to why not; they'd been courting for months. But she couldn't help the twinge of relief she felt. The woman was admirable for her choice to work rather than play at being a high society lady, and yet she was also distastefully superior.

A moment later, Leo found what she was looking for in the directory. "Here it is. Mr. Lawrence Wilkes. And even better." She thrust the directory into Jasper's hands and pointed to the listing. "Look at his profession."

On top of listing addresses and telephone exchanges, the directory also included each person's occupation.

"He's a chemist," Jasper read aloud, the interest back in his tone.

"Gabriela was poisoned," Leo added. "What if Mr. Wilkes didn't handle her marrying another man well?"

Jasper sighed and closed the directory. "All right. I'll track him down."

She threw up her arms. "That's it? No *thank you, Leo? What a remarkable memory you have, Leo?*"

Despite his withering glance, Jasper couldn't quite conceal the twitch of his mouth as he tried not to smile. "Goodnight, Leo."

Chapter Six

The London Polytechnic on Regent Street was not a fashionable institution, unlike Cambridge or Oxford or the University of London. Its students were generally middle or working class, their focus on attaining vocational skills rather than studying philosophy, law, history, languages, and theology. Had Jasper attended university after finishing at Cheltenham Boys School, the Poly would have been a good choice. However, he'd been rubbish at school and restless to *do* rather than to sit, read, learn, and read some more. So, he'd gone straight into the Met, determined not to cost the Inspector another penny—even though Gregory Reid had claimed to have enough set by to send him.

After the conversation with Mr. Stockton and the revelation of the Charles Street home's obscenely high property taxes, Jasper could not fathom how his father had been able to afford the tuition for Cheltenham. If he'd been an alms case, the boys at school would have reminded him of it tirelessly, just as they had the two other boys in their year who were there on charity. A part of Jasper now wondered if the Viscount Cowper had not rescinded the whole of his daughter's dowry. Or if there was some other way his father had held on to a portion of it.

Jasper put off the befuddling thoughts as he entered the Poly. He felt out of place in the halls. A bit long in the tooth too. The students rushing to their next classes appeared youthful and soft, even though they were likely no more than ten years his junior. They had a tender, untested look to them that he'd lost a long time ago, if he'd ever had it at all.

Jasper knew he was rough around the edges. He could be curt and impatient, and he couldn't place the blame on being a police officer. It was simply how he was built. Leo, of all people, understood that, but she'd still left the house in a huff last evening when he hadn't thanked her for the lead she'd supplied. He'd tried to ignore it but ended up stewing in a rare bit of guilt for the rest of the night. He should have said something, if not an outright thank you. Her exceptional memory had, once again, provided an avenue of inquiry, one that he wanted to believe would have shown itself during his investigation. However, it wasn't at all guaranteed. The lead had been helpful, and Jasper knew he had to acknowledge it—and simply grit his teeth and bear her gloating.

With some assistance from a passing student, he found his way to Lawrence Wilkes's office in the chemistry wing. After knocking, a voice from within called for him to enter. The office was small and cluttered, just as Jasper figured it would be. There were tables holding glass flasks and cylinders, racks and beakers and tubing. A few concoctions bubbling in crucibles above Bunsen burners gave the room a distinct sulfuric odor. A man in a worn tweed suit sat at his desk, busily writing. He was in his early thirties, with black hair swept away from his face and a liberal amount of pomade applied to hold it in place. He wore a pair of wire-rimmed spectacles on the tip of his nose, and he kept his eyes aimed at his notebook.

"Yes, what is it?" he asked with the tone of a beleaguered professor.

"Mr. Lawrence Wilkes?" Jasper had his warrant card open and ready when the chemist looked up to see that it wasn't a student who had entered his office.

He removed his spectacles and stood, wearing an instant expression of resignation. "You're here to speak about Gabriela."

Jasper folded the leather case holding his warrant card as the man came forward, gesturing for Jasper to enter and take a seat.

"I thought the police might come. Can I get you anything? Tea?"

"No, thank you, though I do have some questions to put to you."

"I figured you would. I saw the newspapers this morning. They said she'd been poisoned." He gestured to his table of chemical mixtures. "I am a chemist, after all, and I had every reason to be furious with her."

"Were you?" Jasper asked.

Mr. Wilkes frowned. "Yes. At least, I was at first."

Jasper took a few more steps into the office, still cautious. But this man wasn't Gabriela's killer. He was far too welcoming and eager to talk.

"Because she ended your engagement," Jasper presumed.

Mr. Wilkes nodded, his wounded pride still plain on his face. "I'd been employed by Mr. Henderson for a handful of years, and I'd spent most of that time admiring Gabriela from afar." He smiled sadly. "It was only when her father promoted me to his lead developer that she noticed me."

"You proposed?"

"Not right away, of course. We courted for several months before I worked up the courage."

"You thought she might refuse?"

Mr. Wilkes laughed at the question. "Of course, I did. She was the beautiful daughter of a wealthy businessman, and I was a lowly chemist. We weren't evenly matched."

A fleeting thought of Constance momentarily impeded Jasper's focus. Their match was uneven too. But he suspected that if he were to propose, she would accept. That might have been the reason why he was putting it off.

"But she did accept," Mr. Wilkes went on. "And we were happy. Until she met *him*."

Jasper caught on. "Andrew Carter."

Wilkes's face twisted into a knot of enmity. "A friend took her to a party. He was there. He became obsessed with her. Gabriela...she did try to resist him. I could see it. But really, I was no match for him. He was suave, confident, handsome. Dangerous, too, which made him even more alluring, I'm sure. He could offer her so much more."

And evidently, she'd given in to the temptation.

Wilkes had been leaning against his desk as he gave his account, his shoulders slowly drooping inward in defeat. But then, with a surge of determination, he pushed them back and stood taller. "As much as she hurt me, I didn't want her dead. If I was going to poison anyone, it would have been that bastard, Andrew Carter."

The thought had already crossed Jasper's mind: that the intended victim might not have been Gabriela, but her husband, a man who'd already cultivated an abundance of enemies.

"I have to ask where you were the night before last, around half past ten," Jasper said.

Wilkes slumped again. "Of course you do. I wasn't out poisoning anyone. I was at my lodgings at that time. My landlady can attest to it, as can the man who rooms across the landing. He complained about my playing the violin."

"At ten o'clock at night? I'd complain too," Jasper replied. Then, "You said you were the lead developer at Henderson & Son. What were you developing?"

The abrupt shift in topic was intentional. The Inspector had once told Jasper when he'd been new to the Met that questioning a suspect was much more effective when you kept spinning the focus from one subject to another. There was more opportunity for them to trip up and fall on their faces.

Wilkes took a moment to adjust. "New pigments for wallpaper. That's Henderson's business, as I'm sure you know."

He did, but only after reading the gossip column Leo

had given him the night before. "Were you let go after Gabriela changed her mind about your engagement?"

Wilkes flipped his hand in the air, waving off the question. "No, I left of my own accord after a disagreement with Jack Henderson."

"What was the disagreement about?"

The chemist went back to his chair and lowered himself into it as if exhausted. "It had nothing to do with Gabriela. It was about pigment. Scheele's green, specifically." Wilkes shifted in his seat as though thinking of something he hadn't considered before. "Oddly enough, the problem with Scheele's green has to do with arsenic. Jack refused to stop using it for his wallpaper. That specific green pigment is toxic, and some workers in the factory were being exposed to it and becoming ill. Customers too. Not that Jack cared."

The tingling of a suspicion lit up the base of Jasper's skull. He paid attention to it. The use of arsenic in things like paints and cleaning liquids, and for pest control was not unheard of, nor were the tales of accidental deaths. But for Henderson's daughter to die of arsenic poisoning was a link he couldn't overlook as coincidental.

"After several complaints were made against the company, none of which convinced him to change his mind, I knew I could no longer work for him," Wilkes finished. "So, here I am."

Jasper wasn't aware if this was a step down from being lead developer at a wallpaper manufacturing business, but he did know Wilkes wasn't lying. He could sniff out a lie like a hound might a fox. At least, he'd always thought he could. Sir Nathaniel Vickers had certainly fooled him. The man had been the Inspector's closest friend, and yet he'd sent his deputy assistant-cum-henchman, Benjamin Munson, after Jasper and Leo. The man had cornered them in the crypt beneath the morgue, intending to kill them and take the evidence they'd discovered. In the several minutes he'd spent trying to talk Munson back from the ledge followed by the brawl that ensued between them, Jasper experienced a fury unlike anything he'd known before. Sir Nathaniel's betrayal had cut him bone-deep.

He saw no such fury in Wilkes's eyes. Only sadness and acceptance.

"Thank you for your time, Mr. Wilkes," he said. But as Jasper walked toward the door, past the bubbling crucibles, he thought of one last question. "Did you have any contact with Gabriela or Andrew Carter after she called things off with you?"

"No." But he looked pensive, like he was thinking of something else.

"What is it?"

"It's probably nothing. I'd forgotten about it until now, but after Gabriela chose Carter, a woman came to see me. She worked at Henderson & Son. In fact, she was the one who introduced Gabriela to Carter, and it so happened that he threw her over in favor of my fiancée. She was distraught, and I think she wished to commiserate. But I wasn't inclined. I wanted nothing more to do with any of them."

Jasper took out his notebook and pencil. "Her name?"

"Miss Morris. Though, I don't know her first name. You should ask Carter. You've spoken to him too, I hope? The man is slime. A low-life thug."

His hatred for Andrew Carter turned the tips of his

ears red. If anything should happen to the East Rip in the near future, Jasper wouldn't hesitate to put Lawrence Wilkes on his list of suspects.

"Trust me, I know what he is." And in just a short while, Jasper would be coming face to face with him for the first time in sixteen years.

Chapter Seven

There were times—many of them, if Leo was being honest with herself—that she wished she did not have a perfect memory. A cutting remark, an embarrassing moment, a frightening event...these were all things regular people with regular memories could forget with the passage of time. The clarity of the memories would fade, turning them hazy at the edges, perhaps even lapsing entirely. While Leo never wished to suffer as her Aunt Flora did, she often envied other people their ability to forget.

However, there were other times when she was quite pleased her mind worked the way it did. Like yesterday, for example, when she'd recalled the gossip column and provided Jasper with a new suspect to question. He'd acted ungrateful for the tip, but that's all it was—an act. His competitive spirit might have been quiet for the most part, but it was nevertheless consistent.

At around noon, she reached the Yard, wondering how the interview with Mr. Wilkes had unfolded and what

Jasper had learned. However, she wasn't at headquarters just to see the detective inspector. An unidentified corpse had arrived at the morgue overnight, taken in by the night attendant, Mr. Sampson. Despite the ungainliness of her last brief interaction with Constable Elias Murray, they did have an arrangement, so she'd catalogued the details regarding the John Doe for a description in the *Gazette*. As soon as Claude had finished the postmortem—cleverly inviting Mr. Higgins to close with sutures to avoid any display of his own trembling hands—Leo had typed the report and the victim's description, then started for the Yard.

Upon arrival there, the call of the detective department was like a siren's song. If Jasper had returned from the Polytechnic, she could potentially needle him until he told her what Mr. Wilkes had conveyed in his interview. She turned away from the stairs leading toward the *Gazette* office, and went instead to the corridor leading to the C.I.D.

Much to her delight, Constable Wiley wasn't at his desk, guarding the premises from hysterical and over-imaginative females. Leo passed the unmanned desk and walked straight into the department room, which was occupied by a handful of desks, at which sat a few conversing detective constables and sergeants. Eyes turned in her direction. Usually, no one approached or spoke to her, and they didn't now, either. But she couldn't help but notice the glimpses were harsher than normal… and they lingered longer than usual too. Leo kept her eyes forward as she passed Detective Sergeant Lewis's desk. He wasn't there, but she didn't think he would have offered her any warmer of a welcome had he been.

After a perfunctory knock on Jasper's closed door, she turned the knob and whisked inside.

"I have a postmortem report for you, but I also—" Leo came to an abrupt halt.

Constable Wiley pushed off from Jasper's desk, where he'd been leaning casually, his arms crossed. Jasper wasn't present, but three other men were. One was seated in the chair placed in front of the desk, and two more stood, flanking him at his shoulders like stone pillars.

"What are you doing in here?" Constable Wiley hissed as he came toward her.

"Had you been at your own desk, constable, you might have asked then," she answered, her interest solely in the man who, upon her arrival, had unfolded himself from the chair.

Mr. Andrew Carter cocked his head as he took in the sight of her. Recognition lit his pale blue irises, but Constable Wiley snagged her arm and tried to hustle her toward the door.

"The lady can stay," Mr. Carter said, the command a clear admonishment for the constable's manhandling. "And you can leave."

It wasn't a suggestion. One of the two pillars next to Mr. Carter strode forward, and Constable Wiley all but tossed down her arm. He glared at her. "Inspector Reid's late. If he doesn't show up soon, the chief will hand him his own backside."

He spared Mr. Carter an uncertain and subservient grin and left the office, though he kept the door open. Leo was slightly comforted by that as she laid the folder with the John Doe's postmortem on the desk. The two men with Mr. Carter were large and muscled; she presumed they were his protective guards. Mr. Carter himself remained on his feet, his hawklike eyes fixed on her with an intensity she could only describe as dangerous.

"You were at Bloom's club," he stated. "You're the one who said Gabriela was poisoned."

She merely nodded. It wasn't like her to be so easily ruffled, but this was a Carter. A higher-up of the East Rips gang. She'd crossed paths with him at Striker's the other night, of course, but they hadn't conversed. He'd been anguished by his wife's death, utterly preoccupied. He hadn't stared at Leo then as he was now…like he suspected her of something.

Mr. Carter's eyes slid toward the folder she'd placed on Jasper's desk. "Who are you?"

"I…" She licked her lips. He didn't seem to know her name, and she was wary of giving it. Though she couldn't articulate why. "I'm early for my appointment with Inspector Reid. He wished to go over my statement about your wife's…death."

Murder had been on the tip of her tongue, but she'd thought it might provoke him. Barely concealed malevolence lingered in his icy blue stare. The man was furious, as any husband whose wife had been murdered would be.

"I'm told you saw a woman in a hooded cloak running away from my table," he said.

"I did, and I followed her," she said, "but she disappeared into the fog on the wharf."

Mr. Carter came a step closer, his intensity building. "What more can you remember about her?"

"Nothing."

"Her face?"

"As I already said, nothing." Belatedly, she realized

she'd been terse. The arch of his brow indicated he wasn't happy with her tone.

Still, Leo wasn't practiced at backing down, even when she was intimidated. "I do, however, recall that you were not with your wife when she became afflicted. It was only after I returned from trying to follow the cloaked woman that you arrived at your wife's side."

He flattened his arched brow and considered her observation for several seconds. "That's right," he said finally. "I was called away from our table for a short while."

"For what reason?" The question was out before she could think to withhold it. Incredulity flashed in his eyes. A perilous moment passed, her breathing quitting entirely. She expected one of his thugs to step forward in a threatening manner, as had happened with Constable Wiley. But slowly, Mr. Carter's lips peeled back into a sharp grin.

"I didn't realize you were a Scotland Yard detective." He laughed, but he wasn't trying to jest. He was pushing back, warning her against asking more questions.

Leo's initial apprehension of him withered under the challenge. She didn't like being bullied by anyone. Even a well-known criminal.

"I'm not, but I can't help but wonder if the woman in the hooded cloak waited until you'd left to approach the table and your wife." Another thought struck her just then. "You were called away from your table, you say? Might it not have been a coincidence?"

She'd already seen malevolence in his eyes, but now, a sudden savagery set her back on her heels. It drove him another alarming step closer.

"Are you suggesting I was drawn away from my table so that someone could poison my wife?"

The succinct theory gave her as much of a chill as the daunting Mr. Carter, who now loomed over her. "That depends on why you left and with whom you were meeting," she replied despite beginning to feel like tiny insects were crawling over the surface of her skin. "Who was it?"

He peered down his nose at her. "I don't discuss my private business with women I'm unacquainted with. So, tell me, what is your name, miss?"

Leo still wasn't inclined to give it. However, Mr. Carter looked as though he wouldn't stand for no answer from her.

In the corner of her vision, a figure filled the open office doorway.

"What is going on in here?"

At Jasper's raspy voice, Leo drew breath again. Slightly dizzy, she took a step in reverse, putting much needed space between herself and Mr. Carter. Purposefully, Jasper put himself into that space, his back to Leo, and his stare hinged on Andrew Carter.

Mr. Carter abandoned his harsh expression for one of mild amusement. "I was just making the acquaintance of Miss…?"

"The lady is leaving," Jasper said. He turned toward her, his sooty green eyes blazing with admonishment. He ushered her toward the door without laying a finger on her, although Leo was certain he wished to take her by the arm and toss her from the office just as Constable Wiley had tried to do.

"*Go*," he said under his breath, the muscles along his jaw jumping.

"I left a report on your desk—"

Jasper shut the door in her face. Leo bristled at the rude dismissal. But as she walked back through the detective department on somewhat shaky legs, she couldn't deny the surge of relief to be gone from Mr. Carter's presence. Being near him had felt like getting caught in a sticky web.

Passing a snidely smirking Constable Wiley at his desk, Leo thought of something more: Jasper had referred to her as 'the lady'. He hadn't wanted to give Mr. Carter her name any more than she did, and for that, she was grateful—and curious to know why.

Chapter Eight

Jasper waited to speak until his thundering heart slowed and the flash of his temper reduced to a simmer. He filled those seconds by removing his double-breasted coat and hat and sizing up Andrew Carter's hired muscle on his way to his desk. Carter likely went nowhere without protection.

"Thank you for waiting," Jasper said. He wouldn't apologize or give excuses for being late. To a man like Andrew Carter, it would signal submission.

A carriage accident on the way back from Regent Street had snarled traffic. Though he'd arrived at the Yard only ten minutes late, it put him at a disadvantage. Then, walking into his office to find Andrew standing over Leo in an intimidating posture had pulled the rug out from under him. She shouldn't have been there, alone with him. He'd wring Wiley's neck for allowing it, and then he'd hunt Leo down at the morgue and wring hers for good measure.

"Not to worry, Inspector. The young lady kept me

entertained," he said as he moved back toward a chair. "I didn't catch her name."

"She'll remain nameless." He met Andrew's cold, inspective stare. Jasper waited for a strike of recognition in the other man's eyes. Some glimmer of recollection. None came, and he exhaled discreetly.

"That's mysterious," Andrew replied. "You should know, it only deepens my interest in her."

Jasper clenched his jaw. If Andrew had seen that sodding article in the *Illustrated Police News*, he would have known her identity right off. The illustration of Leo had been well-done, and it had taken every ounce of Jasper's willpower that morning not to go to the weekly's offices first thing and demand to know who had drawn it. It would have been a shortsighted move. A visit from a Metropolitan Police detective would only indicate to the paper's editors that the short article had worth, and a follow-up piece would soon be printed. So instead, he'd gone about his morning, stewing, though hopeful that one article would be the last of it. Whoever the artist was, they'd observed Leo, as had whoever wrote the article. The idea of some faceless man watching her, digging for information about her, made him want to hit something. *Hard.*

The weekly tabloid had been among the other papers Mrs. Zhao laid out in his study last night, but his instinct had been to keep it hidden from Leo. It would upset her, to be sure, though he didn't think it likely she would remain oblivious much longer. Someone was bound to tell her about it.

"Lose your interest, Mr. Carter. She is an innocent

bystander in this case, and we'll speak no more of her," Jasper said.

Andrew chuckled as he sat and crossed a leg over his knee. "Innocent? She has more bollocks than most of you bobbies put together. Asked me a few pointed questions."

Jasper groaned quietly. Of course, she had.

"Well, now I will be asking you some pointed questions. I hope you'll cooperate, as I'm leading the investigation into your wife's murder."

He dropped his ingenuine grin. "I'll cooperate, Inspector. Not that I have any faith Scotland Yard will find the person who poisoned her, but I'll give you ten minutes to ask your questions."

"How generous of you," Jasper replied. "Where were you when your wife fell ill at the table?"

Andrew rubbed his chin. "A meeting."

No doubt some sort of criminal underworld dealing. "At Bloom's?"

"In the casino there."

Jasper hadn't known the club had a casino. It was likely a back room, closed off to anyone who didn't intend to wager seriously.

"What kind of meeting was this?"

If Bloom found out an East Rip had been doing business in his club, he'd have a problem with it.

"The friendly kind," Andrew answered, purposefully vague.

Jasper hadn't expected him to be as eager to help as Lawrence Wilkes had been. More than likely, he knew the husband was always the police's first suspect. And since most murdered women were killed by their husbands,

Jasper would not set aside the possibility that Andrew Carter was any different.

"How long did your meeting last?"

He shrugged. "I didn't keep tabs on the clock."

Leo's statement had been detailed, and knowing her as he did, it had also been accurate. "You returned to your table approximately three minutes after your wife's first signs of distress. Did you hear the commotion from inside in the casino?"

"I must have."

Impatience crawled along Jasper's limbs, but outwardly, he remained unflappable. "Who arranged for this meeting?"

Andrew sat forward, his elbows on the arms of the chair. "The mysterious lady you seek to protect asked the same question. Even suggested I was drawn away from my wife on purpose."

Jasper masked his surprise at Leo's shrewd theory. "Were you?"

"I don't take your meaning."

"Did the meeting go as planned? Was there something suspicious about it?"

If he'd been lured away from the table, the person who arranged for it might've had something to do with the poisoning. Andrew was intelligent enough to realize that.

"No comment," he answered.

Jasper knew how the East Rips operated. They meted out their own justice. If Andrew hadn't killed his wife, he would be actively hunting down the person he believed responsible. Sharing information with a Scotland Yard inspector would not happen.

"Had anyone been bothering Mrs. Carter lately?" he

asked next. "Is there anyone you can think of who might have wished her harm?"

Andrew huffed a laugh. "If anyone had been bothering my wife, I'd have taken care of it, Inspector."

"Is there anyone who'd wish to harm you through her? Any enemies of your own?"

The next laugh was the only genuine thing Andrew Carter had expressed since the interview began. "What do you think? Of course, I've got enemies."

"Anyone specific come to mind?"

"If someone does, I'll be sure to let you know," he replied, not even trying to mask his sarcasm.

"Were you and your wife having any difficulties lately?"

Andrew scoffed. "I didn't kill her. Whether you think me capable of it or not, I loved Gabriela. I'd just married her, for Christ's sake."

"Maybe you regretted that. Wanted out."

"Divorce is permitted these days, Inspector. A man doesn't have to resort to murder to get out of his marriage."

That morning, Jasper had sent Lewis to Barnaby & Davis, the Carters' solicitor in Pimlico, with a warrant to view the Carters' life insurance policies. Recently, an increase in policies being purchased in the city had proven a direct link to a surge of husbands killing their wives for a payout, and vice versa. There were even parents who took out policies on their children, then killed them for the money. However, what the common men and women who were intent on such evil had failed to understand was that coroners like Claude Feldman could detect what was and wasn't an accidental death. Their deeds were almost always discovered. And they made a hell of a lot of work for detectives like Jasper.

Andrew Carter checked his fob watch, counting down the seconds until his pledged ten minutes were up. He tucked it away, then cocked his head as he peered at Jasper.

"Have we met before? I don't usually forget a face."

Jasper's pulse slowed, the way it often did whenever he was preparing for a challenge. He'd worried about a moment like this, but he schooled his pulse, refusing to let it unravel at a wild pace. Logic calmed him. Sixteen years had passed since he'd last seen Andrew Carter, and Jasper looked nothing like he had back then as a thirteen-year-old boy. Neither did Andrew, who'd been roughly eight years old at the time. Jasper doubted their limited interactions had been all that memorable.

"We haven't," he answered shortly. "Tell me about Miss Morris."

The unexpected question creased Andrew's forehead. "Who?"

"The woman you were courting when you met Gabriela Henderson."

His confusion cleared. "Regina? I wasn't courting her. What does she have to do with any of this?"

Regina Morris. Jasper filed away the woman's full name.

"What was your relationship with her?" he asked.

Andrew frowned. "That's personal."

"It's a question I want answered," Jasper said. "Were you lovers?"

The East Rip sighed. "Yes. But we weren't anything

official, and I made it clear from the start that it wouldn't ever be that way."

"Why not?"

He waved a hand through the air. "I needed to make a stronger match when it came to marriage."

Jasper understood. "More lucrative, you mean."

"If you want to make it about money," Andrew said with a dismissive shrug.

Of course, it was about money. Jack Henderson and his business had to be worth a great deal, and he'd also have connections the Carters could exploit.

"Was Miss Morris upset about your marriage to Gabriela Henderson?" Jasper asked.

Andrew drew a deep breath, his fingers drumming on the arms of the chair. "You think she's the cloaked woman your mystery lady saw at Bloom's club?"

Jasper battled against showing a grimace. The last thing Leo should have been doing was discussing the case with the dead woman's husband, let alone giving a criminal someone on whom to focus his wrath.

"I didn't say that. When did you last see or speak to Miss Morris?"

"November. I ended things when I decided to marry Gabriela."

"How did she take the news?"

Andrew's expression said the answer should be obvious. "Sure, she was upset. But it was never anything serious with Regina. Hell, she's the one who introduced me to Gabriela."

It corroborated what Mr. Wilkes had told Jasper earlier. If Miss Morris had worked at the wallpaper factory and become friends with her employer's daughter, only to have the wealthy, beautiful Gabriela steal the attention and affection of the man she loved, that gave her quite the motive to exact revenge.

If Regina had approached Mr. Wilkes, wanting to commiserate together, the jilting must have affected her more deeply than Andrew seemed to realize. Deep enough for her anger to simmer for months until she finally developed a plan of revenge? Arsenic, according to Mr. Wilkes, was in ready supply at the wallpaper factory. Easy enough for Miss Morris to access.

"Your ten minutes are done." Andrew stood, but Jasper wasn't finished yet.

"They're done when I say they are." He took the photograph of the two dead children on the rocking horse from the case folder on his desk. "This was found in your wife's handbag."

Andrew scowled at the photograph. The two silent thugs at his side each peered at it with distaste too. "I've never seen it before."

Jasper didn't think he was lying. "Do the children look familiar?"

"I have no idea who these kiddies are, all right?" He pushed the photograph back, as if to get away from it. "If it was in her purse, I can't begin to tell you why."

Andrew started for the door, one hired man walking ahead of him and one behind.

Jasper raised his voice. "The waiter at Bloom's said there was already a drink on the table when he came over to take your orders. You told him not to clear it away. Why?"

Andrew sighed heavily and turned back, his impatience palpable. "Because Gabriela was still sipping it.

Listen, I know she was poisoned. The arsenic was in one of her drinks—"

Jasper came alert. "Who delivered that first drink? It wasn't Harry, who brought your whisky sour and her Spanish claret."

A look of concentration slid over Andrew Carter's sharp features. "I didn't look closely at the waiter, and I sure as hell don't know the names of Bloom's servers. They're all dressed alike anyhow."

"It was a man?" Jasper pressed.

"Yes," he answered tightly.

According to the postmortem report, it would have taken twenty minutes or so for the poison to take effect. Meaning the arsenic had been in Gabriela Carter's first drink, the one delivered by the mystery waiter. Andrew seemed to come to that conclusion at the same time.

"If you can remember anything about this first waiter—"

"He was big. Tall." He thought for a moment. "His hands barely fit into his white gloves. And he said the drink was compliments of Eddie Bloom."

"I don't believe Bloom sent that drink," Jasper said.

"I suppose we'll find out, won't we?"

"Mr. Carter, I'm going to find the person who poisoned your wife and bring them to justice within the bounds of the law," Jasper assured him as Andrew signaled his men that they were leaving. "I need you to not mete out your own brand of vigilante justice."

"Sure thing, Inspector," Andrew called over his shoulder, and then he was gone before Jasper could blink.

He let the tension out of his shoulders. Briefly, he considered sending Bloom a message that Andrew Carter might be paying him an unfriendly visit but then let it go. If two criminals came to blows, he wouldn't get in the middle of it. His focus lay in finding that first waiter and speaking to Miss Regina Morris.

Shortly after Andrew left the department, Lewis returned from Carter's solicitor in Pimlico. He shook his head as he came into Jasper's office. "Andrew Carter's not our man. He took out an insurance policy on himself to benefit Gabriela if anything happened to him. There's nothing on her though."

Without a policy in place on his wife, Carter had no motive to kill her for an insurance payout. Andrew claimed to have loved his wife, and it seemed he might have been telling the truth.

Jasper sat back in his chair, ruminating. "All right. But after my conversation with him, I think he knows more than he's saying."

He might even have leads that eluded Scotland Yard at the moment.

"We could ask Bridget what she's hearing," the detective sergeant suggested.

Bridget O'Mara was the owner of The Jugger, a pub near the St. Katharine Docks, right in the heart of East Rip territory. She was also one of the C.I.D.'s confidential informants. Whenever they wished to speak to her, they would purchase a deboned saddle of mutton, insert a note —giving a day and time—into the rolled-up loin, and send it to her at the pub. The meeting place was always the same: Trinity Square near Tower Hill. The joint of mutton was both a summons and a form of payment for her troubles.

Jasper nodded. "Tomorrow. Dawn. Send it."

"What do you think, ladies? If we were dead bodies, would Jasper be more interested in us?"

Lord Oliver Hayes received a gasp of amusement from the woman seated to his left, a Miss Helen Derring, and one of disapproval from the woman to his right, his cousin, Miss Constance Hayes.

"It is revolting to mention dead bodies at a dinner table, Oliver," Constance said with a shiver of disgust.

Apparently, Jasper had been staring into his cut crystal snifter of whisky for too long while the others had been in conversation. He couldn't recall anything that they'd said. Rouget's on Leicester Square was a far cry from the chophouses and taverns he'd frequented before he'd become friends with Oliver Hayes. At first, he'd rejected the viscount's invitations to dine with him at gentlemen's clubs and fine restaurants in the West End, preferring to eat among his own kind whenever he did go out.

However, when Jasper became acquainted with Constance and started to see her more regularly, he'd known a woman like her did not visit chophouses or dining rooms. So he'd fallen in line, eating at one fine restaurant after another, no matter how out of place he felt or how deeply the cost carved into his pockets. Most of the time, however, Oliver took care of the bill.

"Won't you try your soup?" Constance asked him. "It's crème d'asperges."

Jasper eyed the unappetizing, pale green puree in the bowl before him. "I'm not very hungry."

"I'm sure you would be if Mrs. Zhao were the chef

here," Oliver said with a laugh as he sat back in his chair, relaxing as he sipped his drink.

He didn't appear interested in the food either; his attention was thoroughly ensnared by Miss Derring. Despite the suggestive glances being exchanged between them, Jasper doubted he would see Miss Derring on Oliver's arm again after this evening; the viscount fell in love on a weekly basis. Sometimes nightly.

"What does that housekeeper of yours cook for you?" Constance asked as she spooned up her soup. "I do so look forward to meeting her and asking what your favorite foods are."

The levity of his dinner companions' conversation didn't usually rub him the wrong way. Tonight, however, Jasper felt ill at ease in their company.

Shifting in his seat, he queried, "Why? Do you plan to cook them for me?"

He doubted Constance had ever cooked a meal from scratch in her life.

Across the table, Miss Derring's eyes flashed and cut to Constance, whose expression instantly cooled.

He sighed. "Forgive me, that was rude."

She made no reply, pretending instead that he hadn't spoken.

The murmuring of the restaurant's other guests and the soft strains of a violin grew louder as silence engulfed their table. Oliver raised a brow at him in lighthearted reproach.

"Our Inspector Reid, always so serious."

He was correct; Jasper tended to be serious, not easy-going and affable like them. It didn't win him many friends, or even acquaintances. He had yet to determine what someone like Constance saw in him. She was as beautiful and charming as she was lively and modern. Her job at *The Times* was a dramatic break from her expected role of an aristocratic lady. As was courting a police inspector. Jasper keenly felt the differences in their backgrounds, with his always on full display.

Oftentimes, when he and Constance went out together, she was able to distract him from whatever miserable case he was investigating at the Yard. With her cheery disposition and glib humor, she was adept at drawing people to her, Jasper among them. Spending time with her felt like a retreat from reality, and ordinarily, he enjoyed the escape. Lately, however, he'd started to feel torn between the world Constance lived in and the one he inhabited.

He'd learned to stop talking about his work, as she had made it clear that she did not enjoy hearing about the grittier side of London. And yet, it was what his life revolved around; he spent more time at Scotland Yard than he did in his own home.

Thinking of 23 Charles Street now, he suddenly longed for the comfort and solitude of his study—though he knew he very well might find Leo there again. He pictured her seated in the Inspector's large chair, as she had been last night, her legs tucked up underneath her as she stared at her family's case file on the desk. She'd taken it with her this time. Though, he was nearly certain she still hadn't opened it.

"I'd wager Jasper's far too practical for favorite dishes, Connie," Oliver went on. "If he could, he'd exist on criminal cases alone. And whisky."

Oliver toasted them before taking another sip. It was

enough humor to move along the conversation, and Constance joined in, first telling her cousin not to call her Connie, and then discussing the gossip column she'd typed that day for *The Times*. Jasper followed the first few comments but soon lost interest as his mind turned toward Gabriela Carter's murder.

He'd spent the afternoon going through the list of employees Bloom had sent to the Yard. He, Lewis, and Constable Warnock had divided up the names and called on the waiters, even the ones who had not been working the night of Gabriela's poisoning.

None of them—seven in all—had been noticeably big or tall, with large hands ill-suited to serving gloves, as Andrew Carter had described. None had heard of a Regina Morris, and all had given explanations of where they'd been and the names of witnesses who'd confirm their alibis. It was looking more likely that the poisoner had stolen a bundle of black and white livery from either a storeroom at Bloom's club or from another waiter on staff. However, all waiters could produce their liveries when asked to do so.

By the time Jasper had turned his mind to visiting Miss Morris at Henderson & Son Manufacturing, it was already five o'clock. The trip to Wapping would have put him there past five thirty, and the young woman, whatever her position there, would have likely left for the day.

And then there had been his dinner with Constance and Oliver to prepare for this evening.

Jasper kept his hand on his snifter, slowly swirling the light amber liquid inside. It caught the glittering gaslights from the chandeliers and glowed. So did Constance, Oliver, and Miss Derring, it seemed. The three of them looked relaxed and merry inside this posh restaurant, while he, as usual, felt like a dark rain cloud about to split open on their sunny afternoon.

"I take it the Carter poisoning is what has you in a twist," Oliver said.

His friend was correct, but Gabriela's wasn't the only murder troubling him. There were some leads for her case and plenty of pressure from the Met to solve it. The same could not be said for the murder of the Jane Doe that continued to preoccupy him.

The Inspector had kept a desk drawer full of files belonging to unsolved cases that had haunted him, Leo's included. That the Jane Doe had been bludgeoned to death was horrific, but that she'd also been carrying a child had disturbed him even more deeply. He was cognizant as to why. Jasper had lost his mother in much the same way—a brutal beating. And while the Jane Doe hadn't yet been visibly with child, his own mother had been. The baby that would have been Jasper's sibling had died as well.

"The poor woman," Constance said, dabbing the corner of her mouth with her napkin. "I typed the notice of her wedding last month, though I thought she was mad for wanting to marry a known criminal. I'd wager the poisoned drink was meant for him."

"I considered that possibility," Jasper said. "But it doesn't line up with what we know so far."

He expected them to ask what that was. Then, he would have to tell them he wasn't at liberty to say. But their interests rested elsewhere.

"I can't believe it happened at Striker's Wharf," Miss

Derring said. "Have you been, Constance? It's an exciting place. The Blue Monsoon is to die for."

"The flaming punch? Isn't it divine?" Constance replied, taking a furtive glance at Jasper. She still hadn't forgiven him for that night in January and their argument afterward.

The two women settled into discussing the different entertainment venues they'd attended recently, and Jasper realized he hadn't accompanied Constance to any of them. He wondered, fleetingly, if any other gentleman had.

"Did I hear correctly that Miss Spencer was there at the time of Mrs. Carter's death?" Oliver asked while Miss Derring was speaking about a stuffy assembly room to which she refused to return.

Constance severed her attention from Miss Derring to ask, "What was she doing there?"

"She was with a friend," Jasper replied.

"Who is this Miss Spencer?" Miss Derring asked. "Do I know her?"

"Gracious, no," Constance replied, nearly choking on her sip of wine. "She isn't part of our set."

Jasper sat up straighter and addressed Oliver across the table. "Where did you hear she was at the club?"

"I had a drink with Commissioner Danvers last night," he answered with a blasé shrug. "He mentioned that she drew some attention to herself."

As Leo had helped depose the former police commissioner, Jasper imagined the new one was well aware of who she was. Sir Frederick Danvers had quietly praised Jasper for his work bringing his predecessor's crimes to light, but publicly, he'd been silent. He wanted the Met to move on and forget the entire debacle.

"You must tell me who she is," Miss Derring said, intrigued.

"While we are eating?" Oliver replied with a devilish grin. "You might regret asking."

"You can read all about her, Helen," Constance said with a rigid arch of her brow. "In this week's *Illustrated Police News*."

"What?" Oliver asked with a laugh of disbelief.

Miss Derring's mouth popped open. "What is she doing in that horrid rag?"

Jasper groaned. He'd expected talk about it would circulate. If Leo had not already learned of it, he'd be stunned.

"It's a profile of sorts," Constance answered. "Though I cannot understand what she was thinking by agreeing to such a thing."

"She didn't agree to anything," Jasper said. "Whoever wrote it did so without her knowledge." He was certain of it.

"What does the article say?" Miss Derring asked.

Before Constance could reply, Jasper interjected, "Miss Spencer assists the city coroner at the Spring Street Morgue." It did little to allay the woman's expected reaction.

"How gruesome!"

"The article mentioned that she assists in investigations at Scotland Yard as a sort of female detective," Constance said, looking pointedly at him. "I thought it was only that one time at the beginning of this year."

She assists in investigations at Scotland Yard—that particular sentence was a thorn in Jasper's side, and it would not have been well received at the Yard—*if* anyone there took the melodramatic news rag with any seriousness.

"She was involved in one of my cases, but otherwise, she types postmortem reports for the city coroner, that is all," Jasper said.

Her name had been kept to a minimum in the newspapers after the scandal with Sir Nathaniel, though everyone within the Metropolitan Police knew of the role she'd played in unmasking the commissioner's crimes. Why would anyone be writing about it and Leo now? He considered whether there was anyone new in her life. Mr. Higgins, the medical student, had been at the morgue for about two weeks, according to Leo. Plenty of time to gather information on her. But why would he wish to? And why write for a tabloid when he was studying medicine? Then, there was Flora Feldman's newest nurse. Mrs. Boardman, was it?

"How can she stand to work in such a wretched place?" Miss Derring asked. "She must be very strange."

"She isn't strange," Jasper said, becoming more and more irritated. "She has a different temperament than most ladies do."

Constance smirked and took another sip of her wine. Lowering her glass, she said, "I wonder if that temperament has anything to do with what happened to her family."

Miss Derring gasped. "What about her fam—?"

"We are finished speaking about Miss Spencer," Jasper cut in. The table went quiet. Oliver smothered a bemused grin as he drank his whisky.

"You're in a surly mood tonight, Jasper," Constance

remarked, her lips pouting. "The article on her has upset you."

"My bad mood has nothing to do with her or that bloody article."

It wasn't wholly true. The anonymous profile bothered him; it would only draw attention to Leo and to the unsolved murders of her family again. But his surly mood, as Constance had called it, also stemmed from having found Leo with Andrew Carter in his office earlier that day. She shouldn't have been anywhere near him, asking pointed questions. At least she'd had the foresight not to give him her name.

"I'm investigating a young woman's murder," Jasper clarified. "Forgive me if I'm not in the best humor."

"I've been thinking," Oliver said promptly, attempting to pierce the tension building between Jasper and Constance. "Now that your father is gone—God rest his soul—I don't see why you must continue as if he is still here. He was the one who cared for Miss Spencer all these years, wasn't he?"

Jasper suspected where the viscount was headed with his question and clenched his jaw, remaining silent.

"You are not family to her. I don't see why you should feel any sort of responsibility toward her." He finished his thought with a wave of his fingers.

The suggestion that Jasper should cast Leo off without thought or care slammed into him. He sat back in his chair. "I assure you I don't feel responsible for her at all."

It wasn't *responsibility* that he felt toward Leo. Jasper wasn't entirely sure what he felt, but he knew without question that it would never be indifference.

"Good. You shouldn't," Oliver replied. "Treat her as

you would any witness to a crime and be done with her." He raised a hand to signal the waiter. "Another bottle of wine."

Jasper threw his napkin on the table, no longer able to sit still. "None for me. In fact, I think I'll take my leave for the evening. You're right—I'm not good company at the moment."

It was rude to leave before dinner ended, but he didn't think he could endure any more speculative conversation. Especially if it had to do with Leonora Spencer. He'd only lose his temper and say things he regretted later.

"You are leaving?" Constance's mouth parted in obvious dismay. "We haven't been served the main course yet."

"You stay," Jasper said as he stood. "Oliver will take you home, I'm sure."

"Of course," the viscount replied, though he, too, appeared taken aback by Jasper's unceremonious departure.

Constance twisted away from him, refusing to meet his eyes as he bid them a good evening. He didn't blame her. She had every right to be peeved. Yet, as he left Rouget's, he found he didn't feel the slightest bit guilty. All he felt was relief.

Chapter Nine

Leo had counted on the day not ending without a visit and a verbal thrashing from Jasper. However, as the clock at the front of the house downstairs chimed the ten o'clock hour, she couldn't deny her surprise.

He hadn't come.

Not to the morgue after she'd left the detective department, nor to the house on Duke Street that evening. He was busy, to be sure. And she *should* have been relieved to have been spared one of his infuriatingly high-handed rebukes. But the truth was, she would have gritted her teeth and stomached it if it meant being able to hear what Jasper had learned from Mr. Wilkes at the Polytechnic and from Mr. Carter too.

Warm under the blanket on her bed, Leo still felt uneasy about her encounter with Gabriela's husband earlier that day. She'd never met one of the infamous Carters in person, though she could recall how Gregory Reid had once likened the East Rips family to cockroaches. *There is never just one,* he'd said with a roll of his eyes. The Carter family tree ran broad and deep, with tangled roots throughout London.

Andrew, the youngest brother of the gang's current leader, Sean, was undoubtedly a dangerous man. And yet, there had also been something slightly mesmerizing about him. Leo thought she might understand what had attracted Gabriela to him. Andrew Carter radiated power and confidence, and paired with his good looks, she imagined it could be an undeniable trifecta. Leo had been both repulsed and compelled by the man in the few minutes before Jasper had entered his office and summarily tossed her out.

She'd been so out of sorts from her encounter with him that she'd been halfway back to the morgue when she realized she'd entirely forgotten to bring the description of the John Doe to Elias Murray at the *Police Gazette* office. Strangely uninterested in returning to the Yard, she'd flagged a messenger boy and given him a penny to deliver it for her.

She couldn't sleep, so she picked up one of the books on her bedside table, a volume of travel memoirs penned by the wife of an archaeologist. The trouble was, Leo was vastly more interested in what the husband might have been excavating from the ancient layers of earth than the author's insipid descriptions of the Egyptian landscape and architecture.

A rapping on a door downstairs cut through the quiet house. Lowering the book, she slid out of bed and into her nightrobe and slippers. Halfway down the stairs, another round of knocking came, sounding more impatient this time. The visitor was at the back door, not the front. Immediately, she knew who it was. She groaned, wishing she hadn't put her hair up in curling wrappers, which made her appear all of twelve years old instead of twenty-five.

She hurried into the kitchen before another rapping on the door woke her aunt. Flora and Claude had turned in some time ago, but by routine, Leo left a paraffin lamp lit downstairs in the kitchen. Claude never rested easily and by midnight, he'd come downstairs for some warm milk and a biscuit before returning to bed.

Leo unlatched the chain, turned the bolt on the lock, and peeled the back door open a half inch. Her stomach somehow managed to lift and dive at the same time.

"Oh, so now you decide to show up," she said as she pulled the door open all the way. Jasper stood on the back step, his hands in his pockets, his frock coat unbuttoned.

He pressed down one brow, taking in the state of her. "Did I neglect an appointment we had tonight?"

Leo gestured for him to come inside. He carried with him a light scent of perfume and smoking tobacco. Paired with the black hat in his hand, the fine black, worsted wool suit he wore, and the silk tie speared with a silver stick pin in the center, it was obvious he'd been out that evening with either Constance Hayes or Lord Hayes, or both. She bit her tongue against asking; it wasn't her business.

Leo closed and locked the door again, but before she could make a reply, she felt a tug on one of her curling wrappers. She slapped Jasper's hand away and was startled when he cracked a rare, playful grin.

"Don't tease me," she said. "And don't wake Flora. She's had a difficult day."

It seemed all her days were difficult as of late. She'd

called Mrs. Boardman, her new nurse, by Leo's mother's name, Andromeda, for most of the day and raged incoherently as if in a one-sided argument.

She placed the kettle on the hob. "I suppose you're here to chastise me."

Jasper set his hat on the small wooden table, which she and Claude used for preparing meals and most nights, to sit around while eating. They rarely used the small dining room at the front of the house, preferring instead the simplicity of the kitchen.

Jasper kept his coat on and lowered himself into a chair, stretching his back into an arch as he sat. "I didn't like finding you in my office with Andrew Carter."

His voice was unexpectedly docile. Leo looked over her shoulder at him. "Is that all?"

"Isn't it enough? You asked him questions about the case. That is my job, not yours. You work in a morgue. You type reports. You do not question suspects in a murder investigation."

Now, *that* sounded more like his usual exasperation. She returned to scooping tight, folded leaves into the teapot and poured in hot water to steep.

"Yes, well, I'm not certain how much longer Claude and I will be at the morgue," she said as she pulled out a chair adjacent to his. She folded her arms on the table. "I believe Mr. Pritchard has placed this apprentice under my uncle's training for a reason: to replace him."

And once Claude was ejected from the morgue, Leo would no longer be welcome there either.

"Have you interacted much with him? Higgins, I mean," Jasper asked.

"Why do you ask that?"

He shook his head. "Just curious. When I saw him, he seemed uninterested in working at a morgue."

She watched him for a moment, skeptical. Jasper wasn't ever *just* curious. There was always some larger purpose for any inquiry he made. "I think Mr. Higgins is uninterested in working anywhere. Not that the chief coroner will care. The man is young and a family friend."

Mr. Pritchard, who oversaw several of the city's mortuaries, would support Chief Coroner Giles's appointment of Higgins in a heartbeat.

"What will you do if he takes over?" Jasper asked. She appreciated that he didn't try to tell her all would be well or that she was worrying for no reason.

"I'm not sure. I suppose I could apply to a funeral service like Hogarth and Tipson." Not being squeamish with the dead was a prerequisite she could meet, though she worried she might lack the necessary compassion and care for family members of the newly deceased. And then there would be the scent of white lilies to contend with. Funeral services were often overrun with them, and their sickly-sweet fragrance never failed to bring her back to the day her family had been interred at All Saints.

Jasper leaned forward, his elbows resting on the table. "You could be a matron at the Yard like Miss Brooks—*if* you could keep your nose out of the detective department."

She sent him a withering look. Becoming a matron was something she'd considered before, but it wouldn't work. "I've no interest in guarding women. And I've no ability with children. Dita tells me about her days, and I can't blame her for looking forward to giving up her post."

Jasper spun the empty teacup on its saucer before him. "She is leaving?"

"Not right away. But soon. She wants to marry and start a family."

Leo kept her lips sealed that Dita's prospective husband was PC Lloyd. Jasper wouldn't intend to say anything, but one slip, and Dita would be mortified.

Jasper kept spinning his teacup absentmindedly. Leo picked up the teapot; the leaves had brewed long enough, and besides, he was driving her mad with his fiddling.

"You could do that too," he said.

Leo placed a mesh strainer over his cup and poured. "Do what?"

"Marry."

Her wrist jerked involuntarily, and she nearly spilled the tea. She pulled the teapot back and stared at him. "I told you not to tease me."

"I'm not teasing."

She sighed and poured her cup next. "It's not in the cards for me."

He lifted his cup but didn't sip. "Why not?"

"Because I'm odd. You already know that," she replied, perhaps a touch more aggressively than was warranted. Leo lowered her voice. "I'm more comfortable around the dead than the living, and men don't like that in a lady, or so I'm told."

Jasper made no comment. Likely because he knew it was true.

"You're supposed to be shouting at me," she said, wanting to change the subject.

"I can't shout at someone wearing her hair the way you are."

She lowered her teacup to glare at him and found him smiling again. Two grins in one night? She wondered what was going on with him.

"They are curling wrappers, and most women wear them to bed. Now, tell me what Mr. Carter said after you threw me out."

He leaned back in his chair and sipped his tea. "I shouldn't say."

"But you're going to anyway?"

Jasper shook his head, but it was in defeat, not defiance. "He said the waiter who delivered the first drink to Gabriela—the one that had the arsenic in it—announced that it was compliments of Eddie Bloom."

"But you don't think Mr. Bloom sent it over," she guessed.

"No. Killing the wife of someone in an opposing gang would be reckless. Bloom is scum, but he isn't stupid. We questioned all of Bloom's waiters, but none of them knew who this man was."

"He was posing as a waiter in uniform?" Leo asked.

Jasper canted his head as if to say yes, probably.

"You don't suspect Mr. Carter, do you?" Leo hadn't. Not really. But she was suspicious of the meeting that had called him away from the table. Then again, if the arsenic was in Gabriela's first drink, the woman who came to sit with her arrived *after* she'd been poisoned.

"No." Jasper set his cup on its saucer. His hand looked too big for the delicate bone china. "I can't think of what he'd stand to gain by it. Not money, as she didn't have a life insurance policy attached to her. Plus, he's taken it upon himself to hunt the killer."

"I suspected that," Leo said. "He's quite intimidating, isn't he?"

It was the wrong thing to say. Jasper's expression darkened. "He'll do whatever it takes to get what he wants. I don't want him believing you know more than you do."

She adjusted her position in the chair, her legs beginning to feel a bit tingly.

"And Mr. Wilkes? Do you suspect him at all?" she asked, again to change the topic and erase his baleful expression.

"I don't." He then explained how Lawrence Wilkes had met Gabriela and how he'd lost her to Andrew Carter. As she listened to the sorry tale, Leo reached for the top hat Jasper had set on the table between them. She picked it up, running her fingers along the brushed midnight-black felt of the brim.

"It's odd, don't you think," Leo said, tracing the edges of his hat, "that Mr. Wilkes said arsenic was a contested chemical being used in Mr. Henderson's wallpaper pigments, and yet that is also how Gabriela died?"

"It might not be odd at all," Jasper replied. "Regina Morris made the mistake of introducing Gabriela to her beau. He threw over Regina, and she was upset enough to seek out Wilkes, wanting to commiserate. She was distraught. And working at the factory, she would've had access to the chemical."

Leo pictured the poor young woman, tossed aside like she was nothing. She felt sorry for her. But she knew why Jasper had now focused on her.

"You think she was the woman in the hooded cloak at Striker's Wharf."

He nodded, then sat forward, leaning his elbows on the table again. "Don't let this go to your head, Leo, but I think it would be permissible for you to come with me to Henderson & Son Manufacturing tomorrow when I speak to Miss Morris. I want to know if you recognize her from the club."

Even with his plea not to let it go to her head, elation lit through her at the invitation. She then deflated a little. "I didn't see her face. Dita saw her more fully than I did."

"Miss Brooks can come with us," he replied.

Above their heads, a floorboard creaked in Flora and Claude's room. At the sound, Jasper stood. He eyed his hat, still in Leo's hands.

She stood and handed it over. "It's quite a nice hat."

"Thank you," he said, without putting it on.

"Were you out dining with Miss Hayes?"

Jasper took a long breath, seeming uncomfortable with the question.

"Forgive me, I shouldn't have asked." Leo started away from the table, wishing she'd held her tongue. He always grumbled when she brought up Constance.

Jasper caught her wrist as she passed him. The surprising touch brought her to a stop, though more than just her feet went still. Everything inside her went quiet too.

"I'm not upset you asked." His fingers flexed lightly around her wrist. They were warm and unexpectedly coarse. "It just wasn't an enjoyable dinner."

"Oh?" Leo's interest in what had happened piqued as Jasper frowned. She grew increasingly aware of his hand on her wrist as he continued to hold it.

"It's nothing," he said after a moment. His grip lightened, then let go. As her arm fell back to her side, the pads of his fingertips brushed past her palm. A bewildering shiver raced along her spine.

Jasper held her gaze, and she wondered if he'd witnessed the shudder. But then, he moved past her. "I'll go out through the back."

It would, after all, be unseemly for a gentleman to enter or leave through the front door at so late an hour and with Leo in her nightrobe too. She suddenly felt discomfited at having had tea with Jasper while wearing her night things. And her hair in wrappers, for heaven's sake!

"I'll come around tomorrow at nine o'clock," he said as he opened the kitchen door, which emptied into a narrow lane used for deliveries.

"Goodnight," she said, but he'd already closed the door behind him.

Chapter Ten

It had been a clear, cold night, and as Jasper took a seat on a bench inside Trinity Square just before dawn, the pale face of the moon still hung on the horizon, surrounded by sharp stars. He'd barely slept, and not just because he'd had to set out well before sunrise to make his meeting with Bridget O'Mara. Dawn was the only time of day she could leave her busy tavern without anyone observing, and he didn't want her to be caught.

No, he'd barely slept because of his visit with Leo the night before.

Jasper had left Rouget's in a hansom cab, fully intending to return home. But as he'd sorted through the Carter case and plotted out his next moves, he'd redirected the cabbie. He needed to speak to Regina Morris, and as Leo had seen the woman in the hooded cloak at Striker's, it made sense to bring her along with the hope she might recognize her. He'd also planned to scold her for questioning Andrew Carter. But when Leo let him into the kitchen, wearing her nightrobe, slippers, and hair wrappers, his bad mood had transformed into amusement.

At the kitchen table, conversation between them had been easy. He'd been transfixed by her fingers as they slid along the brim of his hat while she mused over the case. But he'd made a mistake. He shouldn't have touched her to stop her from pushing past him. Hell, he'd practically been holding her hand. He'd been surprised at how small and delicate her wrist had been within his grasp. Leo hardly ever gave the impression of being fragile, but now and then, she let down her guard, and he could see it.

The chill of the pre-dawn air helped to drive out the disturbance he'd felt just under his skin since leaving her a handful of hours ago. He sat on the bench, his hands deep in his pockets to stave off total numbness. The gardens of the square had grown bleak and brittle over the winter, and from where Jasper sat, the equally austere Tower of London was a gray stamp against the coming dawn. The fortress, surrounded by tall walls and a dry ditch, had held scores of prisoners over the years, most of them accused of treason to the Crown. There was some irony that the meeting point with Bridget O'Mara took place within view of the notorious Tower Green, where those found guilty of treason were relieved of their heads.

Should anyone from within the East Rips ever learn the Jugger's doyenne whispered their secrets to Scotland Yard, she could very well meet a similar end. It wasn't as if she took the risk out of the goodness of her own heart. She'd only agreed to the deceit when her own life had hung in the balance.

A few years ago, she'd been taken into custody for killing her husband. Billy O'Mara, ex-convict and all-around rotten apple, had broken his neck after being pushed down a flight of steps at the tavern he owned. A tearful and shocked Bridget had confessed to giving him the shove. He'd been knocking her about, as he usually did, and she'd finally had enough. Detective Chief Inspector Coughlan didn't have any reason not to book her and send her to what would be a quick and damning trial. But instead, he'd given her a second option. Keep her eyes and ears open to news of the East Rips and the Carter family and agree to assist the police on an occasional basis, and all charges would be dropped. Billy O'Mara's death would be ruled accidental, and she would be free to return home to her young son.

Jasper didn't like summoning her. He would have rather let her go about her life. However, she was an informant, and he needed to know what the chatter was among the East Rips regarding the poisoning of Gabriela Carter.

A woman, cloaked and hooded, appeared across the square. Jasper stood. With the sky still a bruised blue, and only a few streaks of orange to hint at the coming sun, he couldn't make out her face, but it was certainly Bridget. She was tall for a woman, standing at nearly six feet, and was generously figured. She possessed a distinctive sway of her hips when she walked too, and now she cut through the lawn and toward his bench, direct and blunt as usual.

"I got five minutes," she said upon greeting him. "My boy's feverish, and some sailor is out back of my pub, half-pissed. What do the bobbies want with me this time?"

Bridget was as stern as any East End woman who owned an alehouse would need to be, but Jasper thought he knew why Chief Coughlan had softened toward her. Despite being a little older, around forty, she was striking in appearance. Perhaps her finest feature was her big, doe-like brown eyes, which constantly looked to be pleading for mercy. He imagined they could easily mesmerize any man with half a heart, especially when they shone with tears.

"Andrew Carter's wife," Jasper said, getting to the point, just as she preferred. "You've heard what happened?"

Bridget nodded. "'Course."

"What have you been hearing?"

She drew the flannel wrap she wore closer around her and shrugged. "Nothin' much. Everyone's too scared of sayin' the wrong thing, what with him actin' half-mad."

Jasper nodded, understanding. Drawing Andrew Carter's attention at any time was unwise; while he was mourning his wife and hunting her killer, it would be downright stupid.

"But you've heard some talk?" he pressed, knowing she had. The Jugger was a popular place near the St. Katharine Docks and was busy all day and night, except for these early morning hours.

Bridget sighed, her breath clouding the air. "Aye, some. He thought some bloke, what drew him into a game of cards at that club, might've lured him from his table so's that his wife could be offed."

It was the theory Leo had posed to Andrew, and then Andrew to Jasper.

"And?" Jasper said.

"And the bloke lost two fingers to an East Rip

bladesman before Carter was convinced he had naught to do with it."

Jasper's stomach dove. "Christ."

Bridget snorted a laugh. "I say he's lucky. He's still breathin', ain't he?"

A pair of old men shuffled into the garden square, and a lamplighter was making his way along the street, climbing his ladder to extinguish the gas jets. Dawn slid up on the horizon.

"Has he questioned anyone else that you know of?" Jasper asked.

Bridget nodded, looking fatigued. "Her old beau."

With a twinge of concern for the chemist, Jasper asked, "What happened to him?"

"I hear he's still alive too."

"Hopefully with all his appendages intact," he muttered, furious with Andrew's violent approach. How could he count on the veracity of the answers he received if they were given under duress? It was bloody and brutish, not to mention dishonorable.

Bridget shrugged, as if not caring one way or another if anyone lost a finger or two. She couldn't afford to be concerned with anyone or anything if it didn't have to do with her, her business, or her son.

"He's been searchin' for a woman, I hear," she said. "Someone he used to step out with. Can't find her though."

"Regina Morris?"

She shrugged. "That could be the name, yeah."

If Andrew couldn't find her, Jasper wondered if she'd gone into hiding. If she had, then she was certainly guilty of something. And his trip to Wapping later that morning with Leo and Nivedita Brooks might not bear any fruit after all.

As the rising sun hit the peaks of the White Tower's four turrets, Bridget cocked her head. "You remind me of someone, copper."

Jasper never liked to hear that line. "Do I?"

"A woman I knew, went by the name of Vera."

His spine went rigid, his muscles locking up tight as a heat flashed through him, followed by a surge of cold. *Vera*. He hadn't heard that name spoken in a long time.

"Been dead nigh on twenty years," Bridget continued, still studying his face. "But you've got the look of her, you do. I've been tryin' to place it the last few times we met."

"I don't know anyone by that name," he said, swallowing the bitter lie with practiced ease.

"Like I said, she's dead. Killed, she was. Had herself a boy and a babe on the way when it happened."

The cold, thin air turned thick and stifling. With a feeling of suffocation, Jasper stepped away from Bridget. He reached into his pocket for his watch, the urge to leave overwhelming.

"What does this have to do with Andrew Carter?" he asked brusquely.

Her doe eyes continued to peer at him inquisitively. "Nothin', I suppose. Just thought you looked like her."

He put away his watch. "All right, thank you for your time, Mrs. O'Mara." He tipped the brim of his hat. "Enjoy the mutton."

"Always do," she replied. This time, she wasn't the first to turn and walk away. Jasper was, and he felt her eyes between his shoulder blades as he left.

His stomach had yet to uncoil by the time he entered the East End for the second time that morning. Though it was only after ten o'clock, his eyes burned from fatigue. His back ached from traveling the roads to Trinity Square, back to Westminster, and then to Wapping. When they arrived, he alighted from the hired cab, relieved to stand and stretch.

Situated on the north bank of the Thames near the London Docks, the air there had a salty flavor. Wapping was primarily occupied by trades dedicated to seafarers who docked their ships in the harbor's man-made pools, but other businesses and factories had set up in the area too, attracting laborers and tradesmen—among them, Henderson & Son Manufacturing.

Jasper helped Leo and Miss Brooks descend from the cab, the latter of whom was wearing her matron's uniform and an irrepressible expression of interest. Dita, as Leo called her, had been more than willing to come along to Henderson's factory in the hope of identifying the lady in the hooded cloak.

"I didn't see her face, mind you," she'd said when Jasper had collected them both at Leo's house on Duke Street. "But the light blue embroidery on her cloak should be recognizable, if she has worn it to work."

It would at least be enough to bring Miss Morris down to Scotland Yard for questioning. That was, if they could find her there. The factory would certainly have been among the places Andrew Carter would have looked for his former lover. If she was laying low, she might also be avoiding her place of work. Still, it was worth a try.

The ride to the East End docklands had been relatively quiet, with Miss Brooks carrying most of the conversation. As outgoing and gregarious as the police matron was, it only served to highlight Leo's own reserved and cautious personality. And his own. They were traits Jasper understood and respected, and it was why his blunder with Bridget O'Mara earlier weighed so heavily. He hadn't been cautious enough. Hell, he should have sent Lewis to meet with her, not gone himself.

Vera. His mother's name had always seemed too elegant and strong for her. She'd been quiet and submissive, afraid of her own shadow, it seemed to him when he'd been young. After his father's death, which Jasper didn't remember, she'd remained tied to her husband's family. Specifically, to his cousin, Robert. Jasper had called him *uncle*, though he wasn't that.

It had been imprudent of him not to consider that he might have grown to resemble his mother. But what were the chances that the C.I.D.'s informant, of all people, would remember Vera enough to draw a connection between them?

She had a boy and a babe on the way. Damn it. He needed to focus on the investigation, not Bridget O'Mara's words.

Jasper asked the driver to wait and then started for the large brick building. A wide, gated yard ran alongside it, packed with drays and crates and laborers. Black smoke pumped from twin stacks on the roof of the factory. Lettering carved from wood and painted black, hung on the exterior brick, spelling out the company name.

The front entrance brought them into a lobby. It also appeared to be a showroom for wallpaper designs. Samples hung on accordion racks, and a wall of cubed recesses held rolls upon rolls of wallpaper, many of them featuring bright green pigments. A woman stood from a desk to greet them.

"May I help you?"

Jasper showed her his warrant card as he first introduced himself, then Leo and Miss Brooks. The woman's friendly expression dissipated.

"You're here about Miss Henderson. I mean, Mrs. Carter," she said, correcting herself quickly.

Jasper took in the woman's appearance. She appeared a decade too old to be Regina Morris. Lawrence Wilkes had described her as younger than twenty-five and pretty. This woman was handsome, but she was at least thirty-five, perhaps forty. Gray streaked her blond hair, and the first lines of age surrounded her mouth and eyes.

"We'd like to speak to Mr. Henderson," he told her. "Is he in?"

The woman winced. "He is, but he's in quite a state."

It might have been hard-hearted of him, but Gabriela's father being in 'a state' was exactly what Jasper had been hoping for. He'd yet to speak to Jack Henderson; Carter, Wilkes, and Bloom's waiters all had stronger motives and opportunities to have lashed out. Regina Morris too. However, it was his duty to consider all those who were known to Gabriela.

"Let him know we're here, thank you, Miss…?" Jasper instructed.

She faltered, not understanding that he was asking for her name. But then, she jumped with the realization. "Geary, Inspector. Miss Geary."

She bobbed her head and left the showroom through a

door behind her desk. Jasper turned toward Leo and Miss Brooks. "When we are speaking with Mr. Henderson—"

"Let you do the talking," Leo recited as she rolled her eyes. "Yes, I know."

Miss Brooks bit back a smile at Leo's exasperation.

The secretary returned to show them into an office encumbered by what looked to be years of accumulated possessions: papers, trinkets, framed photographs and paintings, boxes of rolled wallpaper, shelves of ledgers, all arranged haphazardly. A haze of cigar smoke lingered near the wattle and daub ceiling. A large man with a ring of silver-speckled black hair, combed around a liver-spotted pate, waited for them in front of his desk, the top of which could not be seen beneath the detritus.

"Either tell me you've arrested the bastard who killed my daughter or get out."

Disgruntled family members were no rare thing. By now, Jasper knew not to show his belly by bowing and scraping nor to be too high in the instep.

"No one has been placed under arrest yet, Mr. Henderson—"

"Bloody incompetent fools!" he shouted before popping a lit cigar back into his mouth.

"However, the investigation is progressing," Jasper went on, as if the man had not spoken. "May I introduce Miss Spencer and Miss Brooks. They were both at the dance hall at the time of your daughter's death."

The man frowned at Leo and Dita. "Why have you come?"

Leo parted her lips to answer, but Jasper beat her to it. "I've some questions for you and for one of your employees."

Mr. Henderson removed the cigar. "You should be questioning that damnable Carter. All of this is his doing. I didn't want my Gabriela to marry the bastard in the first place!" He gesticulated wildly toward Miss Geary in dismissal, who scuttled out of the office, closing the door behind her.

"You aren't on good terms with your son-in-law?" Jasper presumed.

The man scoffed and returned to puffing on his cigar, giving no answer.

"Were you on good terms with Gabriela?" he tried next.

At this, Mr. Henderson seemed to deflate. After pausing, he answered, "We hadn't spoken since the wedding."

Jasper sensed he felt sadness for that, rather than anger.

"Can you think of any enemies Mr. Carter has, or those your daughter might have had? Anyone who may have wished her harm?"

The answer to this standard question was almost always *no*, which was less than helpful.

"Andrew Carter doesn't go anywhere without forming a new enemy," Henderson said with a huff of derision. "However, Gabriela was kindness itself. The girl was unfailingly sweet and caring. All I can think is that he took advantage of her natural disposition. Manipulated her into marrying him."

Mr. Henderson's hatred for Andrew sparked Jasper's interest; it might have led him to attempt to be rid of his son-in-law entirely. All they had was Andrew's word that the drink had been meant for Gabriela, *compliments of Mr. Bloom*. It was entirely possible the drink had been delivered to *him*, and Gabriela had taken it. Then, when she died as a result, Andrew realized he'd been the original target. His animosity toward the police would lead him to keep this information to himself and seek vengeance all on his own, outside the bounds of the law. It was, after all, how the East Rips and every other gang in the city operated.

But Mr. Henderson would have been risking much by arranging for a deadly drink to be delivered to his daughter's table. Who was to say she wouldn't sip it? There were other, more direct ways to be rid of someone. Besides, men usually did not select poison as their murder weapon of choice.

"I'd like to speak to a woman you employ here, Miss Regina Morris," Jasper said. "It's possible she was seen at Striker's Wharf that evening, sitting with your daughter just before her death. Miss Spencer and Miss Brooks can verify her presence, if indeed it was her."

The cigar smoke was clouding the room more rapidly, with no window through which to vent it. The haze reminded him of the gentlemen's clubs Oliver brought him to, where upper-class men smoked, drank, boxed, and whored. Jasper partook in the first three without compunction, and the fourth only irregularly before he'd started seeing Constance, always with a bit of self-reproach afterward. It had been some time since he'd indulged at a club with Oliver. Though it wasn't a thought he should be entertaining just now.

Mr. Henderson stubbed out his cigar. "Miss Morris was my son's secretary. You say she was with Gabriela that night?"

"Was? You mean to say she is no longer employed here?" Leo asked, speaking up before Jasper could.

"She certainly isn't," Mr. Henderson answered. "She quit her position without so much as a say-so in person. Left a note on David's desk! A note—after two years of employment here. My son was utterly staggered."

"When was this?" Leo asked, again cutting off Jasper. He sent her a quelling look, which she pretended not to see.

"Last month."

She'd disappeared *last month*? Jasper frowned.

"Around the same time as your daughter's wedding to Mr. Carter?" he asked.

"I suppose so, yes. Why?"

"Were you aware Miss Morris was courting Mr. Carter before he met Gabriela?" Leo asked, again not paying any mind to Jasper's look of reprimand.

"Of course, I wasn't bloody aware! I don't keep tabs on my employees' love lives. Do I look like a gossip column in the godforsaken newspapers?"

Jasper raised his hand, having had enough of the man's blustering. "Mr. Henderson, you're entitled to your grief, but I'll ask you to hold your tongue against any more outbursts. We are here to help. Now, I'll need Miss Morris's home address."

The manufacturer fumed as though wanting to command him to leave, but his temper lowered enough for him to decipher the reason for Jasper's request.

"You think she has something to do with Gabriela's death?"

"We're following all leads and possibilities," Jasper

replied, giving the standard, vague reply to keep anyone from jumping to conclusions.

Mr. Henderson shouted for his secretary through the closed door, and a moment later, she rushed inside.

Leo turned to Jasper. "Show him the photograph."

"What photograph is this?" Miss Brooks asked.

"I'd planned to show it to him, thank you," Jasper grumbled, reaching into his coat pocket while Mr. Henderson ordered Regina Morris's employment file to be brought forward.

As soon as the secretary left on her task, Jasper turned the death portrait outward for Mr. Henderson to view.

"Any idea why your daughter would have had this in her handbag?"

The man tucked his chin and grimaced. "Absolutely not. Who are those children?"

"Someone may have given it to her the night she was poisoned," Leo answered. Jasper gritted his molars and gave up; the woman was unbiddable. "Possibly Miss Morris. She and Gabriela were friends, were they not?"

He tossed up a hand. "If she was friends with Miss Morris, it wasn't brought to my attention. I say, if Carter gave my son's secretary the old heave-ho, she would've had her nose out of joint about the marriage, wouldn't she? And since you're looking into her, you should also find Lawrence Wilkes. He and Gabriela were due to marry, but she threw the poor sod over when Carter started coming around. The man was furious."

"I've already found and spoken to Mr. Wilkes," Jasper replied as Miss Brooks came up beside him for a glimpse of the photograph. She gasped in dismay and quickly stepped away again. "I don't believe he was involved. He also has an alibi for the night of Gabriela's death."

"Well, look into him again, Inspector. Wilkes hates this family. Tried to get my business shut down entirely."

Jasper shook his head. "Mr. Wilkes was concerned about your business because of the complaints made against your wallpapers. It wasn't about Gabriela's rejection of him."

Miss Brooks, who still appeared nauseated by the photograph of the two children, perked. "What sort of complaints?"

"The green pigments in the paper are toxic," Leo explained. "They've made some people ill."

"Utterly unfounded," Henderson said. "Manufacturers have been using chemicals to brighten the color green for decades. If it was really as bad as they say, everyone would be ill and dying, wouldn't they?"

Leo caught Miss Brooks's eye. "Arsenic, specifically."

Her friend raised a brow, understanding the link now.

"I'm telling you, Wilkes is your man. I don't care what he claims; he never had a problem with the way this factory operated until after Gabriela threw him over."

The photograph of the two unknown children on Mr. Henderson's desk seemed to glow as an idea formed. Jasper asked, "Do you keep records of these complaints, Mr. Henderson?"

The man grumbled again. "My solicitor tells me I must, so I do. But you are wasting your time."

Miss Geary returned with a piece of paper. "The address we have on file for Miss Morris, sir." She handed it directly to Jasper. Her attention landed on the death photography, and her eyes widened with shock.

"Apologies, madam." Jasper swiftly collected the photograph and pocketed it, along with the proffered address. "Mr. Henderson, I'd like all the complaints your business has received for the last five years."

Mr. Henderson drilled him with a glare, then shot it toward his secretary. "Pull the complaints file."

"The complaints?" Miss Geary asked, looking between her employer and Jasper.

"Yes! The company complaints, as I said. All the settlements and what have you. They're on a shelf in here somewhere. If the Inspector would like them, he may have them, though little good they will do in finding my daughter's killer."

Miss Geary hurried to the wall of shelves as if her heels had been lit on fire. Jasper's patience was quickly wearing thin with this man. It seemed to him that Gabriela may have had a good reason for not speaking to her father; then again, Jasper might have broiled with the same frustrated anger if he ever had a daughter who elected to marry into a crime family.

While Leo had stayed at Jasper's side, Miss Brooks had turned to have a look around the small office. She'd come to a stop at one of the framed photographs on the wall. It was a panorama of what appeared to be employees gathered for a pose in front of the factory.

"Is Miss Morris in this photograph?" she asked. "Perhaps we can recognize her from it."

Leo started for the framed photograph, as did Mr. Henderson while muttering under his breath. Looking greatly hassled, he peered at the picture, then tapped a spot on the glass.

"Right here."

He dropped his hand, and Leo took a closer look. Her pointer finger rose to the glass. "*This* woman is Regina Morris?"

"Yes, as I said," he huffed before striding back to his desk.

Alarm brightened her hazel irises, and when she turned them onto Jasper, the small hairs along his forearms stood on end.

"What is it?" he asked.

"Come look," she replied.

Approaching the panorama, Jasper saw the joined smudges of Henderson's and Leo's fingerprints resting at the feet of a woman in the front row. Her dark hair was pulled up into a stylish bun, and her lips were pursed into a straight line as she waited impatiently for the photographer to capture the panoramic image. Jasper's pulse stuttered. His skin tightened. He knew this woman. She had lingered in his mind, haunting him for the last four weeks.

"Will someone bloody well tell me what is going on?" Mr. Henderson's voice sounded far away under the rush of blood swirling through Jasper's ears.

"I'm sorry, Mr. Henderson," Jasper said. "But your son's secretary didn't just quit. She was killed."

The Jane Doe he'd been investigating, found bludgeoned to death a month ago, now had a name: Miss Regina Morris.

Chapter Eleven

Leo placed the small, green enamel cup in front of Miss Geary. The black tea inside sent up a cloud of steam. The secretary had been pulling a thick folder from one of Mr. Henderson's office shelves when Jasper announced Miss Morris had been killed. The folder had slapped onto the floor, papers spilling free, as the secretary, already frazzled by her employer's curt demands, lost her grip. Her palms had flown to her cheeks, her shock unchecked. Such a strong reaction could only mean one thing—she'd been close to Regina Morris. Perhaps even a friend.

Jasper had quickly explained about the young woman found dead, killed by a severe blow to the skull, roughly four weeks ago. They'd been unable to identify her and thus, unable to arrest a suspect, but thanks to the photograph in the frame, he could now reopen the case. "I'm going to need to speak to your son," he'd told Mr. Henderson.

Even more inflamed than before, the man stormed

from his office. Dita had immediately gone to help Miss Geary, who was crouching to pick up the contents of the dropped folder. Pausing next to Leo's shoulder, Jasper had leaned close, lowering his mouth to her ear. "The secretary," he'd whispered. With a prickling down her back and along her scalp, she'd nodded in understanding.

As Jasper followed Mr. Henderson from the office, Leo asked Miss Geary if the factory had a canteen where she might be able to sit and have a cup of tea to calm her. With trembling hands, the woman gave the recovered folder to Dita and led them deeper into the building. The workers had a lunchroom near the production floor, where the drone of machines could be heard printing wallpaper. The tangy, mixed odors of oil, smoke, and paint threatened to make Leo's head dizzy as they took seats at one of the four long wooden tables in the room. A hatch in the wall opened to a small kitchen, where Leo purchased a pot of tea for the three of them from an unsmiling older woman in a headscarf.

Now, Miss Geary held the cup between her palms and breathed evenly. "Yes, I knew Regina. Not very well, but we were friendly," she said, answering the first of Leo's questions.

Her inquiries were lined up, ready to fly, and yet Leo knew she was in a precarious spot. Jasper expected her to come away with helpful information from Miss Geary; if she succeeded, perhaps he would be less inclined to complain and stonewall her whenever she offered to lend a hand. That meant she needed to proceed with patience and care.

"You worked with her for two years?" Leo asked,

recalling the length of time Mr. Henderson said Miss Morris had been employed.

"No, just these last six months that I've been here."

Dita crossed her arms over the complaints folder and listened intently, her dark brown eyes meeting Leo's with awareness. She knew what Leo was doing.

"She left her position rather abruptly," Dita commented. "It must have surprised you."

"It surprised everyone," Miss Geary replied. "Mr. Henderson, especially. The younger, I mean. David."

"Do you think it had to do with Gabriela winning Mr. Carter's affections?" Leo asked, thinking of the element in the Jane Doe case that had most affected Jasper: she'd been with child. Leo hadn't understood why he'd been so disturbed by this finding; they'd both seen their share of dead children. Including babies. It was always heartbreaking, and yet this Jane Doe had shaken him more deeply when he'd come to view the body and discuss the autopsy findings.

Miss Geary nodded. "It must have. I didn't realize Regina had been seeing one of the Carters, but when rumors struck up that Gabriela had ended her engagement and was marrying Andrew Carter instead...well, Regina was inconsolable."

Taking into consideration the approximate gestation of the unborn baby—between thirteen and fifteen weeks at postmortem—it was possible Andrew Carter had been the father. Had Regina only discovered she was expecting after he'd become engaged to another woman? It would be a strong motive for wanting to be rid of Gabriela—but as she had been dead for over a month now, Regina could not have poisoned her, nor could she have been the woman in the hooded cloak at Striker's.

"I should tell you that he was here," Miss Geary sighed resignedly. "Yesterday, in fact."

Leo blinked. "Mr. Carter was here?"

At her nod, a spate of cold dread spiraled from Leo's chest down into her stomach. Just the thought of Andrew Carter seemed to affect her with an uneasy chill.

"He asked to see Regina," Miss Geary said. "I told him she quit a month ago, but he didn't believe me. I finally had to ask Mr. Henderson—David, that is—to come confirm it. Only then did he leave."

Leo bit the inside of her cheek. As she and Jasper had, Mr. Carter must have believed Regina was the woman who'd sat with his wife at Striker's. If he was searching for her, he didn't yet know she was dead.

"Miss Geary," Leo said, inching forward with a question, afraid of revealing too much, but also of holding back. "Regina was…in the family way," she said softly, aware that there were other factory workers seated at the tables around them: a few men in greasy coveralls, and three women in utilitarian dresses and patterned kerchiefs tied up in their hair to keep the strands safely tucked away from spinning machine parts.

Miss Geary's expression of astonishment, then another one of sadness, were genuine. She hadn't known. "Oh, no. Oh, how awful." She covered her mouth with quivering fingers, her nails trimmed short, her knuckles chapped.

Dita turned to Leo. "You said she wasn't very visibly pregnant?"

She'd mentioned the Jane Doe to Dita in passing after the corpse first arrived in the morgue, but as usual, her friend couldn't stand to hear about dead people—she found it almost as nauseating as seeing them in person. So, it was a bit surprising to know Dita had remembered this detail.

"Yes, why?"

"I just wonder…what if Miss Morris left her position so swiftly because she'd started to notice herself increasing and feared she couldn't hide it for much longer? She might have gone to stay with family until after the baby was born." The suggestion made sense. Her family might not have taken the news well.

"Did she have any relatives that you know of?" Leo asked Miss Geary. "Anyone she could have turned to?"

The woman hadn't yet sipped her tea; she just continued to hold it, letting it warm her hands. They no longer shook, at least. "She never mentioned anyone."

"Did she ever mention a beau of any sort?" Leo asked. Miss Geary had only said she didn't know Regina had been courting a Carter, not that she hadn't been courting at all.

When the secretary hesitated, Leo and Dita exchanged a glance. Dita, whom Leo could admit was much warmer and reassuring than she herself, put a gentle hand on Miss Geary's shoulder.

"Anything you tell us will be in confidence," she said. "We only want to help Inspector Reid solve Regina's murder."

"Are you quite positive it *was* murder?" Miss Geary lowered her voice with a surreptitious look over her shoulder. "People can fall, crack their skulls…"

"She was bludgeoned with a heavy object," Leo said. "A mallet, most likely."

The secretary's coloring leeched entirely from her face, and Leo realized too late that she had been too blunt. Though Miss Geary already had dark circles under her eyes and lines bracketing her mouth, she appeared more aged as she took in this revelation. She nodded jerkily.

"I...I could have been imagining it, but I noticed Mr. Henderson—David—had become more...solicitous toward Regina since the autumn."

Leo sat up, alert. "Before or after Gabriela announced her engagement to Mr. Carter?"

Miss Geary twisted her lips, as though trying to recall the exact timing. "Before. Shortly before."

"Solicitous in what way?" Dita asked.

Miss Geary waited to reply until a pair of women in canvas pinafores streaked with colorful paint had passed behind them. "A vase on her desk was filled with a new bouquet twice a week, sometimes more often. It was David. I saw him one morning refreshing the vase with new flowers. He'd blushed, as though I'd caught him out. And then there were the looks they shared. Smiles." She shrugged. "I didn't ask Regina because I didn't want to know the truth. He's a married man, you see."

Leo did see. If David Henderson had come to suspect Regina was carrying his child, he might have wanted to eliminate the inconvenient problem. She supposed his wife might have felt the same way, if she'd found out about the affair. Right then, Jasper was questioning the man. Leo trusted he would come to the same suspicion.

As if her thoughts had summoned him, the detective inspector appeared in the canteen entrance. Aggravation tensed the corners of his mouth. Leo thanked Miss Geary for her time, and when they rejoined Jasper, he wasted no time leaving the factory.

"The interview with the younger Mr. Henderson didn't go well, I assume?" Leo asked as they walked along the street toward a cab stand.

Jasper whisked off his bowler and ran a hand through his golden hair. "He seemed genuinely upset, and when I informed him about the baby, his legs went out from underneath him. The man all but toppled into his chair."

"They were having an affair," Leo said.

"Miss Geary suspected it," Dita added. She'd brought the complaints folder upon their exit and now handed it to Jasper.

He nodded. "I figured as much and pressed him, but he wouldn't admit to anything."

"Well, now we know Regina Morris couldn't have been the woman in the hooded cloak I followed at Striker's," Leo said. No other theories of who it could have been came to mind either.

What a tangle this case had become. Had the Inspector still been alive, Leo would have brought all the pieces to him to sort through with her. Frustration had been an emotion that always eluded Gregory Reid, even in the most perplexing of cases, or ones that never gave answers or resolutions. He would remove all emotion completely, it seemed, instead treating the elements like an arithmetic equation that had been disarranged and in need of reordering. She could hear his voice now, musing to himself, *"Are these two separate cases, or are they one?"*

"Did you show David Henderson that awful photograph?" Dita asked Jasper. He nodded.

"Like everyone else, he couldn't imagine why his sister had it with her or why anyone would have given it to her."

They arrived at the cab stand, where two hansoms waited for hire. Jasper opened the door to one and handed up Dita. He paused before extending his hand to Leo.

"I won't be traveling back with you. Since both victims were connected to the wallpaper factory and to Andrew Carter, I need to speak to him again." His brow crinkled in distaste. "I'll take another cab to his address."

He rolled his shoulders and neck as though trying to stretch out a knotted muscle. Unlike the Inspector, Jasper often experienced the emotion of frustration. However, it usually seemed to spur him on rather than defeat him.

She gestured toward the folder in his hand. "May I read the complaints file? I don't know if it will help, but I can memorize them and then summarize the findings."

He peered at the folder for a long moment, deliberating. Then, he handed it to her. "I suppose there's no harm in it."

Leo held the complaints file to her chest, somewhat stunned that Jasper had agreed to her request, as he helped her into the cab. He told the driver to take them to Scotland Yard, then nodded in parting as they merged into traffic.

"Oh, good, he isn't coming with us," Dita said.

Leo gaped at her. "I know he can be disagreeable, but I didn't think his behavior was overly terrible today."

"That's not what I meant," she replied while reaching into her cloak pocket. "I wanted the chance to speak to you alone." She withdrew a folded-up newspaper. "My father brought it home last night. He wasn't sure if you'd seen it yet."

Intrigued, Leo took the newspaper when Dita extended it. It was this week's *Illustrated Police News*. She had read the tabloid more devotedly when the Inspector had been alive, as it was delivered every week on subscription. Lately, however, she hadn't paid it much attention.

"Page three," Dita advised, and Leo, now concerned, turned to it.

Her fingers tightened, clamping the edges of the paper when she saw her own face, drawn in black ink, staring out at her. She inhaled the caption and the headline, and then the two small columns of text describing who she was, what had happened to her family, and how she was now working in a city morgue. Even that she had assisted in an investigation at Scotland Yard.

"Who wrote this?" Leo asked, out of breath even though she sat perfectly still.

"It doesn't say," Dita said. "But whoever wrote it knows you worked with Inspector Reid on a case."

The article didn't name Jasper, and thankfully, it also did not name the city morgue where she worked. There were at least a dozen in London.

Leo folded the newspaper, her mind reeling. "I suppose there are many people who know about me, and police officers accept bribes from newspapers all the time to provide secrets and details about cases, but...who would do this?"

Someone had observed her closely enough to draw her likeness and that made her uneasy. Not to mention they'd also dragged her most profound tragedy back into the limelight. And for what purpose?

She tried to hand the paper back to Dita, but her friend indicated for her to keep it. Leo would, if only to burn it.

She reassessed the sutures she'd placed in Mr. Howard Barnston's chest and nodded in approval. Leo had been careful to duplicate her uncle's usual stitching with the black catgut, each suture placed a half inch apart. It was the first time since Mr. Higgins's arrival that she'd been able to assist Claude, and as she closed the postmortem incision, she found she'd missed the quiet focus the procedure required.

Claude had determined none of the four stab wounds inflicted upon Mr. Barnston's abdomen and chest had been the cause of death. They'd all missed vital organs and arteries, though they would have most likely been fatal if left untreated. Rather, the blow to the top of the victim's cranium, which had crushed his skull, had been what killed him. The perpetrator had already been taken into custody, as he'd gone into a pub afterward and bragged about the deed to the bartender loud enough for several people to hear and become concerned.

If only Regina Morris's bludgeoning could have been so easily solved.

Satisfied with her work, Leo re-covered the dead man with a sheet. Mr. Higgins had taken his sullen self from the morgue an hour earlier than usual, claiming indigestion, and once he'd gone, Claude had sunk into a chair in the back room, exhausted. He'd rubbed his hands and wrists.

"They're worse than usual today," he commented, his disappointment in his palsy more bitter than usual. It was on the tip of her tongue to bring up her idea of applying to Hogarth and Tipson and to suggest they consider telling the deputy coroner that the time had come for Claude to retire. But when she parted her lips, she wound up saying that she would take care of things for the rest of the day, if he wished to rest. He stood and, with a sad nod, prepared to return home.

To make sure no one entered the morgue while she was at work on Mr. Barnston, as had happened back in January when a criminal broke into the morgue and found Leo suturing a cadaver, she locked the front and back doors. They were still locked at six o'clock when she was at the sink, washing and sterilizing the basins Claude used earlier to hold Mr. Barnston's internal organs. Unlike when she was suturing, Leo could let her mind wander as she sterilized the equipment with phenol, the sweet, rotten-fruit odor something she'd become accustomed to.

Immediately, her thoughts turned to the article Dita had shown her that morning. Just as she'd intended, upon her return to the morgue, Leo fed the weekly to the cottage range in the corner of the back office. Her uncle didn't read the *Illustrated Police News*, and she didn't want him to see it. The humiliation of being exposed as an oddity on the pages of one of the city's most popular publications wasn't something she wished to discuss with anyone. It had to be why she'd fielded even more curious glances at the Yard over the last few days. Had *Jasper* seen it?

She scrubbed harder at a white enamel-glazed basin as heat filled her cheeks and lit the tips of her ears. There wasn't anything she could do about it now, she supposed, and dwelling on it would only tie her up in knots.

Leo forced it from her mind and turned instead to the file of complaints against Henderson & Son Manufacturing that she'd read earlier. The stories were disturbing and heartbreaking. Everything from laborers who became ill after touching the wallpapers and then using their unwashed hands to eat, to multiple factory employees who suffered rashes, other skin lesions, and respiratory illnesses after handling the pigments and wallpapers daily. One customer, an older woman, had become so ill after installing the papers in her home herself, she'd been admitted to a hospital where she'd died.

However, it was the account of two tots—a brother and a sister—who, while unsupervised, ripped down the new wallpaper in their nursery and gummed it, that had most affected Leo. The wallpaper pattern had been one of fruit, green grapes and green apples specifically, and they'd apparently wanted to taste them. Their small bodies had not been able to fight off the poisoning from the arsenic. Both children had died.

Mr. and Mrs. Terrence Nelson were the grieving parents, and their file showed Mr. Nelson accepted a lump sum payment from Henderson & Son Manufacturing to cease any further legal action. In fact, almost all the claimants were offered, and had accepted, lump sums to settle out of court.

Leo was thinking about the death portrait of the two

young children propped on a rocking horse, when a knock echoed through the postmortem room.

She came to attention while drying the equipment with a linen towel and realized the late hour. Another few knocks sounded, and she traced them to the lobby door. Removing her canvas apron and hanging it on a peg, Leo checked to be sure all was in order before going to answer it. An officer in blue uniform stood on the step. He doffed his hat.

"Constable Murray," she said, her voice high with obvious surprise at seeing the officer from the *Police Gazette*.

"Miss Spencer, I didn't know if I might find you here this late, but I thought I'd take the chance."

She held still, confused as to why he'd come. For a moment, she worried she'd forgotten an appointment she'd made with him. But then she recalled at their last meeting that he'd asked if they might dine again sometime. *Oh, gracious.* Her stomach flipped.

"I'm just about to lock up and leave for the evening. My uncle is already gone," she said, though unnecessarily. He hadn't come to see Claude.

"Of course. I won't keep you. I just wanted to inform you that the description of the John Doe you sent over yesterday has already proved successful. He's been identified as a man missing from Clerkenwell, a Mr. Norrell. I'm told his family should be here tomorrow to view and claim his body."

The John Doe had fallen to the very recesses of her mind over the last twenty-four hours.

"That is wonderful news," Leo said, then rethought her

words. "Not that Mr. Norrell would think so, but I am glad his family will know what happened to him."

When Mr. Norrell had been found dead in an alley, his pockets had been empty. Anything that could identify him had already been stolen by street vagrants. Claude determined the cause of death had been a heart attack, as he'd found large blood clots in the ventricles of the man's heart, with no apparent signs of trauma.

"If you're leaving for the evening, allow me to flag a cab for you," Constable Murray offered.

"That's not necessary. I live close enough, and I usually walk."

"At this hour? It's getting dark. Please, allow me to escort you."

She hadn't been expecting the offer, and her initial reaction was to refuse it. "It isn't a dangerous route."

"I'll simply walk several paces behind you if you say no, so you may as well accept."

She was uncertain if she should feel annoyed or warmed by his insistence as she went inside to gather her things and the folder of complaints, then put out the gasoliers. He was grinning victoriously when she stepped back outside and locked the lobby door.

"Don't look so smug," she warned. "It isn't becoming."

Constable Murray laughed good-naturedly. It wasn't a sound she was accustomed to, not when her world orbited around a morgue and Scotland Yard. Jasper most certainly didn't laugh. In fact, she tried to imagine what it might sound like coming from his throat and failed.

They started out into the chilly March evening, and the constable fell into step beside her.

"I'm curious, Miss Spencer, as to how much longer you plan to work with your uncle."

She slowed, a suspicion spiraling in alongside his question. Had he read the article about her?

"Why do you ask?"

"He is…growing older," he replied, sounding as if he was choosing his words carefully. "Might you be thinking about what happens after he retires from the profession?"

It seemed the topic was on everyone's minds as of late. Hers, Jasper's, Claude's, the Chief Coroner's, and now, Constable Murray's. She gave him the same answer she had given Jasper the previous night, that she might consider employment at a funeral service.

He peered at her quizzically. "You enjoy working with the dead."

It was a statement, not a question. The article had insinuated as much too.

"I don't know if enjoyment is a factor," she replied tightly. "But I'm not ashamed to say it doesn't bother me."

She'd already said as much at their dinner the week before. He could only be asking again because of that blasted article.

"You don't mind the sights?" he asked. "The smells?"

Leo came to a stop, and he halted a step or two after her. "Constable Murray," she began. "I have seen the newspaper article, and it seems you have as well."

He appeared contrite as he clasped his hands behind his back. "I thought it was well-done."

She huffed and began walking again, this time at a faster clip. "It was an invasion of privacy! The author did not ask for permission to write about me, and now, all of

London knows that I am a strange young woman working in a morgue."

He caught up to her. "Not at all. I think you are fascinating."

Slowing again, she peered at him, unsure if she should believe the compliment. But he did look and sound sincere.

The few times an officer from Scotland Yard had shown her any interest, she would soon learn it was her peculiar work that intrigued him. After she and Constable Murray had dined at the chophouse, she'd started to think perhaps that wasn't the reason for his interest. She didn't wish to be proven wrong.

"You are in the minority, Constable, I'm sure," she said. "Though, it's kind of you to say."

"I'm not being kind. I'm being honest. And please, call me Elias."

She didn't know what to say in response. Wasn't it possible to be both kind and honest? And did she wish to call him by his given name? It wouldn't be so intimate, she supposed, but then, it would be only right to invite him to call her Leonora. Or perhaps, Leo, as she more preferred.

But she pinned her lower lip with her teeth, keeping silent.

"You truly thought the article ungenerous toward you?" he asked after a moment's quiet while they waited for a few cabs and horses to pass on the Strand.

On a second reading, she'd calmed enough to see that it was mostly factual. What bothered her most was the mystery surrounding the inspiration for the article in the first place.

"I merely thought it was cowardly of the author not to name himself. Or herself, I suppose," she replied.

"It's common practice for a newspaper when they haven't paid for an article," he said.

"How do you mean?"

An opening in traffic allowed them the chance to cross, and as they did, he explained, "Editors will try out new writers from time to time. Think of it as an audition of sorts."

Leo stepped up onto the pavement. "How do you know this?"

Constable Murray shrugged bashfully. "When I was younger, my friend's father owned a printing press and published a small journal. His work was always more intriguing to me than my own father's and grandfather's—that of maintaining law and order," he said with a self-effacing grin. "It's why I'm at the *Gazette*."

"At least the *Gazette* is a respectable publication," she said.

He nodded, keeping his hands clasped behind him as he walked. It made him look very much like a beat constable. "Perhaps, though it is rather mundane. I should think a real newspaper would be more exciting."

"Is writing what you are interested in?" she asked.

He bobbed his head. "More than policing, if I am honest."

Leo slowed as they approached Duke Street. After reading the complaints file, specifically the account of Mr. and Mrs. Nelson's dead children, she'd considered going to *The Times* to see if they'd run any stories about the sorry tale. She had the date of the children's deaths—August of last year—and she also had a contact there. Mr. Fordham Graves wrote the paper's police columns.

"I know someone at *The Times*," she said as they walked along Duke Street. "I could recommend you to him."

A slow grin formed on Constable Murray's lips. He was rather handsome, she supposed. But was the flustered state of her stomach and nerves attraction? Leo wasn't sure. As he thanked her but told her that wasn't necessary, she began to feel uneasy about this walk home and the attention he'd been paying her. Gracious, what if he was about to ask her to dine with him again? He couldn't possibly wish to *court* her. Could he?

She was grateful when her terrace house came into view. And even more so when a hansom pulled up along the curb, the driver calling to his horses to stop. The door to the cab opened, and Jasper emerged. His attention went first to Leo, then speared the constable next.

"Inspector Reid," Constable Murray said, his voice cracking in surprise to see the detective here.

Jasper was, to Leo's astonishment, an inch or two shorter than the constable. And yet, it was Constable Murray who appeared cowed. Jasper looked at the man skeptically as though trying to place him. "You work in the office of the *Gazette*."

"Yes, sir. PC Elias Murray, sir."

Wordlessly, Jasper hitched his chin and looked between the constable and Leo.

"Constable Murray was walking me home," she said, unnecessarily. Then, even more unnecessarily, "And now, we are here."

The constable swiveled on his heel to face her, bobbed his head, and bid her a good evening. He did the same to

Jasper and then started back the way they'd come, his gait brisk.

"I think you scared him," Leo said as she approached the front door. She unlocked it and let herself in, and Jasper entered the front hall on her heels.

"How do you know the *Gazette* officer?" he asked.

"The unidentified corpses, remember? I'm giving him descriptions for printing." She handed him the folder of complaints and then removed her coat, hat, and gloves. When she'd hung up her things, she took the folder back to allow Jasper to remove his own coat and hat. However, he didn't.

"Why was he walking you home?"

For a moment, she considered he might be upset. But then, Jasper was always scowling about one thing or another.

"He wanted to share that a John Doe has been identified based on my description of the body," she said, biting her tongue against saying anything more. She hadn't divulged to Jasper that she'd dined out with Constable Murray and didn't intend to discuss it now.

"He hardly needed to walk you home to tell you that," he grumbled, then took back the folder without removing his outer trappings. He seemed perturbed, and Leo perked up.

"What is it? Something you found out from Mr. Carter? Or at Miss Morris's address?"

Jasper didn't answer straightaway. Instead, he tapped the folder against his palm.

"Have you eaten?" he asked.

The strange question spun her about. "Of course, I haven't. I've only just arrived home."

At the back of the hall, Claude appeared, having come from the kitchen. "Ah, Inspector. I wondered whose voice that was alongside my niece's."

"Uncle Claude, Jasper wants to know if we've eaten."

Now that the danger of Constable Murray asking her to dine had passed, she realized she was rather hungry. She hadn't had more than a few biscuits for tea, and that had been hours ago.

Her uncle cast a look toward the back of the house. "No. There was an...incident this afternoon with Mrs. Boardman. Things have been out of sorts here ever since."

Leo's heart dropped. The nurse had been getting on so well with Flora, but Leo knew how erratic her aunt could be. She only hoped Mrs. Boardman hadn't given her notice.

"Not to worry. I can make something, I'm sure," Leo said, her mind casting about for anything she could prepare that wasn't eggs, toast, and kippers. The breakfast items were just about the only things she could cook that were halfway decent.

"Would Mrs. Feldman be able to make a trip to Charles Street?" Jasper asked. Again, he'd set Leo back on her heels. "Mrs. Zhao prepares too much for me alone. We could eat there."

Leo blinked, speechless. He wanted them *all* to dine at his home? It was a generous and wholly unexpected invitation, and it took Claude by surprise too. Her uncle's silver brows shot up, his face taking on the same expression he wore whenever someone complimented him or said something that he didn't quite know how to respond to.

"Is that Mr. Dibley?" Flora shuffled into the hall.

Claude must have left her in the kitchen alone—something that could have proved disastrous.

She took small, waddling steps forward, her dress one of the black beaded mourning gowns she had stored in her cedar chest. Leo hadn't seen it in years, and she presumed it had something to do with the trouble with Mrs. Boardman today.

"Not Mr. Dibley, my darling," Claude said, taking her arm gently.

Mr. Dibley had been Flora's piano teacher when she was a child. For some reason, she had begun to think every visitor that came knocking was her long-dead instructor.

"Mrs. Feldman." Jasper removed his hat, and as if that alone had been concealing his whole face, Flora gasped in surprise.

"Jasper Reid!" A smile crinkled her crepey cheeks as she sang his name, knowing him at once. Of course, she would. With a bittersweet smile, Leo thought of how her aunt had adored Jasper from the start. *Such a handsome young man,* she had said countless times over the years. *And such manners,* she would add, *for a boy come in off the streets.*

Flora's affection for the Inspector's ward, compared to her utter indifference for her own niece, whom she had been forced to take in, had baffled Leo. It still did. She'd felt pangs of envy in the past, but no longer. In fact, Flora's warmth toward Jasper was a relief; any opportunity to see her aunt happy was reassuring, especially these days.

"Inspector Reid has invited us to dine with him tonight," Claude explained to his wife.

"Oh, dear me," Flora said, her faded blue eyes glittering. "How lovely."

"I have a cab waiting," Jasper said, taking down Leo's coat from the stand. He held it up, indicating that he meant to help her into it. She inserted her arms, the assistance peculiar yet comforting.

"This isn't necessary," she whispered while Claude helped Flora into her coat and hat. "I'm not totally inept in the kitchen."

"Am I to believe you would prefer your own cooking to Mrs. Zhao's?"

Leo relented. "Very well, no."

He opened the door. "Besides, you can tell me over dinner what you found in that complaints file."

"That is hardly appropriate dinner conversation." Especially the story about the Nelsons' poor children.

"All right then, we'll wait until after dinner, over a cherry cordial," he said. She peered at him, now utterly confounded. A mischievous smile tucked the corner of his mouth. "Don't worry, I still can't stand the stuff. I'll be drinking whisky."

Leo exited the house after Claude and Flora, smothering a grin. "You know, you can be rather charming when you aren't being such a scowling bear."

Chapter Twelve

The understated elegance of 23 Charles Street never failed to impress itself upon Leo. The signs of wealth were obvious, though they were masked somewhat by time and a touch of neglect. The wine-red carpet had faded toward pink; the floral wallpaper was out-of-date; the furnishings were aged, though polished to a high shine by the scrupulous Mrs. Zhao. The Inspector had kept things exactly as they'd been when his wife and children had been alive. In some ways, the inside of the house felt like it had been trapped in amber, isolated from the rest of the world.

Located just off St. James's Square, it was an affluent area, home to wealthy aristocrats, politicians, and businessmen. The Inspector must have felt out of place here, surrounded by none of his contemporaries and instead by those who would look down on him for being a member of the working class. As Mrs. Zhao greeted their party gaily, Leo wondered whether Jasper, too, felt the snub of his neighbors. Might that be why he'd nurtured a friendship with Lord Hayes? Or why he'd been courting Constance, an aristocrat herself?

Mrs. Zhao, pleased by their unanticipated arrival, assured them that she had indeed cooked a meal that could provide for them all. She ushered them into the little-used sitting room to await her summons to dinner. Jasper left the room soon thereafter to deliver the complaints file to the study and, presumably, to prepare for dinner. Claude made small conversation with Flora, who needed a few reminders of where they were and why. Leo felt at home in the sitting room as they waited for the meal, yet also a twinge of friction. It might have just been due to the presence of her aunt and uncle here at the house on Charles Street. She'd had two worlds from the age of nine onwards. In one, she had her beloved uncle and reluctantly accepting aunt; and in the other, she'd had the Inspector and Jasper. They didn't often mix.

Things eased a little after sitting down to eat. Jasper ignored the chair at the head of the table where the Inspector had always sat and took the one at the opposite end, with Flora and Claude settling into chairs to his left and Leo to his right. As Mrs. Zhao brought in a tureen of soup, Claude and Jasper turned to business. They discussed an emerging theory that the whorls and ridges of a person's fingerprints, which were known to be individual to every person in the world, might be used to identify and connect criminals to their crimes.

"I could begin pressing the fingertips of unidentified corpses onto a stamp pad and then transferring them onto paper to include in their postmortem report," Leo said with a spike of excitement.

Flora, who'd been spooning up her soup, then letting it

spill back into her bowl again and again, made a disgusted noise in the base of her throat. She dropped her spoon against the rim of the bowl, muttering to herself, "Corpses, corpses."

Leo held still, aware of her blunder. Claude hushed his wife and helped her to grasp her spoon again before guiding it to her mouth. It was a caring, yet heartbreaking, display. Perhaps feeling as if he was intruding on the moment, Jasper turned to Leo.

"Sergeant Lewis and I visited Miss Morris's address," he said, his voice low. Leo was glad for the change in conversation. She'd been curious as to what he'd learned after leaving Mr. Henderson's factory.

"The landlady confirmed Regina Morris hasn't been there in a month. She had shared her room with another young woman, a Miss Putnam, who has since taken on a new roommate."

"What did Miss Putnam have to say?" Surely, the roommate would have known Regina was pregnant. She might even be able to identify the baby's father.

"She wasn't in. I sent Lewis to the coffeehouse where Miss Putnam works. I should receive his report in the morning." Jasper set down his spoon; he'd begun to dally with it as Flora had been.

"And you met with Mr. Carter?" He nodded but hesitated to give anything more. She wasn't about to let it stand. "Well? How did he react when he heard Regina was dead?"

Jasper sat back in his chair. "He's like a reptile. Cold, unblinking. I don't know if he felt anything at all."

From her one conversation at Scotland Yard with Andrew Carter, Leo agreed. He guarded his thoughts and feelings better than anyone she'd ever met, even better than Jasper, whose own expressions were so often unyielding.

"Did he know about the baby?" Leo asked softly.

"If he's to be believed, no. He did mention Miss Morris had family. An aunt in Liverpool. I have the address."

Although Regina had already been buried in a pauper's grave, Jasper would contact Regina's aunt to inform her about her niece. To question her as well, she imagined. Anyone with a connection to Regina would have to be.

Mrs. Zhao arrived with the main course of roasted veal, potatoes, and carrots, and for several minutes, Flora held court, explaining—more than once—that it was exactly as her mother used to make for their family. Leo tensed as she ate. Any mention of Flora's family often led to talk of her sister, Andromeda, and then, ultimately, to the murders. Thankfully, they made it through the meal, and the four of them retired to the study for after-dinner drinks.

As Jasper poured glasses of cherry cordial, Leo looked to the low table, where Mrs. Zhao made a habit of placing the newspapers. The *Illustrated Police News* wasn't there, even though she presumed Jasper hadn't canceled the Inspector's subscription. Had he removed it from the table on purpose, so she wouldn't see it?

She said nothing as Jasper brought two glasses of cordial to Claude and Flora, who were busy inspecting the bookshelves.

"All right," he said upon his return to Leo's side. "Tell me what you found in the complaints file."

Putting the bothersome article from her mind, Leo focused on the typed reports she'd memorized earlier.

Quietly, she recounted the stories of the most serious complaints against Henderson & Son Manufacturing, starting with the older woman who died after putting up her own wallpaper.

"Her son accepted the settlement from Mr. Henderson's solicitor and signed a contract to never seek more compensation or to sell his story to the newspapers," she said. "But his recorded statements did imply that he was unsatisfied and was only accepting the conditions because Mr. Henderson was a powerful and connected man, and he, a middle-class, unconnected one. He thought the courts would automatically side with Henderson."

"So, he might hold a grudge?" Jasper suggested after he sipped his whisky.

"Maybe. But it's been three years since his mother's death. Why would he enact his revenge now?" Leo moved on. "However, there is a much more compelling complaint, filed by a Mr. and Mrs. Terrence Nelson."

As Jasper listened to the tale of the Nelsons' two children ripping down their recently-installed wallpaper—the color scheme heavily pigmented with the iridescent green of fruits and vegetables—his interest built. She noted it in the lowering of his drink and the lift of his chin.

"When was this?" he asked.

"Last year," Claude answered.

Leo had parted her lips to say the same thing, but her uncle had been listening. He had led Flora to the leather Chesterfield, her hands petting the cover of a book she'd taken from a shelf.

"You recall the case?" Leo frowned. "But it wasn't reported in the news. At least that is what the agreement in the settlement indicated."

"No, no, I heard it from Richard Durant, the coroner at Kennington morgue," he answered, coming closer to the sideboard while casting a look back at Flora to be sure she was settled. "We meet for a pint every now and then."

Leo recalled him mentioning Mr. Durant over the years. "You met last summer. August, wasn't it?"

She'd had supper with Flora that evening, just the two of them. Her aunt had been slipping, but not as severely as she was now.

"That's right," Claude confirmed, his glass of cordial untouched. Leo knew he was only being polite; he preferred small beer, and that only sparingly.

"It affected him, the death of those two children. We coroners accept the fact that we must deal with dead children and infants, but these two…Richard said the green pigment that stained their mouths and tongues gave him nightmares. He even decided to hire a man to come take down the wallpaper in his own house. Grandchildren, he said. Didn't want to risk it."

"There was no police investigation?" Jasper asked.

Claude shrugged. "The postmortem was straightforward. Arsenic poisoning. Accidental."

"But the Nelsons may have filed a report with the police," Leo suggested. "They clearly held Henderson & Son accountable for their children's deaths and wished to press charges."

"However, they accepted Henderson's private settlement of one hundred pounds," Jasper said. "And a contract of silence as well?"

Leo nodded. If they were a poor family, as Mr. Nelson's employment as an ironmonger indicated, the sum would be life-changing. However, so would be the loss of their two children.

"The death portrait," Leo said. Jasper nodded, understanding her suggestion without her needing to say more. The children upon that rocking horse might very well be the Nelsons'.

"Those poor babies."

Leo's eardrums buzzed at her aunt's voice. Their conversation had slowly risen from a whisper as they'd been speaking. Flora, still seated on the sofa, clutched the book to her chest. Her eyes were distant.

"Killed. Murdered," she said, her voice high.

Claude started back to his wife's side.

"This was an accident, Aunt Flora," Leo said, wanting to kick herself. She'd assumed her aunt hadn't been paying attention.

Her distant gaze sharpened and locked on Leo. "She told me. She wrote to me, telling me about the business. The bloody, bloody business."

Leo held her aunt's stare, her curiosity rising. This was something she had never said before. "Who wrote? My mother, do you mean? She wrote to you?"

Not once had Flora mentioned correspondence with Andromeda. Claude had never mentioned letters either. Flora shook off his hand when he attempted to grasp her shoulder and got to her feet with surprising rapidity and balance. "It was you. *You* did it. You killed them!"

The words had been slung at her before, but Leo felt the heat of embarrassment consume her cheeks even more fiercely now that Jasper was listening. Flora continued to mumble the words again and again—*You did it. You killed them!*—as Claude tried to soothe and distract her. Leo set her cordial glass down, avoiding Jasper's eyes.

"Mrs. Feldman, why don't you take the book with you?" he suggested, joining Claude in his efforts of distraction.

She stopped chanting and thanked him profusely before then inquiring where they were and what they were doing there. Leo's throat cinched up tight as they left the study and met Mrs. Zhao in the foyer to collect their coats and hats.

Jasper pulled her aside after she hastily put on her own coat. She hadn't wanted him to help her again, as he had earlier. She was too agitated. Too desperate to leave.

"Are you all right?" he asked. Ridiculously, his concern caused her eyes to mist over perilously.

She forced a cheery nod. "Of course. She doesn't mean what she says." Leo put on her hat, still unable to look him in the eye. "Thank you for dinner. It was kind of you to invite us."

Jasper exhaled as if unsatisfied with her response. But he left it alone and said, "I'll hail a cab for you."

"That isn't necessary." Leo opened the front door. "We'll go to the cab stand."

He caught the edge of the door with his hand. "I will hail a cab, Leo." The terse command was successful in dragging her eyes to his at last. In them, she saw resolve. And a touch of sympathy. "Wait here."

With that, he went outside and closed the door behind him.

She glanced toward Flora and Claude, who were saying their goodbyes to Mrs. Zhao. As sorry as she was that the evening had concluded on such an unsettling note, Leo was at least grateful for one thing: her aunt's strange comment about the letters from Andromeda Spencer. *The bloody, bloody business.* What business could she have meant? Leo would ask Claude once they were alone. But there was also another way to find out.

If Flora had received letters from her mother, they could be somewhere at their home on Duke Street. If they were, Leo would find them.

Chapter Thirteen

"Five days, Reid. Five goddamned days, and you've not brought a single suspect into custody!" Chief Coughlan ran his palm across his forehead. "I told you this case needed to be handled swiftly. This is not swiftly!"

Jasper stood before the chief's desk, hands clasped behind his back and waited for Coughlan to conclude—or continue—his ticking off. As the investigation had lengthened, and the chief's temper had grown shorter, Jasper had come to expect the chief's wrath during his daily briefings.

Stories about Gabriela Carter's murder had been making it into every newspaper in London for days, and with no suspects named, no arrests made, and no more facts available to the ravenous reporters lingering outside the Yard, some of the more questionable papers had resorted to printing pure fiction and theory. Most were calling it a retaliation killing. A few named Eddie Bloom, as it had all taken place inside his club. And as usual, the papers were accusing the Metropolitan Police of inept investigating and more corruption.

"Do you know what this looks like, Reid?" Coughlan went on. "It looks like we're turning a blind eye. Like we might not want to capture the killer."

Jasper could listen to no more.

"Sir, I'm following promising leads. And the new connection to Regina Morris's murder could provide more—"

"You are not investigating that woman's murder any longer," the chief cut in. His voice cracked loud enough to reach through the walls and the closed door. No doubt, the whole detective department was listening. "I want you focused on the Carter murder and nothing else."

Jasper clenched his jaw, suppressing the urge to shout that it was shortsighted to ignore the link to Regina Morris. Should he do that, Coughlan's brittle patience would shatter entirely.

"You need to find the waiter who delivered that drink to Gabriela Carter, and you need to arrest him," Coughlan ordered.

The chief, though easily irritated and often vexed, had a firm understanding of the many elements of this case. He also knew the hellfire that would rain down upon him and his department if they failed to pin the crime on someone. What Jasper would not do, however, was select someone to blame and arrest him just to get the public and the Home Office off their backs. Others at the C.I.D might, but not him.

"I believe Andrew Carter is searching for that waiter too, Chief, and plans to deliver his own justice."

Coughlan scoffed. "That is unacceptable. You cannot allow him to do that."

"How do you propose I prevent him, sir?" The sarcastic retort was out of his mouth and touching off a firestorm before he could stop himself. The chief's skin began to boil toward pink, then red.

"By finding the murderer first, of course! Or is that too much of a challenge for you?" He came around his desk, his tall, thick-chested body suddenly seeming several inches wider. "You've landed at the C.I.D faster than others, Reid, and don't think I don't know why or how. Reid is an influential name around here. But by God, you will prove you deserved that promotion, or you will find yourself back where many people say you belong."

Jasper flexed his fists, his blood roiling. Never had he felt the urge to strike someone so fiercely. He'd assumed there were some in the department who didn't believe merit alone had earned him the promotion to detective inspector. And now, the chief had confirmed it.

He released his fingers from their clenched fists. "Yes, sir," he gritted out, then left the office before he could be dismissed, and before he could do or say something more to enrage the chief.

Jasper kept the door to his office in his line of sight, ignoring the glimpses and smirks the others in the department were certainly giving him as he stormed by. Most detectives would dodge high-profile cases for this very reason. If all went well, the detective would shine, but if it didn't, he would become an object of pity.

Roy Lewis rose from his desk and followed him.

"Tell me what you learned from Miss Putnam," Jasper

barked as the detective sergeant closed the office door quietly. Lewis tucked his chin, not reacting to his temper.

"She was at the coffeehouse, like the landlady said. Regina kept to herself mostly, but she had been seeing someone recently."

"How recently?"

"December or thereabouts. But here's where it gets interesting—Regina admitted to her roommate that it was a married man. After Carter cut her loose, the only place she ever went to anymore was work at the factory, so Miss Putnam assumed she met the new bloke there."

Jasper had started to consider whether Lawrence Wilkes had, in fact, taken up Regina Morris's offer to commiserate over their mutual losses. Seeking comfort in each other's arms, he could have gotten her with child. But he wasn't married, and he would've had no motive to then get rid of her.

However, David Henderson was married, and the secretary Leo spoke to, Miss Geary, had suspected something romantic between him and Regina.

"Did she give names?" Jasper asked, but Lewis shook his head.

"Regina only said he was already yoked. Miss Putnam did suspect she was carrying a babe, though. *There were signs*, was what she said."

Jasper sat down hard enough to send his swivel chair rolling backward. Coughlan had just finished telling him to forget Regina Morris's murder and to focus on Gabriela. It would be impossible to do, considering the two were connected. He had no evidence of it yet, but he knew it in his blood.

"The chief is under pressure from the new commissioner to get this tied up," Lewis said, as if to explain Coughlan's harsh scolding. But that wasn't what was weighing on Jasper.

Briefly, he explained to the detective sergeant what the complaints file had turned up, though he bit his tongue about the fact that it had been Leo who had done the footwork and memorized each report. He felt a pang of guilt for omitting it, but he was already under enough scrutiny as it was. To his astonishment, Chief Coughlan hadn't brought up that sodding article saying she'd assisted at Scotland Yard. But he suspected it was on his mind and waiting in the wings to be tossed into Jasper's face at just the right moment.

"The death portrait found in Gabriela's handbag was unknown to everyone I questioned. No one could understand who the children were or why she would be carrying such a thing," Jasper said.

"You think they're the tots that were killed by Henderson's wallpaper?" Lewis asked, catching on.

"Possibly. I want you to find an address for Mr. and Mrs. Terrence Nelson. It wasn't included in the complaint report, just that they were from Lambeth."

Lewis nodded and stepped out on his task, but before he could close the door, Constable Wiley's puffed-up chest filled the frame.

"Inspector, there is a woman here to see you—"

Leo shoved past his shoulder and stepped inside the office. "Honestly, Constable, you know my name."

Jasper got to his feet as the desk officer glowered. His unabashed dislike of Leo Spencer was as thorough as hers was of him.

"Thank you, Wiley," Jasper said, gesturing for him to

leave. The door shut, and Leo didn't bother to hide her small grin of pleasure.

Jasper didn't match it, even if he did enjoy seeing Wiley, a man who was bloated on his own unwarranted sense of self-importance, being hassled. Still, he didn't need word of his visitor spreading around the Yard.

"Why are you here?"

Leo flicked him a look of reproach as she removed her gloves. "Back to being a scowling bear, I see. So much for the charming gentleman you pulled out of your magician's hat last evening."

Inviting Leo and the Feldmans to his home for dinner had been a spontaneous decision, and one he'd come to regret when Flora turned on her niece at the end of the night. Afterward, he realized he'd doubted Leo's earlier claims that the cruel things her aunt was saying—casting blame on her for her family's murders—were truly that bad. He should have known better than to assume Leo was exaggerating the truth, and now he felt like a horse's arse for not believing her.

Before that, however, when they'd simply been dining, Jasper had enjoyed himself. It had been lonely at the dinner table since the Inspector's death. He could not have Leo over for dinner, not alone, however her uncle and aunt's presence had mitigated the impropriety.

"Answer the question, please," he said as he retook his chair with a groan.

She slapped her gloves onto his desk. "Happily. I've been to *The Times* to speak with Mr. Fordham Graves."

Jasper rubbed the back of his neck. "Do I want to know why?"

The reporter despised the police, and he'd made it his

role at the newspaper to write pieces maligning them. Graves had, however, supplied Jasper and Leo with some helpful information during their investigation into the murder of Samuel Barrett and the accidental death of his sister, Hannah, in January.

"Trust me, you do want to know," Leo replied. "I wanted to ask if he recalled any story similar to the one described in the complaint report involving the Nelsons. I'm aware they signed a contract of silence with Mr. Henderson," she said, raising her hand to stave off what Jasper was about to remind her of. "However, I thought it entirely likely that before the contract was signed and the settlement reached the story might have made it to the papers."

"And had it?"

Leo grinned and leaned a hip against his desk. Jasper's attention went to the curve of dark purple wool. It lingered only a second before he came to his senses and got to his feet.

"A fellow reporter took the report from the grieving mother," Leo explained, oblivious to his momentary distraction. Unquestionably, dinner last night had been a mistake. Even with the Feldmans there.

"I spoke to the reporter, who said Mrs. Evelyn Nelson was adamant that Henderson & Son must be held responsible. She wanted to warn other parents of young children about the dangers of installing wallpaper pigmented with Scheele's green. However, before the reporter could even finish the article, it was pulled. He was told there wasn't space for it, but he suspected that wasn't true. He found out later that the publisher is an acquaintance of Mr. Henderson's."

And an article that could sully Jack Henderson's name wasn't going to make it into his publication, especially if Henderson happened to offer a timely donation to either the paper or its publisher. Sometimes, Jasper hated to be cynical. But he had yet to find a reason not to be.

"Anyway, the reporter had the address for Mrs. Nelson." Leo took a small, folded slip of paper from her dress pocket and held it aloft between her fingers. Her goading grin conveyed exactly what it was she wanted in exchange for the address.

"You're not coming with me this time, Leo," Jasper said. "Chief Coughlan is currently fashioning a noose for me in his office and is ready to use it if I don't get this case solved and do it by the books."

Lewis knocked before entering. "Got the address for the Nelsons, guv."

Jasper went to get his coat and hat. Leo followed on their heels as they left the department. "I was thinking…if the Nelsons felt they never got justice for the deaths of their children and wanted revenge, why would they target Gabriela? She had no say in her father's business. Why wouldn't they poison Mr. Henderson instead?"

"Could be an eye for an eye," Lewis suggested. "Henderson's child for theirs."

To a rational person, it would be an untenable thought. But to two parents in anguish, Jasper supposed rational thoughts could be few and far between.

They passed the telegraph room on their way to the lobby. The door was open, and inside, several uniformed officers were receiving communications from other divisions in London. A public telephone had been installed a few years ago, however, it had almost immediately been removed when most calls coming in had been frivolous in nature, beleaguering the officers and preventing more serious crimes from being reported. One woman had even called to complain that her maid had burned off a lock of her hair while using curling tongs, and she wanted to put her in a jail cell overnight to punish her. The return to telegraph lines between police divisions around the city had been a relief for the operators.

A few strides past the room, an officer rushed into the corridor behind them. "Inspector Reid, there's something here for you."

He turned back and accepted the slip of paper. The typed words barreled into him with a slap to his senses.

"Christ," he muttered, crumpling the paper. "A body has been found at Henderson & Son Manufacturing."

Leo took in a small gasp of air. "Do you have a name for the victim?"

He shook his head. "Just a request that I get there as fast as I can."

They hurried out the back of the building into the yard, where several hansoms were lined up, waiting for business. It was a popular spot for cabbies who were always ready to be hired by any police officer or visitor to the Yard.

"Might I come along?" Leo asked, still on Jasper's heels. "I can speak to Miss Geary again."

Lewis flagged a cab, and while the detective sergeant was busy, Jasper pulled her aside. "Please, Leo, go back to the morgue. If this is another murder, I can't have you there."

The lines of her jaw rippled as she clenched her teeth in defiance. But in the end, she didn't argue. Her unexpected compliance might have been why he heard himself saying, "Thank you for bringing me the Nelsons' address and for going to *The Times*. You didn't need to do that. In fact, you probably shouldn't have."

Her dark brow lifted. "Your cab is waiting," she said sharply, then she turned on her heel and began to walk toward the stone arch leading out of the yard.

As soon as he joined Lewis in the single-bench cab, their driver, who sat perched high behind them, urged the horses forward. As they did, Leo could be seen approaching another cab. Comprehension smacked into Jasper like an anvil.

The insufferable woman. He called for the driver to stop.

"What are you doing?" Lewis asked as Jasper opened the half-door and called for Leo.

"She has the Nelsons' address. She'll just go there on her own while we are dealing with the body at Henderson's factory," he explained as Leo straightened her back and grinned at his summons. Dismissing the cab driver she'd been speaking to, she walked briskly toward their hansom, leaving a trail of triumph in her wake.

Lewis whistled softly. "Someone ought to put a leash on her."

Jasper darted a sharp look of reprimand at him as Leo reached the open door, still smiling smugly.

"Get in," Jasper barked, extending his hand. "You bloody pest."

Chapter Fourteen

Sergeant Lewis shifted his weight on the cab's seat, his brow creased. He and Jasper would have had plenty of room on the single, forward-facing bench, however with Leo squeezed between them, the fit was tight.

She was certain Sergeant Lewis didn't approve of her accompanying them on official police business to Henderson & Son, and by the increasing chafe of Jasper's sidelong glances, he didn't either. He'd only invited her because he'd seen her approaching a hansom—something she would not have needed had she just been going to Spring Street.

However, he knew she had the Nelsons' address, and to him, she must have appeared to be about to hire a driver to take her there. Of course, she'd merely been asking the driver for the time and then complimenting his horses while she waited for the detective inspector to see her and deduce her plan.

Leo would confess her ruse later. It would be naïve and reckless to visit the home of a possible murderer, and it irked her somewhat that Jasper had believed she would do it on her own. Alas, she was now where she'd wanted to be—on her way to view the body at the wallpaper factory.

No, she wasn't a detective, and truly, she had no role at a crime scene. However, if the local police had sent for Inspector Reid, it was because this body had to do with his current case. Having been present at the time of Gabriela Carter's death, having seen the woman in the hooded cloak rushing away from the scene of the crime, Leo felt tied to the investigation.

Besides, she could be of use. She'd gained Miss Geary's trust. If there was anything the secretary knew about this new event, she would confide it in Leo.

The three of them didn't speak for the entirety of the drive. Had Sergeant Lewis not been with them, Leo suspected Jasper would have had plenty to say, likely spending the half hour grumbling at her. Instead, they arrived at the Wapping factory and only then did Jasper take her aside while the detective sergeant paid the cab fare.

"Please, Leo, follow protocol while we are in there," he said, sounding utterly harassed.

"Stop worrying, Inspector. I will be the epitome of proper protocol," she promised, and with good intentions too. She knew the potential wrath he could suffer if she were to do or say something that made its way back to Chief Coughlan. She wouldn't risk that.

They met uniformed constables posted at the entrance to the cobble-surfaced work yard, and only after Jasper and Sergeant Lewis had shown them their warrant cards were they permitted into the area. A uniformed officer saw them and came forward swiftly.

"Constable Harding," he said, introducing himself. "My superior suggested we call you, in case this is related to the Carter poisoning."

Constable Harding led them into the yard, where the discovery of a body had not kept the employees from their work. Men were still unloading and loading drays, and inside the open doors to the building, Leo heard the steady hum of machinery.

"What can you tell me, Constable?" Jasper asked as the senior Mr. Henderson spotted their approach.

He stood at the opening to a recess between buildings. Overhead, a covered passageway connected the two buildings. A handful of workers had gathered there, smoking cigarettes as they leaned over the railing to view the commotion below.

"The body's that of a woman," Constable Harding provided. "The foreman, name of Stephen Bridges, found her first thing this morning."

Several more uniformed constables gathered around a blanket-covered figure. Another man stood close by, his eyes red, his mouth fixed in a tight grimace. He looked like a much younger version of Jack Henderson. Leo presumed this was his son, David.

Her hopes began to sink as a premonition crawled through her, and when they joined the group, they dropped completely.

"It is my secretary, Miss Geary," Jack Henderson announced, a wave of his arm toward the covered figure.

Shock stilled Leo completely. She stared at the blanket. It didn't fully cover Miss Geary's feet. The worn soles of a pair of brown shoes were visible, and from their positioning, Leo ascertained she was lying on her front.

Right then, a memory, sharp and vibrant, burst into her mind, unbidden: another sheeted body, although smaller in size. Leo's perspective had been from over Inspector Gregory Reid's shoulder as he carried her past her sister's bedroom, the door ajar. It could have been no more than a half-second glimpse, but it was as though time had stood still, allowing her brain to imprint everything she saw in that breath of a moment: Agnes, in bed, her arms raised by her head as she lay on her stomach—it was the only way she had ever been able to fall sleep. Her blanket had been drawn up high to cover her, but her forearms and hands were still visible. Her fingers, so little and still.

Leo dragged in a breath and blinked hard. Her head went dizzy.

Leaning toward her, Jasper whispered, "Are you all right?"

Mr. Henderson noticed.

"What is this woman doing here again? You aren't from the press, are you? No reporters are allowed back here. Constable, what did I tell you? No reporters!" he barked as he rounded on Constable Harding.

"I'm not a reporter," Leo was quick to say, though her breathing wasn't yet normal. Perhaps it was the momentary lack of oxygen that made her then add, "I assist the coroner at the Spring Street Morgue."

Mr. Henderson goggled. "A woman, assisting a coroner? That is insupportable."

"Many would agree with you," Leo said tightly. "Be that as it may, it is what I do. Might we see the victim?"

She regretted the request instantly. Jasper had just finished telling her to follow protocol, to avoid doing or saying anything that might get back to Chief Coughlan. This most certainly would.

After a concise glare of reproof, Jasper signaled a much younger constable to pull aside the blanket. The young man crouched to do so. Leo felt a pang of sadness at seeing the corpse of someone she'd known, however briefly, but tried not to let it show on her expression. A moment ago, she'd been gripped out of the blue by a staggering memory involving her little sister. It had likely been revived thanks to the Inspector's file on her family's unsolved case. Dormant memories had been coming to the surface ever since.

"You're that lady in the paper," the young constable said. "The deadhouse lady."

Leo felt all eyes snap onto her.

"Concentrate on the victim, Constable," Jasper said, without a flicker of confusion over the policeman's comment. His dusky green eyes met hers, then skidded away.

So, he *had* read it after all.

Leo let it go for the moment and moved to the side to view Miss Geary's head more closely. Bone fragments and blood darkened the back of her skull, matting her ashy blonde hair.

"When was she found?" Jasper asked.

"Five-thirty this morning," a man in a gray cap answered. "I open the factory every morning at that hour. I find the occasional vagrant passed out by the gate, but never here," he said, gesturing to the green-painted double doors Miss Geary had fallen beside. "Haven't ever found something like this."

"Has the body been moved since you found it?"

"No, Inspector."

It was now nearly nine in the morning. Any number of people could have touched the body or walked around it, disturbing the scene.

"Who closes the factory each night?" Lewis asked next.

The foreman, Mr. Bridges, claimed responsibility for that too. When asked, he said no, Miss Geary had not been there when he'd locked up and left the building at seven o'clock the prior evening. The place had been empty.

Leo crouched next to the secretary's head. It was turned away, so that her face wasn't visible, however she could easily spot a significant indentation in the top right side of the woman's skull.

"Her parietal bone has been crushed." In the silence that followed, she looked up to find several pairs of eyes staring at her quizzically. Jasper, however, only peered closely at poor Miss Geary. He crouched next to Leo.

"A killing blow?"

"Most likely." With her fingers still encased in gloves, Leo moved aside some of Miss Geary's blood-crusted hair. "Jas—" She caught herself. "Inspector Reid, look at the shape of the depression."

"It's difficult to make out. All I see is blood and…" He didn't finish his comment. There was a good amount of gray matter exposed, which surely disturbed him. But Leo was looking past that to the wound itself.

"It's almost perfectly round," she said, tracing the shape with her fingertip.

Leo recalled another woman's crushed skull from the month before, and the round indentation the murder weapon had made in her temporal bone. Claude had determined that a heavy mallet had been used to kill Regina Morris, then known as Jane Doe. With the crystal-clear memory of Miss Morris's skull during her postmortem in mind, and with Miss Geary now in front of her on the cobbles, Leo was almost positive the wounds would prove to be a match.

Above them, Mr. Henderson groaned. "Can we please hurry this along? Her body cannot stay here much longer. As soon as reporters hear of this, it will be an utter spectacle."

Jasper straightened and ignored the owner's comment. "When did Miss Geary leave work last night?"

David Henderson had been standing outside the circle surrounding the body, holding his arms tightly around his middle, as if he had a stomachache. "Five o'clock, like always," he said.

And yet she'd been found here again at five-thirty in the morning. She'd returned at some point during the night or early morning. Bracing herself for a round of objections, she removed her glove and reached for Miss Geary's arm.

"What do you think are you doing?" Constable Harding asked incredulously.

"Determining how long she has been deceased," Leo replied. She lifted the woman's arm and felt hard resistance. The muscles were rigid, as were her fingers, which would not easily move when Leo tried to manipulate them. Ignoring the murmurs of shock around her, she stood and went to Miss Geary's feet. Lifting her ankle, she felt the same rigidity. "She is in full rigor. You see, the larger muscles stiffen considerably about six hours after death and can remain that way for well over twelve hours, though no more than twenty-four. Considering it is now nine-thirty in the morning, I would place her death anywhere between seven o'clock last night, after the foreman left, and three o'clock in the morning."

After a moment of silence, the elder Mr. Henderson barked out a mocking laugh. "I daresay that is for a coroner himself to determine, not you."

Leo stood, her own muscles tight with irritation. "Correct, the coroner will determine it, and I believe he will agree with my estimation."

Jasper cut her a warning look but nodded to Lewis, who wrote a note on his small pad of paper. The approximate time of death, Leo hoped.

"If she was killed between those hours, that means she returned for some reason. Was it usual for her to come here late at night?" Jasper asked.

"Of course not," Jack Henderson said. "Clearly, she was up to some trouble."

David withdrew from the circle again, his expression drawn. He rubbed the back of his neck, his brows pinched in misery. He appeared to be handling Miss Geary's murder much more appropriately than his blustering and pitiless father.

Disappointed in the older man's lack of sympathy, Leo returned to inspecting Miss Geary. The bludgeoned skull had captured her focus at first, but now she took in more of the woman's position on the ground. Her hands were up and splayed at either side of her head. She wore a black glove on her left hand, with its match on the ground near her right. She must have dropped it when her attacker had come from behind and struck her.

"Miss Geary looks to have removed her glove," Leo said. "Perhaps to handle a key more deftly."

"She shouldn't have had keys to the yard or to the building," David said, though he lacked the same ire his father was boiling over with.

"If Mr. Bridges had locked up for the night, she must have had them," Leo replied as she lifted her eyes to search the nearby cobbles and the ground surrounding the green double doors. "Or perhaps someone let her in."

"Who else has keys to the gate and the building?" Jasper asked.

David spluttered for a moment before answering, "Mr. Bridges, of course. And my father and I."

"As Mr. Henderson's personal secretary, it might not have been too difficult for Miss Geary to get her hands on a set," Leo offered as her eyes caught on a small metal object that lay between a pair of large steel barrels, pushed up against the exterior of the building. She stood and drew closer. It was exactly as she'd hoped: a pair of brass keys on a small ring.

Lewis came forward to collect it. "She must have dropped it when she was attacked."

"Was the door still locked this morning when you arrived?" Jasper asked the foreman, who nodded.

"What does any of this matter?" Mr. Henderson turned to Constable Harding. "Call for a wagon. We need to remove her from the premises."

"It matters," Jasper replied, raising his voice and stopping the constable in his tracks as he prepared to do as told, "because a woman has been murdered. A second secretary employed by your business has been bludgeoned to death, and that in no way can be a coincidence, Mr. Henderson."

Leo bit back a grin of satisfaction to see the blustering old man cowed. She returned to taking in the state of Miss Geary's body and the details it might provide. Blood had leached into the high, ivory lace collar of her blouse, where a brooch had been pinned at the notch of her throat. Enclosed within the rectangular frame of white enamel, the brooch displayed a pattern of what appeared to be two different colors of thread. The threads had been expertly woven together to create a checked pattern. Leo crouched again for a closer look as Mr. Henderson accused Jasper of inciting a vicious rumor that someone was killing secretaries at Henderson & Son.

Strung on a long chain around her neck, and now lying on the cobblestone, was a thin, circular gold band. A lady's wedding ring?

"Does Miss Geary have family?" Leo asked, presuming the ring might have belonged to someone special, like her mother.

"Not that I am aware of," David Henderson replied. "Father?"

But Mr. Henderson only grumbled and said the information might be within the employee records in Miss Geary's desk. He then drew away to speak to the foreman and shouted at two of the other constables on hand to go block anyone, especially reporters, from entering the work yard.

"Constable Harding, summon a wagon and have the body delivered to the Spring Street Morgue," Jasper said, then turned to David Henderson. "What is Miss Geary's given name?"

"Andrea," he answered, his voice rough and rasping.

Leo stood from her crouch, pleased that the body—*Andrea*—would be sent to Claude rather than a deadhouse in Wapping. Jasper must have wanted confirmation that the death blows to the skulls of Andrea Geary and Regina Morris were inflicted by the same weapon, and thus, the same killer.

"Lewis." Jasper turned to the detective sergeant. "You're in charge here. Speak to the other employees and see if you can find anything that links Miss Morris and Miss Geary. Find her address within the employee files and pay it a visit. If she has no family, it's likely a boardinghouse. Speak to the landlady, her roommate, whomever you can. Find out what she could have been doing here at such a late hour."

Lewis's forehead crinkled with surprise. It was, Leo thought, quite a lot to put upon his shoulders. Jasper leaned toward Lewis and said something else inaudible. She tried to listen but couldn't hear a word, and with his mouth turned from her vision, she couldn't read his lips either. Lewis nodded tightly.

"Where will you be, guv?" he asked.

Jasper glanced toward Leo before answering, his mouth a grim slash. "I need to pay a call on the Nelsons. I've no proof yet that they were involved, but they had a legitimate grievance with Henderson & Son, and now three women connected to the company are dead. I need to speak to them."

Sergeant Lewis nodded before sending Leo a suspicious look, evidently still curious about what she was doing here with them. As he cut away to follow David Henderson into the building, Jasper took another searching look at the body on the cobbles. He then started back for the street. Leo stayed with him.

"Am I going with you, then?" she asked.

"Isn't that what you wanted?"

"Yes, but I expected you to tell me I'm not part of this investigation."

They reached the street, where the carts, drays, and horse traffic had thickened with the addition of curious onlookers. Mr. Henderson had been correct; reporters would soon be flocking to the factory.

"You aren't," Jasper replied, signaling one of the black cabs within traffic. "But as you would go there on your own—"

"I wouldn't have," she confessed. "I was only tricking you into believing I'd go so that you might take me here with you."

His jaw loosened as he scowled at her this time. "You're impossible."

The driver pulled along the pavement, and Jasper gave him the Nelsons' address. Then, he extended his hand. "Get in."

Leo slid her fingers into his palm. "With pleasure."

Chapter Fifteen

After several minutes of being stuck in the congestion building up outside Henderson & Son, the cabbie started for London Bridge and across the river, their destination Wake Street in Lambeth. Jasper felt the scowl on his face as he stared out the window but, try as he did, he could not erase the expression.

Andrea Geary had been killed in the same manner as her fellow secretary. Leo was almost certainly correct—the two skull wounds would prove identical. As Miss Geary had just confessed the previous day that she believed David Henderson and Regina Morris had been having an affair, the younger Henderson had a strong motive for both murders—to prevent the truth from reaching his wife. He also possessed keys to the premises and might have opened the gate for Miss Geary, leading her into the deserted factory yard. They could have struggled. He might have dropped his keys. But then, why leave her body to be found? As much as Jasper had wanted to stay to question David, he needed to abide the chief's directive and focus on Gabriela's poisoning. Right then, the Nelsons were of greater interest.

So, he had quietly instructed Lewis to ask David questions and to get his alibi for last night through this morning. But to go lightly. Pressing too hard might tip him off that he was a suspect, and before he placed David under arrest, he wanted more proof. Andrea Geary may have shared her concerns about the affair with a roommate or friend. She might have even told someone why she was going to the factory so late at night. David had looked powerfully affected while standing over her body, but it was a toss-up whether it was from sorrow, shock, or guilt.

How David Henderson could be connected to his sister's poisoning remained unclear. There was a possibility he wasn't involved at all and that Gabriela's murder was isolated from the two bludgeoning deaths. Regina's former relationship with Andrew Carter could merely be coincidental.

Still, Jasper wasn't satisfied.

"Did you see the wedding band she wore on a chain around her neck?" Leo asked as soon as they'd gotten under way. "It could be a family memento, but what if she was previously married?"

"Then even as a widow, she would be Mrs. Geary, not Miss," Jasper said, his eyes on the bridge as they neared. He hadn't seen the wedding band but didn't know how it might matter to the case.

"Or perhaps she went back to using her maiden name. We might be able to learn more about her if—"

"Lewis is handling it."

Leo sealed her lips. "You're angry."

He met her probing gaze from across the cab. "You manipulated me into bringing you along."

She'd claimed that she wouldn't have gone to the Nelsons' address on her own, but he didn't believe her. Had he not fallen for her trick, she might have been incensed enough to try it.

"I did. I'm sorry, but I'm quite useful around dead bodies, you must admit."

"I could easily have determined the time of death to be sometime between the foreman's departure last night and his return this morning without you."

"Yes, but then you would have had to waste time suspecting Mr. Bridges, as you would not have known she died hours before he arrived."

He conceded with a roll of his eyes and returned to looking out the window. They crossed the bridge in silence, but it didn't stretch on for long.

"You were keeping me in the dark about the article in the *Illustrated Police News*," Leo said.

He sighed. "I didn't want to bring it to your attention if you hadn't already seen it, and I'd hoped you hadn't."

"Dita showed me." She paused. "I can only think that this reporter, whoever it is, has a contact at Scotland Yard."

He cut his eyes to her. "When I find out who wrote it, I'll bash him in the head with his own typewriter."

Leo bit her lips against a laugh. "You will not."

He wouldn't promise not to. Frankly, he found the idea of it appealing.

"Jasper, promise me you won't," she said. "If you find out who wrote it, you will tell me, and I will speak to him, or her, myself."

She could defend herself, of course. But that didn't stop him from wanting a hand in it.

When they arrived at the Wake Street address, Jasper descended from the carriage first. "Wait for me here." He began to shut the door, but Leo stuck out her boot, preventing it from closing.

"I am not waiting in the cab."

"Yes, you are." The knot in his gut tightened. "If the Nelsons are involved in Gabriela's murder, it would be irresponsible of me to bring you near them." He shoved her foot back with his hand and latched the door.

It was irresponsible to even have her with him in the cab. Word was bound to get back to Scotland Yard that Leo had been at the factory too. He could only make so many excuses before Coughlan followed through with his threats.

And yet, although he would not admit to it, he did appreciate Leo's ability to determine Miss Geary's possible time of death. It was a large window, but if David Henderson didn't have an alibi for those eight hours, from seven at night until three in the morning, Jasper could indeed place him under arrest for suspicion of murder.

He went to the Nelsons' front door, a narrow building on a lower working-class street, surrounded by other nondescript homes. The people on this street likely spent their wages on food and necessities, not on beautifying the places they leased. Jasper grasped the brass knocker, and the door moved. It wasn't shut completely.

"They've scarpered, they have," a small voice came from behind him. Jasper spun away from the door.

A boy in half trousers and a patched cap stood on the short walk, hands in his pockets. He looked to be about eight or nine years old, one cheek smeared with dirt, the toes of his boots split from the soles.

"This is the home of the Nelsons?"

The boy nodded.

"When did they leave?"

Predictably, the door to the cab opened, and Leo emerged.

The boy kept quiet, holding Jasper's gaze in what could only be described as an enterprising manner. Sighing, he reached into his coat pocket. No sooner had he held out the threepenny bit than it vanished from between his fingers, the boy pocketing the loot in a blink.

"Two nights back," he answered.

"You're certain?"

The boy nodded. "'Course, I'm certain."

"You saw them leave?" Leo asked.

He nodded again. "Heard the missus and mister shoutin', then they come out with a couple o' bags and scarpered."

"What were they arguing about?" Jasper asked.

The boy shrugged. "Just regular shoutin'. The missus says they got to go now, and the mister started cursin' worse than my Uncle Jim, and he's a sailor."

Leo started for the house. Jasper thanked the boy, who was already running off, and overtook her before she could push the door open the rest of the way.

"No one is even at home," she complained as he stepped inside first.

"Unless the boy was lying or wrong."

Inside, the interior was just as bland and uninspired as the exterior. The furnishings were spare, the carpets hadn't been swept, and the walls were unadorned except for faded, out-of-date wallpaper. There was a raw chill to the air, what with no stove having been lit to warm the rooms in at least a day. A shawl and a coat, a couple of large, waxed canvas bags for the market stalls, and a few hats still hung on the pegs of a coat stand. At its base, a lone blue glove lay on the floor.

Jasper glimpsed into a sitting room, then a small dining room. A darker spot on the wallpaper indicated a piece of furniture had been there for some time before being removed.

"They were selling their belongings," he observed, noticing just two chairs at the large table, rather than the six it should have had.

"Even after being awarded a hundred pounds?" Leo opened a hinged door that led to the kitchen. "What did they do with the money?"

The kitchen was also nearly stripped bare. The only thing there seemed to be an abundance of were empty ale jugs and spirits bottles.

"There are any number of ways one could lose that sum of money, especially if Mr. Nelson had been drinking heavily," Jasper replied.

"Or Mrs. Nelson," Leo said.

He nodded. It was possible.

"Two days ago, Henderson's secretary gave us the complaints file," Jasper said as they returned to the front hall and started up the stairs. "It contained the Nelsons' report, which pointed us toward them as suspects."

Leo reached the top stair, her hand lingering on the carved ball of the newel post. Her lips parted in awe. "You're suggesting Mrs. Nelson somehow found out about it?"

"Miss Geary could have informed them that the file had gone with the police." Jasper peered into rooms as he cobbled together a theory. "They may have panicked, thinking their motive for murder would be evident and fled before we could arrive on their doorstep."

The first two bedrooms he peered into were sad and desolate, but the third was utterly forlorn. It was a nursery, and unlike the other rooms in the house that had been whittled away at, this one was untouched.

Two small beds were made up with blankets and pillows; a rag doll laid atop one and a wooden soldier upon the other. A mobile hung from the ceiling, with paper cutouts of rabbits, sheep, and cows dangling from the arms. This room's carpet was swept, the furnishings polished. The green pigmented wallpaper that had poisoned the two young occupants had been scraped loose and taken down. The walls remained bare plaster.

Leo wandered toward a low chest of drawers, painted a pale buttery yellow. "This room is like a memorial to them."

It reminded Jasper of the two rooms on the uppermost floor of his Charles Street residence. They had belonged to Beatrice and Gregory Junior, the two children his father had lost. Out of curiosity, Jasper had only visited the rooms a few times over the years, and only when his father wasn't present. They were much like this one, with beds, toys, and a dresser full of clothing. The drapes in each room had been pulled shut, permanently.

"I cannot bear to go in," his father had confessed when Jasper, newly arrived at Charles Street as his ward, inquired about the rooms. *"I know it is maudlin, but I also cannot bear to clear away their things, their childhood. Parting*

with their clothes, the toys they so loved..." His eyes had shone, his chin trembling, and Jasper had regretted asking.

Even now, their rooms remained untouched. His father's wish to preserve what he had left of his children had been transferred onto Jasper's shoulders. Perhaps that was why he could feel Mr. and Mrs. Nelson's pain still lingering in every room of this house, even though they had left it.

"To think something so innocuous as wallpaper had the power to kill innocent children," he said, peering at the bare walls. Here and there, slivers of green paper had been left behind.

"And yet Mr. Henderson claims no responsibility for the danger using these pigments presents," Leo replied.

"He isn't the only wallpaper manufacturer who uses toxic pigments. Not that I'm forgiving him for turning a blind eye to the problem."

If dead children weren't enough to make him want to change his business practices, nothing would entice him.

"Miss Geary might have felt sympathy for the Nelsons and remained in contact," he suggested as Leo pulled open dresser drawers. Folded clothing was still within them, topped by sachets of lavender. Jasper picked one up. The scent had gone stale.

"There aren't any framed photographs downstairs," Leo murmured. "I imagine Mrs. Nelson took them with her when she and her husband left two days ago."

She likely had. But a loving mother might have kept a cherished photograph somewhere more private. His own mother had kept a framed daguerreotype of him on her bedside table. After her death, when he'd gone to live with his uncle Robert and aunt Myra, his aunt had taken the frame and put it with those of her own children. He'd been shuffled to the back, obscured by other frames. No longer important.

Jasper left the nursery and returned to the room he thought most likely to be Mr. and Mrs. Nelson's. The bed was made, some clothing hung on a rack, and while a vanity dresser had been cleared of a brush and comb, it still held some other things like scent bottles, a few pieces of inexpensive jewelry, and small pots of cosmetics. On the bedside table, there wasn't a framed photograph, but a book and a folded lace kerchief. He picked up the book as Leo entered the room behind him.

"Have you found something?"

"No, I thought perhaps..." He went quiet as he opened to the saved page. The book's marker wasn't a silk ribbon or a more common pronged, enamel-topped spear. It was a photograph, mounted on a photographer's card. Two children, one fair-haired and one dark, sat on a carpet surrounded by bolster pillows and toys. They were positioned in front of a painted backdrop depicting a countryside vista. They appeared close in age. Possibly fraternal twins.

Leo came to his side, her arm brushing against his. "It's them. The children from the death portrait."

He retrieved that photo from his waistcoat pocket where he'd been carrying it and compared the two. There was no question; they were indeed the same children.

"The only person who could have given this death photograph to Gabriela Carter was Mrs. Nelson," Jasper said.

"So, she was the woman in the hooded cloak at Striker's?" Leo asked, shaking her head. "But why give Gabriela something that she must have so treasured? By the state of their living conditions, the Nelsons couldn't have afforded numerous copies of this photograph. Perhaps one or two. To give it to Gabriela...it was an important gesture."

"And not necessarily a threat," Jasper said, recalling that the poisoned drink had already been delivered by a man twenty or so minutes earlier.

They both fell silent. Jasper presumed Leo was doing as he was—attempting to form a plausible reason for Mrs. Nelson's actions. In the drop of quiet, Jasper became aware of a scent. Honeysuckle, he thought it might be. Light and floral, he breathed it in. It was coming from Leo. He couldn't recall her wearing the scent before. Or maybe he just hadn't stood close enough to her before to notice.

"We should go," he said, and at her distracted nod, they started for the door.

A clanging downstairs stilled him. He shot out a hand, barring her from advancing another step. Another rattling sound—of metal or glass—came, and Jasper held a finger to his lips. Someone was in the Nelsons' kitchen.

"The scrappy boy from outside?" Leo whispered.

Jasper didn't think so. He told her to stay where she was but knew from experience that she would do no such thing. He stepped lightly from the room, hoping the floorboards didn't creak. Leo did the same, following him to the top of the stairs. The noises from the kitchen persisted. As Jasper reached the bottom step, a man exited the dining room directly across the narrow hall. Tall, muscled, and impressively broad in the chest and shoulders, the man jolted in surprise. His dark eyes flared.

With the photographs in one hand, Jasper reached for his warrant card in his breast pocket with the other. "Inspector Reid from Scot—"

The man barreled forward and slammed his meaty arms into Jasper, knocking him against the wall and into the coat stand. The sharp blow of a fist cracked across his jaw, and Leo screamed. The strike whipped Jasper's head back, stunning him and spinning his vision for a few crucial seconds.

"Jasper!"

Black darts shot across his vision, blotting out his surroundings. Another strike didn't come, and Jasper suspected the man had fled. Leo gripped his elbow and tried to steady him to his feet. He'd been pummeled at Oliver Hayes's boxing club before but never with a wallop like that. He shook his head, clearing the black specks, and leaped for the open front door. By the time Jasper reached the front walk, the muscled man's dark blue sack coat was disappearing around a corner. He started to give chase but knew he wouldn't be able to keep up. He also wouldn't leave Leo in the house on her own.

"Damn it!" he swore, regret burning through him. He should've been prepared for the man to attack.

"That were the mister!"

The scrappy boy from earlier stood up from where he'd been sitting on another front step two doors down. He pointed after the man, who was now long gone.

"That was Mr. Nelson?" At the boy's nod, Jasper despised himself even more. He felt like an idiot as he turned back to the open door of the abandoned house.

He'd been lucky Mr. Nelson had only come at him. Allowing Leo to join him inside the house had been exactly what he'd known it would be: an irresponsible mistake.

She wasn't paying him any attention as he walked back toward her, the pain in his jaw setting in, the muscles around his mouth stiffening. She held a woman's cloak in one hand and in other, the photographs Jasper had dropped. Her lips parted as she looked between the items she held. The cloak, he noticed, was black and hooded, with blue embroidery along the edges.

"Is that the cloak you saw at Striker's Wharf?" he asked, wincing at the blooming tenderness in his chin.

"It was underneath the coat on the stand," she answered with a nod. "You were right—Mrs. Nelson was the cloaked woman from Striker's. And I think I know where we can find her."

Chapter Sixteen

Leo entered the morgue through the back door, along the dirt lane behind St. Matthew's Church. During the summer months when temperatures rose, she would prop the door open in the hope that any breeze might carry in fresh air. The vestry had been chosen as a site for a city deadhouse in part because of its proximity to Scotland Yard, but also for its stone foundation and exterior. It kept things icy during the winter months and at least partially cool during the summer. However, nothing could prevent corpses from more rapidly decomposing during the warmest times of the year or snuff out the odors that arose from them.

She was grateful for the persistent chill of the morgue right then as she hurried through the back office and into the postmortem room. It cooled the heated flush of her skin, compliments of her racing pulse and Jasper's contrary nature.

"There is no proof to support your theory," he said—*again*—as he entered the room behind her. He'd argued against her possible discovery during the entire carriage ride from Lambeth.

"No, there isn't...*yet*," she replied. Seeing her uncle at one of the autopsy tables occupied by a corpse, she called, "Is that Andrea Geary?"

Claude peered at them from over the top of his spectacles. "It is." He frowned. "Inspector Reid, you've quite a contusion there."

Jasper rubbed his jaw, which had begun to purple on the way to Spring Street. Luckily, Mr. Nelson had not had anything other than his fist to swing at him, although Jasper was certainly furious that the debilitating strike had prevented him from apprehending the suspect. He might have been slightly humiliated too, but Leo suspected he'd never admit to it.

Shedding her coat and hat, Leo tossed them onto an autopsy table along with the hooded cloak she'd found at the Nelsons' home. Tibia, the morgue's gray tabby, had been sleeping upon it in a tightly curled crescent. The cat meowed a complaint, then hissed at Jasper as he passed by.

"It's nothing," he told Claude, scowling at the tabby. "What have you noted about the body so far?"

Leo was glad to see the corpse had so newly arrived that it was still clothed. Her eyes went straight to the brooch pinned at the woman's throat. In the factory yard in Wapping, the checkered pattern had looked to have been done with two colors of fine thread. But now, after taking a second look at the children in both the death portrait and the photograph found inside Mrs. Nelson's bedside book, Leo believed otherwise.

Mr. Higgins exited the supply closet, and she

suppressed a groan. Everything about him was thin and long, from his frame to his face to his mustache, the tapered points of which stretched to the edge of his chin. As usual, he looked perturbed to see her.

"Miss Spencer," he greeted with a sniff of disdain, then, cocking his head, "Inspector," with a touch more respect. The young man was unbearably morose and clearly did not wish for his appointment here as an apprentice to her uncle.

For his part, Jasper ignored him. So did Claude.

"I've yet to complete a thorough inspection, but from what I can see," her uncle noted, as he moved aside clumps of hair matted with blood, "there is significant injury to the parietal bone, inflicted by a heavy object. The impression in the skull is round, indicating the shape of the object used. A single strike."

"That alone would have killed her?" Jasper asked.

"Instantly," Claude confirmed. "But I will look for further injury and evidence, of course."

"Uncle, does this injury remind you of another body that came in recently?" Leo didn't want to lead him too much toward the answer she sought.

Claude furrowed his brow and looked again. "Hmm. Quite. I believe the expecting Jane Doe from last month had a similar skull wound."

Leo exhaled, relieved. She then unpinned Andrea Geary's brooch.

Mr. Higgins, who had returned to his work on another corpse that was open and in the process of a postmortem, sighed heavily at her handling of the body.

Leo held the brooch out to her uncle. "Can you confirm that this is human hair?"

He took it, his hand quivering. Leo shot a look over her shoulder at the apprentice, but he was busy removing a spleen, nearly dropping it back into the open abdominal cavity in the process.

"It is," her uncle said, returning it to her. "The texture is fine and smooth, most assuredly from young children."

Leo offered the brooch to Jasper. He shook his head, not needing to hold it. Or perhaps not wanting to. It was mourning jewelry. Many thought it a fashionable accessory, a way to memorialize a lost loved one. But like death photography, Leo thought it macabre.

"Look again at the hair of the children in the photographs," she urged. Impatiently, she reached into Jasper's coat pocket, where he'd stored them, but he caught her wrist before she could retrieve them.

"I can get them myself, Leo."

Jasper released her and took out the photographs.

"The little boy is fair, and the girl's hair is somewhat darker," she said. Holding the brooch next to the photographs, she touched a light blonde square, then a darker one woven in. "I don't believe this woman is Andrea Geary. I think she is the dead children's mother, Evelyn Nelson."

Jasper scrubbed his jaw, agitated. But at least he wasn't still disputing her theory.

"And you propose that she took a false identity when applying for work at Henderson's factory," he said.

"Six months ago, yes. Her children would have died two months before that."

He continued, "Her motive was to get close to Jack Henderson and decipher a way to seek vengeance?"

"Something that could be more easily done if she was a trusted employee," Leo replied.

It made sense, even if Jasper still appeared skeptical. As a detective inspector he was supposed to be cautious, but at least he was entertaining the possibility.

Claude made a sound of interest. "Didn't you say the Nelsons filed a formal complaint? Surely Mr. Henderson would have recognized her as the mother of the poisoned children and turned her away at once."

Leo had thought of that. "Not if he and his solicitor had only dealt with Mr. Nelson for the complaint. If Mr. Henderson had never set eyes on her before she applied for the position of his secretary, how would he have known who she truly was?"

"So, she took a new name and insinuated herself into the company she detests," Jasper said. "To what end? You saw her. She was meek and skittish around Mr. Henderson. Hardly the conniving woman you're suggesting she was."

Leo refused to back down. The more she thought this theory through, the more accurate it felt.

"What if her conniving wasn't hers alone? Her husband must have been aware of her new position, especially if she was absent from the house for several hours each day of the week. You're right. She was meek and skittish. Perhaps her husband forced her into this scheme, and she felt as though she had no choice but to go along with it."

Jasper braved the autopsy table where Tibia had gone back to sleep and lifted the black cloak. "You're certain this is the same blue embroidery?"

Leo pursed her lips. "Need you truly ask? Yes, I am certain."

"So that night at Striker's, Mrs. Nelson exposed herself and her six months of deceit by giving Gabriela a photograph of her dead children. Why?"

"To warn her?" Leo suggested. "To tell her the truth? That her husband was intent on avenging their children by poisoning Mr. Henderson's own beloved daughter."

But she'd been too late. Gabriela had already consumed the poisoned drink.

At the adjacent examination table, Mr. Higgins snorted a laugh. Leo swiveled on her heel.

"Is there something you'd like to contribute, Mr. Higgins?"

He set the extracted liver into a basin. "What you're saying is all very entertaining, but the body has already been identified as Andrea Geary. There is no evidence to the contrary."

Leo bit her tongue. The man hadn't contributed much in the way of anything, but on this he'd formed an opinion? Even worse was that he was correct. They had only speculation and coincidence to go by. Miss Geary had been the one to pull the complaints file from Mr. Henderson's shelves; if she was truly Mrs. Nelson, she very well could have gone home that evening and warned her husband that the police were likely to visit their address soon, especially after seeing the death portrait Jasper had shown Mr. Henderson.

But as Mr. Higgins had so smugly pointed out, that was only supposition.

Then there was the question of why Andrea Geary, or possibly Evelyn Nelson, had been killed. And apparently, by the same person who'd killed Regina Morris. Leo closed her eyes, overwhelmed by everything she didn't yet know.

"If this is Evelyn Nelson," Jasper said, "we need proof. We need someone to identify her."

Leo brightened. "Like the boy from outside their home?"

Jasper shook his head. "Not a child. But another neighbor will do. I'll send a constable to knock on doors—"

A bell rigged to the lobby door rang, signaling someone's arrival. Claude went to see who it was, leaving Leo and Jasper alone. She lowered her voice to keep Mr. Higgins from overhearing.

"Do you recall Mr. Nelson's occupation from the London Directory?"

"Ironmonger." Jasper shifted his jaw and winced. "He sells tools, hardware, anything made of iron, and I'm sure he's in repairs. That would account for his build."

"He would have ready access to a mallet."

"So might David Henderson," he reminded her. "Think. Why would Terrence Nelson bludgeon Regina Morris and his own wife, but poison Gabriela?"

"Because Gabriela's death was meant to be symbolic. It was meant to be revenge. Death by arsenic is equal retribution."

Jasper continued to shake his head. "No, equal retribution would be the poisoning of Henderson's *two* children. Not just Gabriela. And yet, David is alive and well."

He was also Jasper's top suspect for Regina's murder

and Mrs. Nelson's. She *was* Evelyn Nelson. Leo was certain of it.

Claude returned, and with him was Sergeant Lewis.

"Hoped you'd be here, guv," Lewis said. "The address for Andrea Geary was a sham. The woman who runs the boardinghouse hasn't ever heard of her."

Vindication burst through Leo, and she nearly hopped with glee. Only the fact that they were in a morgue, investigating two murdered women, kept her feet planted to the floor. Jasper took the news with his usual subdued expression.

"And did you speak to David Henderson? Does he have an alibi?"

The other detective grinned impishly. "He says he had dinner with his father, then went straight home at eleven o'clock. However, when I spoke to Jack Henderson separately, he claimed to have dined out with friends at a club on Ludgate Hill. I asked for names. His boy wasn't among them."

Jasper started away from the table, taking out his fob to check the time. "The factory closes at one o'clock on Saturdays. We need to move fast if we're to catch him there and bring him into Scotland Yard for questioning."

Then, as if he'd been yanked by an invisible rope, he turned back toward Leo. His eyes cut to Mrs. Nelson, then away again. "We still need someone to identify her as Evelyn Nelson, but I think you're right. Good work, Leo."

The compliment stunned her, and she watched him and Lewis leave the postmortem room without so much as a peep from her parted lips. She couldn't have asked to go with them. There was no reason for her to accompany them and no way to trick Jasper this time. Besides, a corpse needed seeing to. With Mr. Higgins engaged with another postmortem, Leo could at least serve as a barrier between her uncle and the medical student if his hands shook.

Claude began to remove Mrs. Nelson's clothing, and Leo went to her feet to help with her boots. They had worked together countless times to strip a body in preparation for a postmortem, and now they moved in sequence easily, out of habit and routine. Mr. Higgins had voiced his censure about her assisting her uncle on his first day, but as he was a student, he didn't possess the authority to order her away from the process. Not yet, at least. However, with enough complaints to his professor at the medical college, the chief coroner might have something to say to restrict her efforts.

"You've been busy with the inspector," Claude commented as they rolled the body onto its side to shift her arm out of a coat sleeve.

"I suppose I feel attached to this case in some ways since I was there when Gabriela Carter died."

But that wasn't the only reason. The truth was she enjoyed unraveling the different pieces of information in an investigation, the challenge of deciphering which details were important and which weren't, and the rush of exhilaration she felt when she figured something out. Just as she had now, with the brooch and the revelation that the dead woman was very likely Evelyn Nelson. With a twist of sadness, she thought of how much she'd have liked to tell Gregory Reid all about it. And how much he would have enjoyed listening to her recount her discoveries. She could even envision his proud smile.

"It was kind of him to invite us to dinner last night,"

Claude said. While helping to roll the body onto its opposite side to slip the other arm free from the coat, Leo caught a swift, searching look from her uncle.

"What is it?" she asked.

"I just wonder...is there any reason Jasper might have invited us to his home?"

Leo puzzled at the question. "How do you mean?"

No dinner had been prepared at their own home, and since Mrs. Zhao always made too much for one person, Jasper had kindly invited them. It seemed a straightforward reason. Yes, it had been out of the ordinary, especially for Jasper. He wasn't the spontaneous sort. He also wasn't overly hospitable. But what other motive could he have had?

The memory of his unexpected visit a few nights prior to their dinner and how he'd taken her wrist in his hand skittered through her mind. Jasper's touch had left a prickling sensation on her skin, and she wasn't certain it was due only to the coarseness of his palm. The moment had been...curiously intimate and slightly awkward.

Claude shrugged as if to dismiss the subject from further discussion. But as Leo rolled down one of Mrs. Nelson's stockings, then the other, she continued to think about the gentle press of Jasper's fingers against her wrist.

"Uncle Claude," she said as she folded the wool stockings and set them on a table with the woman's other belongings, "speaking of last night's dinner, I meant to ask you about something Aunt Flora mentioned: the letters she'd received from my mother."

Before she could go on to ask if those letters were real and if Flora still possessed them, Claude finished unbuttoning Mrs. Nelson's blouse. A piece of paper could be seen at the top edge of her exposed corset. It rested between the corset and her cotton chemise, the corner of the paper sticking up from the center busk. Leo pulled it free.

"It appears she kept it there for safekeeping," Claude said.

She unfolded the paper. A woman's dainty handwriting filled the single page. As she devoured each printed word, Leo's skin numbed. Her pulse escalated.

"Leonora?"

She peeled her eyes from the paper, which she gripped in a stranglehold. "Uncle, I need to go."

"Go? Where?" he called as she folded the paper and slid it into her skirt pocket.

"Henderson & Son!" she called as she took up her coat and hat and hurried for the morgue's front door.

Chapter Seventeen

An exodus was underway at the wallpaper factory when Jasper and Lewis arrived. Employees spilled from the factory yard into the street, their workday completed. There were no constables present to keep out reporters, but from the look of it, no reporters were angling to get in either. A woman's body had been found that morning, and yet, time had already marched on.

The front door was locked, so they went into the factory yard, moving against the tide of employees. The foreman, Mr. Bridges, was conversing with a few lingering men but waved them off when he noticed him and his detective sergeant approaching.

"Is there something more, detectives?" he asked. "As you can see, the workers are dispersing. If you want to speak to them, they won't be back until the start of next week."

"We'd like another word with David Henderson," Jasper said.

The foreman waved them into the factory with a nod. "He's in his office, as far as I know."

Jasper and Lewis passed through a storage room that was chock-full of cylindrical containers prepared for shipping and delivery.

"My wife says she wants new coverings for our walls," Lewis remarked as they moved out of the room into a long corridor.

"So long as you avoid those papers with Scheele's green pigment in them," Jasper warned, passing the canteen and turning up a set of stairs toward the office where he'd spoken to David Henderson the previous day.

"Too posh for my purse anyhow," Lewis replied. "And after all that about the poisoned kiddies, I wouldn't trust the wall coverings around my own little ones."

On the way to Wapping, Jasper had informed the detective sergeant about the Nelsons and their possible connection to Gabriela Carter's murder. Possibly because the idea had originated with Leo, Lewis seemed less convinced that Miss Geary was, in fact, Mrs. Nelson. But he agreed that the Nelsons had strong motive to avenge their children's deaths.

Briefly, he and Lewis had stopped in the telegraph room at Scotland Yard before leaving for Henderson & Son to send out notice to all divisions to be on the lookout for Terrence Nelson; now that Jasper had seen him, he'd been able to provide a description of the suspect as well.

"I'll stick to a clean limewash," Lewis went on. "Nothing wrong with—"

At the sound of a thud, then a muffled cry, Jasper held up a hand. Lewis went silent.

"Stop! I'm telling you, that's not how it is!"

David's panicked voice reached through the door to his office just ahead. Jasper rushed toward it while reaching for his revolver holstered at his ribs. Without knocking, he barged in.

Andrew Carter was leaning against David's desk, his arms and ankles crossed, while one of the men he'd brought to Scotland Yard for his questioning pinned David's arms behind his back. The second hired man whirled toward Jasper and Lewis, his meaty fist clenched and streaked with blood. David's lip had been split, as had his brow.

"Inspector!" he wheezed, as though trying to recover from a punch to the gut. "Thank God, Inspector, tell them. Tell them I had nothing to do with it!"

"Release him," Jasper ordered, his palm on his police-issued weapon. He watched for any movement from Andrew or his muscle men, but all the East Rip did was grin and snap his fingers.

David collapsed to the floor, landing on his knees as the man holding him backed away.

"What in hell are you doing, Carter?" Jasper asked, not yet convinced it was safe to remove his hand from his Webley.

Andrew pushed off the desk to stand tall. "Just some family business with my brother-in-law. Nothing to concern yourself with, Inspector Reid."

"I am concerned just the same, so explain yourself," he said.

David staggered to his feet and scurried to the other side of his office. "He has it in his warped mind that I had something to do with my sister's murder."

"Why would he think that?" Jasper asked.

Andrew ambled toward his two men, joining them perhaps to have their protection. "It's simple," he said smoothly. "Gabriela told me her brother was having an affair with his secretary and that she'd threatened to tell his wife unless he put an end to it. Now I hear his secretary is dead."

"Is this true?" Lewis asked David. His hand was also still resting on his weapon, which he kept holstered at his hip.

David's expression folded. "Yes. Gabby knew, and she did say I needed to end things, or she would tell Celia, but I would never have killed my sister—"

"No, just your mistress when she revealed she was carrying your child," Jasper said.

Slowly, he took his hand from his revolver. He didn't trust Andrew Carter or his men, but they were here on the same task, it seemed.

"Never! I didn't kill Regina!" He gripped the edge of his desk, leaning upon it for support. "And I didn't know she was carrying my child. She left a note on my desk, which said she could no longer work at her position here, and I never saw or heard from her again. I certainly had no idea she was dead!"

Andrew took slow steps back toward the desk. "What happened, David? Did Gabriela know what you did? That you bashed in Regina's skull to keep her from going to your wife?"

David scuttled further behind his desk, stammering a denial. "No, she knew nothing because I had done nothing!"

"Stand down, Carter," Jasper warned. Andrew raised his hands, as if to say he wasn't doing anything wrong.

But he'd almost certainly come here to force a confession from his brother-in-law, then mete out his own punishment. Jasper would make sure that didn't happen.

"You admit to the affair," he said to David, who nodded. "Were you aware that Andrea Geary suspected the affair too?"

David closed his eyes, and exhaling, nodded again. "Regina and I, we were here late one evening. We thought everyone had gone for the night, but on her way out, Regina ran into Miss Geary and a man. A beau, Regina thought."

Jasper wondered about this beau. Might it have been Mr. Nelson?

"Why would seeing Regina have been suspicious to Miss Geary?" Lewis asked.

Shamefaced, David answered, "She alerted Regina to the fact that her blouse's buttons weren't properly aligned."

Observing that Regina had stayed late with her employer and afterward appeared rumpled, Miss Geary had made the correct assumption. However, Leo said Miss Geary confessed to seeing David refresh a vase of flowers every few days on Regina's desk; she hadn't made a peep about this much more obvious after-hours encounter.

"Two mornings later, Regina left her note," David said with a helpless shrug. "I didn't see her again."

"And now, this other secretary's turned up dead," Andrew Carter said, his tone sharpening. "Bashed-in skull, just like Regina's. And only one day after Scotland

Yard came here asking questions. Admit it, Davy, you panicked."

David slammed his hands flat onto the desk he hid behind. "No! I haven't bashed in any skulls, and I didn't poison my sister!"

Andrew made a whirling motion with his fingers, and the two hired men bristled to attention. "I don't believe you."

"Tell your brutes to stand down," Jasper ordered, his palm going to his Webley again. "I'm investigating these murders, Carter, not you. I'm aware they're connected, but I don't believe your brother-in-law is behind them. Not anymore."

He had, especially when David lied to Lewis about being at dinner with his father for a short while the previous evening.

"Mr. Henderson, what can you tell me about Terrence Nelson?"

David stared blankly at Jasper. "Who?"

"The father of the two tots who sucked on your company's wallpaper and died," Lewis said. "Arsenic poisoning."

His expression soured. "My goodness. Why do you ask about that horrid business?"

"Because I have reason to believe Andrea Geary was, in fact, Mrs. Evelyn Nelson, the mother of the toddlers," Jasper answered.

David's squinting eyes grew round and large, while Andrew Carter whistled, as if amused. Jasper's irritation with him only increased.

"Why would... No, that's impossible. Miss Geary,

she…she wasn't married," David said, tripping over his words.

"I'm betting Mr. Nelson was the *beau* Regina Morris saw on the night she stayed late," Lewis said as he caught on.

"He didn't like being seen," Jasper said, nodding. "Maybe he thought Regina had heard or discovered something she shouldn't have."

"Like their plan of revenge," Lewis concluded solemnly. "He believed he had to get rid of her."

David raised his hand. "Revenge for what? Father settled their claim. I was there. The man received one hundred pounds, a princely sum for a man of his class."

Jasper nearly recoiled. David spoke as though the children of certain men were less valuable than others. As different to his father as David Henderson had seemed to be, he was still very much cut from the same cloth.

Andrew Carter scoffed. "Their tots were still dead though, weren't they? I'd stuff my pockets full of your daddy's money and still slit his throat."

"No, it wasn't enough for Jack Henderson to suffer his own death," Jasper said. "The Nelsons wanted him to suffer what they had—the deaths of his children. David, I'm assuming you and your father dealt solely with Mr. Nelson, not his wife?"

He confirmed it with a nod. "But Miss Geary? Truly? She tricked her way in here to…to *kill* Gabby and me?"

Andrew rolled his neck, stretching it side to side in the manner Jasper had seen boxers do in the ring before a fight. "That's devious. If my wife hadn't been the target, I'd appreciate that level of treachery." He walked toward a sofa and a table of decanted spirits nearby. It would be where David sat down with other businessmen, plied them with liquor, and made all sorts of deals. It might have even been where Mr. Nelson sat when he'd signed away his right to ever seek justice for his children's deaths.

"If the woman wasn't already dead, I'd do the honors," Andrew said, picking up a glass decanter and pouring himself a liberal splash. "As it is, I'll have to settle for her husband. Inspector, I trust you've reached the same conclusion as me: Nelson was the one dressed in Bloom's livery that night."

He was big, Andrew had said, his recollection of the waiter vague. *His hands barely fit into the white gloves.* Jasper shifted his sore jaw. Terrence Nelson's hands matched that description well.

He agreed with Andrew, but he refused to utter it aloud.

"I'm arresting Mr. Nelson and sending him to trial," he said instead. "He'll hang for his crimes—"

"I'll gut him before he gets to Scotland Yard," Andrew said, raising his glass in a toast.

The door to the office suddenly burst open, and Jasper's hand went to his Webley again. He swore under his breath as he saw Leo standing within the frame, her hand still on the knob.

"What the hell are you doing here?" he thundered.

"Thank goodness," she breathed heavily, flushed as if she'd sprinted to the factory all the way from Spring Street. "We must leave the building—now! I found a confession in Mrs. Nelson's bodice."

"A confession to what?" Lewis asked.

But Jasper was more interested in the reason for Leo's frenzied state. "Why do we need to leave the building?"

"She didn't want to kill Gabriela and David; that was her husband's plan. She argued against it, saying they needed to destroy the *wallpaper*, not two people who had nothing to do with their children's deaths. The book on her bedside table, Jasper!"

He vaguely recalled it. "A guide of some sort," he said. "About mining?"

"A guide to handling dynamite for coal miners, yes. I overlooked it at the time because I cared more about the photograph you found between the pages. But now it makes perfect sense. Hurry, we need to leave before—"

A deafening roar silenced Leo and shook the floor. Jasper's legs disappeared from underneath him as a cracking blast shuddered through his teeth and wiped out his hearing. He reached for Leo, but the ceiling came down, and she was gone.

Chapter Eighteen

"Leo!"

The voice reached through the dark, past a persistent chiming in her ears. *Jasper.* She moved, and a splinter of pain radiated down her torso and along her ribs.

"Leo, goddamn it." His voice drew closer and became clearer, and then all at once, the darkness dispersed. Leo opened her eyes and pushed up from the floor, where she'd been laying. A hand gripped her shoulder as she slid her feet underneath her.

Debris rolled off her skirt to the floor as Jasper helped pull her up. Plaster from the ceiling had come down in chunks, and dust lingered in the air. She could smell smoke. Something was burning.

He looked her over. "Are you badly injured?"

She shook her head and coughed as dust particles shuttled down her throat. Jasper's hat was gone, and his hair hung over his brow, the golden strands coated with white. Blood streaked his temple, and he cradled his left arm to his chest. "You're hurt," she said.

He winced but shook his head. "I'm fine. We need to get out of here."

Looking around, her hearing still muffled, she saw that Andrew Carter and his two men were already gone. David Henderson was crawling out from behind his desk, trying to stand; and Lewis was still on the floor, unmoving. Jasper went to his side.

"Lewis?" he said loudly. "Roy, wake up."

The detective sergeant moaned and twitched. Leo exhaled, relieved he was still alive. Jasper tried to lift him but grunted in pain.

"You *are* hurt," she said. Then, at the odd drooping of his left arm, she guessed, "Your shoulder is dislocated?"

"I'll take care of it later. We need to leave the building. It can't be stable."

Leo winced at the ache in her ribs as she helped Lewis to his feet. He swayed, and Jasper shored him up.

David was attempting to pull himself up from the floor while gripping his bloody head. "Good God, what was that?"

"Dynamite," Leo replied as she moved to help him stand. "Mrs. Nelson was *leaving* the building late last night, not entering it, when she was attacked. She'd already planted the bomb. She confessed everything in her letter, even her husband's deeds."

And then, she'd intended to end her own life. Leo suspected, however, that her husband had beat her to it.

David leaned heavily against her, one of his eyes swollen to a grotesque state, and blood washing over his cheek. "This factory is filled with flammable polymers and chemicals," he said, stumbling over his words. "There could be another explosion."

Jasper grunted again in pain as he positioned one of Lewis's arms over his uninjured shoulder. "Go, Leo," he commanded, his voice strained.

With David's considerable weight leaning against her, she staggered out of the debris-strewn office. In the corridor, a wall had collapsed, and parts of the ceiling had come down. The sharp scent of smoke filled the air. Something was on fire within the building—just as Mrs. Nelson had intended.

The destruction of the wallpaper factory had been Evelyn's sole desire, while her husband had chosen another method of revenge. From her confession letter, Leo learned they'd drifted apart for months while she had worked to acquire dynamite and assemble a timed bomb, and he had planned to hurt Jack Henderson as Terrence had been hurt—with his children's deaths. But Mrs. Nelson hadn't intended to kill anyone. She'd joined Henderson & Son to more easily place the bomb when it was ready.

"She timed the bomb to go off after the employees left for the day," Leo said as they reached the stairwell.

"It doesn't matter. David is right. With the amount of chemicals in this building, the fire could trigger another explosion at any moment," Jasper said.

Lewis was coming to, murmuring that he could walk on his own. David stumbled awkwardly, nearly causing her to fall down the stairs. Sweat rolled down the back of her neck and her ribs were on fire by the time they made it to the bottom step. The foreman came through a wall of dark smoke toward them, and he lifted David's other arm, to Leo's relief.

"This way!" he shouted, then led them to the loading dock and out into the factory yard.

Fresh air flooded Leo's lungs so quickly her head and vision swam. Jasper lowered Lewis onto a crate, and David collapsed onto the cobbles. Drawn by the explosion, people swarmed the factory yard. The blast likely had been felt from several streets away. A bucket brigade had begun to form, and pea whistles trilled in the distance, summoning a proper fire wagon.

Jasper stared at the building, its glass windows blown out and a ragged hole in the wall where bricks had cascaded to the ground. He continued to cradle his arm. "Mrs. Nelson got what she wanted. There must be thousands of pounds worth of wallpaper burning in there right now."

"That was what *she* wanted, yes," Leo said. "It was Terrence who wanted to hurt Jack Henderson more personally."

The confession in Leo's coat pocket made it clear that Mrs. Nelson had still felt responsible for Gabriela's death and for Regina's murder as well. Her husband had become obsessed with his revenge, and she hadn't been able to dissuade him from his plans.

Regina had seen Terrence one night at the factory, arguing with Evelyn. Then, a few days later, when the note from Regina appeared on David's desk, Evelyn had been concerned. She wrote in her confession that the handwriting hadn't looked like Regina's but rationalized that she might have been in a hurry to leave it and be gone from the factory before anyone saw her. It wasn't until

Jasper identified the Jane Doe as Regina Morris that Mrs. Nelson understood her husband had killed the secretary to silence her. She'd known then that he needed to be stopped.

"Why then is David still alive?" Jasper asked, glancing toward the man. He'd been moved from the cobbles to the back of a cart. There, a pair of older women were tending to his bloodied, swollen face. He'd already been injured when Leo arrived in his office, and she suspected Andrew Carter's two hired men had something to do with his condition.

"Maybe Terrence had been counting on his wife to help give him access to David, but she wouldn't agree," Leo suggested.

She removed the letter from her pocket and held it out for Jasper to take. He lifted it from her fingers using his uninjured arm.

"I can help you with that," she said, pointing to his left shoulder.

Many bodies arrived at the morgue with dislocated shoulders, especially those who'd suffered deadly falls or carriage accidents. Claude had shown her how to maneuver the ball of the shoulder back into its socket. However, if Jasper allowed her, it would be her first time performing the motion on a living person. She chose not to tell him as much when he nodded, a tight grimace already on his face in preparation for the shock of pain the maneuver would cause. At least then he'd be able to use his left arm again.

She gripped his forearm, and at the count of three, pulled and pushed the shoulder back into place. A cracking sound accompanied it, and Jasper groaned, hanging his head and cursing under his breath. That was when she saw the tear in his coat along the top of his back and shoulders, and the blood seeping through the fabric.

"You're bleeding quite heavily," she said, wincing. "We need to get you, Sergeant Lewis, and Mr. Henderson to a hospital."

He nodded, his face glistening with sweat and streaked with soot and blood. "The London is closest."

They left Mr. Bridges in charge of the bucket brigade; pails of water were being drawn up from the nearby Basin and rushed to the factory to douse the fire. She and Jasper trundled Lewis and David into one of the factory's wagons. Then Jasper took the reins.

"You've one good arm, and you're bleeding," Leo said, stealing the reins from his hands as she sat on the driver's bench beside him. "I will drive."

"But you're terrible at it," he grumbled.

She balked. "The Inspector taught me, and he said I was marvelous."

Jasper chuffed a laugh. "Of course, he did. When did he ever discourage you from anything? Even the things you were bad at?"

Leo tried to think of an example and failed. "It doesn't matter. I'm still driving."

He gave in to her demand, cradling his still sore arm as she directed the pair of horses toward the hospital. The drive wasn't far, just off Whitechapel Road, and along the way, Lewis began to speak and think more clearly.

"We should have Henderson guarded. At least until Nelson is found and arrested," he said, pressing a hand to the back of his head. His palm came away wet with blood.

"I don't need a guard," David said, his words slurred, as though he'd partaken in too many pints of ale at a pub.

"Your sister's killer still wants you dead," Leo reminded him. "I should think you'd want a phalanx of guards."

He didn't argue, though that might have been because he'd dropped into unconsciousness again.

While she drove, Jasper read the confession Leo had found in Mrs. Nelson's bodice. Once he finished it, he folded the paper, almost reverently, and put it away in his pocket. His forehead continued to bead with sweat, even though it was cold, and they were in an open wagon. His coloring paled, then flushed, and she worried he was losing too much blood. He wouldn't want her to fuss though, so she kept her lips sealed until they arrived at the hospital and entered the front doors.

"You need to see a doctor," she told him as David and Lewis were being collected for treatment.

"I'm fine," he replied, rolling his shoulder. "See? You set my arm."

"No, you're not fine. Your coat is gashed open, and you're bleeding through your shirt." She pulled aside his coat collar, revealing the blood-soaked linen.

"Leo—" He took her wrist and held it down. But an eagle-eyed nurse had seen the blood, and she hastened forward with a wheelchair.

"All right, I give up. I'll go. But I am not sitting in that." He left the lobby on foot with the nurse.

Leo trailed them at a distance. Her only injury was a few bruised ribs; at worst, they may have been broken, but there was nothing to be done except to bind them tightly, and she could attend to that herself once she was home. The nurse showed Jasper down a wide corridor, with curtains hanging to enclose the individual beds.

As Leo waited, she considered Mrs. Nelson's confession letter and the frustrated sadness she'd felt while reading it. The bereft mother had intended to bring public attention to the dangers of the toxins used in wallpaper, and yet instead, her husband had taken the settlement to pay off debts, drink, and gamble heavily. By signing the contract of silence, Mr. Nelson had muffled his wife. After that, she'd felt her only option had been to enact a bolder protest.

Leo didn't know what it was to have a child or to lose one. It would not be the same as losing a brother or sister, or a mother or father. This, she knew instinctively. Her grief over the Inspector's death was also a different breed than the anguish Mrs. Nelson must have endured with the loss of her children.

Leo's family had been taken from her, but unlike Evelyn Nelson, she had never learned who'd killed them. A part of her didn't want to know. What would she do with that information? How could she possibly avenge them? Would she be as single-minded as Evelyn had been in her plans for vengeance? Perhaps. For that reason alone, Leo could not entirely condemn the poor woman. And though he would likely never say as much, she suspected by the careful refolding of Evelyn's letter that Jasper felt much the same way.

She'd settled into a chair in the corridor, her eyes tracing the checked pattern of black and white floor tiles. She didn't know what made her glance up. Some intuition, maybe. When she did, a doctor was passing by. He wore a white, smocked coat as he walked briskly past her and down the corridor. His profile was only visible for a split second, but recognition fired through her brain. Leo sat straight up, watching the man as he carried on toward the other end of the long corridor. His doctor's coat didn't quite fit his broad shoulders; the material pulled between his expansive shoulder blades.

Her heart hammering, she shot to her feet and reached for the curtain enclosing the space into which Jasper had been shown. Her breathing was ragged as she yanked the curtain aside.

Seated on the bed, his shirt discarded next to him, Jasper leaned forward, elbows on his knees. The nurse was sponging dried blood from a long gash that was drawn across his shoulder and upper back. He sat straight up, twisting to glance at Leo.

"Miss, please wait outside," the matronly woman said sternly.

Jasper reached for his shirt and stood from the bed simultaneously. "What's wrong?" he asked, ignoring the nurse's protests.

Stripped to his waist, Leo received a generous view of his bare chest and abdomen. She blinked, momentarily startled. He gingerly slid his arms into his shirt sleeves and brought the panels together.

"Leo?" he pressed, buttoning as he waited for her tongue to unknot.

"Mr. Nelson," she blurted. "He's here."

He went still, buttons forgotten. "Where?"

Leo stepped back out into the corridor and pointed. "That way. He's wearing a white doctor's coat."

Jasper tore past her and stared in the direction she'd indicated. Mr. Nelson was no longer in sight. "He's after

David Henderson," he said and, with his shirt still unbuttoned and untucked, began to run along the hall, ripping open curtains as he went. Leo fell into step alongside him, taking the right-hand side of the corridor, while he took the left, both of them flinging open any of the drawn privacy curtains and receiving gasps and startled admonishments as they went.

But then, as Leo swung the next curtain aside, she jolted to a stop.

David Henderson, his head and eyes bandaged with linen, was seated on a hospital cot. A thick-set doctor was helping him to grasp a drinking glass and raise it to his lips.

"Don't drink that!" Leo shouted.

Terrence Nelson swung toward her, his eyes ablaze with determination.

"The water is poisoned," she said.

David, blinded by the linen over his eyes, tried to pull the glass from his mouth, but Mr. Nelson fought him, attempting to force it up to his lips. Leo shot forward despite knowing she was utterly unqualified to fight a man as large and burly as Mr. Nelson. She only knew she had to help David somehow.

Thankfully, Jasper rushed into the cordoned-off space just then and barreled past her, straight into Mr. Nelson. The impact was enough to dislodge the glass from his hand. Water spilled as the glass fell to the floor, David frantically wiping his lips and face where the water had touched.

Jasper tackled Mr. Nelson, but the brawny man pushed back, punching Jasper in the abdomen, then the side of the head. Their arms locked, they staggered into the freestanding framed curtain, crashed through it, and tumbled into the neighboring bed space. The frame tipped over, and Jasper and Mr. Nelson fell to the floor with it. Mr. Nelson, however, rolled to his side and leapt up with more agility than he looked to possess. His escape route was clear, and the frightened doctors and nurses gathering in the hall didn't look to be interested in stopping him.

Next to Leo, a steel cart on wheels held scissors, gauze, and other medical instruments. She grabbed the edge of it and launched it in front of him just as he started running. The cart and its contents went sailing, but after an initial stumble, Mr. Nelson stayed on his feet. The obstacle had provided enough of a delay, however, for Jasper to get to his feet and tackle him again, throwing Mr. Nelson forward and off-balance. He fell to the floor with a thud, and Jasper delivered two blows to the side of the ironmonger's head before digging his knee into the middle of his back. It wouldn't matter how large or powerful Mr. Nelson was—with enough acute pressure to his lumbar region, he'd be paralyzed by pain.

"Cuffs, Leo! My coat," Jasper shouted.

Running back to the curtained space where he'd been receiving treatment felt more like she was wading through a river of honey. But when she picked up Jasper's coat and holster strap, the Webley still in place, and hurried back to the commotion in the corridor, she found Mr. Nelson still pinned to the floor. She pulled the handcuffs from a coat pocket.

"Terrence Nelson, you're under arrest for the murders of Regina Morris, Gabriela Carter, and Evelyn Nelson," Jasper said, gasping for air, his own pain evident. He closed the cuffs around the man's wrists, then sat back on his haunches, breathing heavily.

"I'm poisoned!" David cried from his bed, still wiping madly at his mouth.

"If you did swallow some water, it was a trace amount, not nearly enough to poison you," Leo assured him, but then stepped aside as a nurse broke from the hovering hospital staff members, all of whom were wide-eyed with shock, and came forward to calm him.

"Guv," Sergeant Lewis called as he staggered through the commotion to join them. "Bloody hell. Is that—"

"Yes." Jasper got to his feet with a deep groan. Leo's heart squeezed at the sight of him, his shirt panels still undone, fresh blood dripping from his collarbone. He looked utterly ragged, but triumphant.

Terrence Nelson lay moaning on the tiled floor in shame and defeat, his forehead and nose pressed against it. Jasper peered down at him in disgust as he resumed buttoning his shirt.

"Doctor, is there a side exit we can take this man through?" Jasper asked once Leo had handed him his holster and coat. "I think we've caused enough of a scene for your other patients."

The doctor readily agreed and gave directions to the hospital's little-used side door. After Jasper and Lewis hoisted Mr. Nelson to his feet, the detective sergeant left to fetch the wagon and horse.

Jasper urged Mr. Nelson forward, but the larger man thrashed his shoulders as if to throw him off.

"Enough, Nelson, it's over," he warned.

"He deserves to die. He killed them!" he shouted, directing a hateful glare toward David Henderson, who was now gagging on a spoonful of syrup being administered to him. Ipecac, Leo presumed.

"He did not kill your children, Mr. Nelson," she said as Jasper kept him moving. "Wallpaper colored with a poisonous green pigment did. Greed and negligence did. Your wife knew that."

Mr. Nelson swung his head, his face glistening with sweat. "She went soft on me. She gave up." He bared his teeth in a grimace. "She forgot what they did to our children."

"No, she didn't forget. She just knew killing two innocent people wouldn't bring them back."

"Innocent!" he roared as Jasper urged him down another corridor. "Do you know how many people, how many babies, their poisoned wallpaper has killed?"

He'd lost his mind to bitter grief, but he spoke honestly. Jack Henderson's file of complaints and settlements contained proof of that.

"Your wife wanted to destroy the factory, but that wasn't enough for you," Leo said as Jasper led him to another turn, then down a flight of steps. "You wanted to inflict pain upon the man you blamed for your children's deaths. The same pain you felt as a father."

Recalling the names Mrs. Nelson had written in her letter, she added, "Do you think Timothy and Greta would have wanted their father to become a murderer, Mr. Nelson?"

He grated out an anguished bellow as they came to the exit. His plan, the only thing he'd likely been living for, had been thwarted. And now, he might be seeing clearly for the first time what he had truly done and how far he had truly fallen.

Leo opened the door and stood aside as Jasper pushed Mr. Nelson through and into the alley that ran alongside the hospital. The narrow lane was bordered by a tall brick wall. Lewis had not yet arrived, but Jasper took his prisoner further along the lane to wait.

Leo moved to close the exit door—but stumbled aside as it was punted open again. Alarm blared through her as Andrew Carter snatched her arm and tugged her hard against him. She struggled in his grasp, but only until the cold tip of a blade kissed the delicate skin underneath her eye.

Leo froze. From where he stood in the lane several feet away, Jasper swore.

"Let him go, Inspector," Mr. Carter ordered, his voice a dead calm. One of his hired men exited the hospital. It was just the two of them, and apparently, they had been following them to this side exit. Leo clenched her back teeth. She and Jasper had been so intent on Mr. Nelson, they'd not even noticed their presence.

"I'm placing him under arrest, Carter. Put that knife down and release her," Jasper said, still holding Mr. Nelson's cuffed arms.

"That man murdered my wife. That makes him mine."

A speeding carriage turned down the slim alley. Leo's heart sank. It wasn't their wagon being guided by Lewis, but Mr. Carter's other hired man driving a covered coach.

Jasper didn't move. "He'll be convicted, and he'll hang; you know he will. I'm not giving him to you. Now lower that knife."

Mr. Carter's grip on Leo's upper arm intensified. A spike of pain pierced her as the blade nicked her skin. She let out a short cry before swallowing it.

"Goddamn it, stop!" Jasper shouted. The carriage rattled to a halt mere feet before it could trample him and Mr. Nelson, but Jasper had not even flinched.

Mr. Carter chuckled. "Somehow, I think you'd like to keep looking into these pretty hazel eyes, Inspector Reid. Now, step aside. You can keep the handcuffs on him, of course."

Jasper hesitated. He clenched his jaw and met Leo's eyes. If he did as Mr. Carter wanted, there would be hell to pay at Scotland Yard. He could not allow vigilante justice, and he could not afford to fail in this arrest.

But then, he swore under his breath again and, in a swift motion, released Terrence Nelson. Jasper held up his hands in surrender as Mr. Nelson stumbled forward. He whipped a panicked look between Mr. Carter, Jasper, and finally, the hired thug who closed in to hustle him toward the waiting carriage.

Andrew Carter urged Leo toward the carriage too, while giving Jasper a wide berth.

"Let her go, Carter. That was the deal. *Now*," he growled.

"Not to worry, Inspector. You've made the right choice." Mr. Carter gave Leo a hard shove, and she nearly tripped on her unsteady legs. Jasper rushed forward, taking her arms and pulling her to him. They lurched aside as the carriage bolted forward, wheels hot, and sped away down the alley.

Her heart was racing when Jasper turned her to face him, his hand tipping up her chin. "Damn it, you're bleeding."

Leo shook her head, ignoring the prick of pain and a

wet drop of blood rolling slowly down her cheek. "I'm fine. I'm sorry. I didn't see him behind us—"

"Neither did I. It isn't your fault." But then, he closed his eyes and backed away from her. It was as if the magnitude of what had just happened hit him full on. It hit her too. She began to tremble as Jasper raked his hands through his hair. "Christ. What am I to tell Coughlan?"

Lewis appeared at the mouth of the alley. He drove the cart and single horse toward them, oblivious to what had unfolded during his absence. Jasper had meant to take Mr. Nelson to the Yard and charge him with murder. An arrest was what Chief Coughlan had wanted. A success to make the police look good. Now, Mr. Nelson was in the hands of an East Rip.

And he would soon be dead, if he wasn't already.

Chapter Nineteen

"You better have a damn good explanation for that woman's presence."

The vein bisecting Detective Chief Inspector Dermot Coughlan's forehead bulged as he glared daggers at Jasper and Lewis. They stood within the chief's office, boots planted to the floor, bracing themselves for more of his wrath.

By the time they had returned to the Yard, Coughlan had already been apprised of the explosion at Henderson & Son. But when Jasper explained, in as few words as possible, each one dislodging from his throat with effort, that their main suspect had been apprehended at the hospital, only to escape several minutes later, the chief had gone stone-faced with his fury.

And at the mention of Leonora Spencer, Chief Coughlan's flinty eyes had blazed.

"Miss Spencer found a letter of confession tucked into Mrs. Nelson's clothing at the morgue," Jasper began. "She then came to the factory yard to warn us about the bomb

Mrs. Nelson had planted there before she was killed. After the explosion—"

"You should have sent her home!"

Jasper bucked his chin, as if it had received a blow from the chief's white-knuckled fist. In the detective department beyond the walls of the chief's office, all was silent as the other officers, along with the Special Irish Branch, listened. After what had happened, it promised to be an explosive telling-off. They might even be waiting to hear the chief sack Jasper entirely. That most of them wanted that outcome was another stake to Jasper's chest.

But Coughlan was right. He should have sent Leo away. She shouldn't have been at the factory in the first place. She hadn't rushed there only to warn the workers or David Henderson. She'd known that he and Lewis were there, and she'd put her own life in danger by entering the building and seeking them out.

Additionally, her bravery had made a difference in saving the life of Jack Henderson's son at the hospital.

"If not for Miss Spencer, David Henderson would be dead right now," Jasper replied, challenging the chief with a direct look. "She is the one who stopped Nelson from poisoning him."

Turning in a frustrated circle, Coughlan crossed his arms. "Yet, she is also the reason you were forced to hand over your prisoner to another criminal."

"You would have had me stand by and watch Carter pluck out a woman's eye?" Jasper shot back. Had Andrew Carter done more than nick Leo's skin, he would have stopped at nothing to kill him. Even that minor injury made Jasper's rage tight as a fist inside his chest.

"Not just any woman. Leonora Spencer," Chief

Coughlan spat out her name. "She has been a pox on this department, and don't think I haven't read the little story about her in the *Illustrated Police News*. Assisted in an investigation, did she? Do you know how that makes us look, Reid?"

Next to him, Lewis shifted his footing and tucked his chin. *Christ*. The detective sergeant probably wished for Jasper's sacking too.

After Carter and his thugs disappeared with Terrence Nelson, Lewis had drawn his cart to a stop, demanding to know where the devil their prisoner had gone. The only thing Jasper could think about then was how to mitigate the disaster. But that would be impossible. There could be no fixing what had happened.

Nelson was a deranged murderer who'd wanted his revenge so fiercely he'd lost all perspective, all sense and logic. He deserved to die—but at the end of a rope after a judge sentenced him to death. Andrew Carter had usurped the law, taking it into his own hands and delivering his own justice.

And it had made Jasper look like an incompetent police officer in the process.

"A warrant for the arrest of Andrew Carter has already gone out to all divisions, although, unless we find Nelson's dead body in his presence, we'll never be able to prove he did more than interfere in an arrest," Coughlan scoffed. "You're off this case, Reid. You as well, detective sergeant. I'm handing it over to Timson."

Jasper withheld a groan, though just barely. The Special Irish Branch detective was a pompous ass and would gloat over his appointment to the case.

"I will not warn you again," Coughlan went on. "Unless

you cease associating with Miss Spencer, you will be dismissed. And not just from the C.I.D. There will be no place for you anywhere within the Met, Reid. Am I understood?"

With a rock settling into his gut, Jasper jerked his chin in a nod.

Coughlan dismissed him and Lewis, and they exited his office into the department room. There, looks of sympathy mixed with cold glowers.

"I'm sorry, Roy," Jasper said to his detective sergeant, who had taken the chief's verbal thrashing without a single word spoken in his own defense. "You didn't deserve to be in there. This is all on me."

Lewis shrugged, scrubbing a hand along the back of his still-tender head. "I figure Carter could've just as easily held me or another officer at the end of his blade, and you would've made the same choice."

It was true. *Hypothetically*. Though Jasper doubted he would have felt the same precipitous plunge of his stomach as when Andrew's knife was pressed against Leo's cheek.

"She's smart, your Miss Spencer. Smart and plucky, I'll give her that," Lewis said. "But the chief's right. She's a liability, and if you're not careful, she's gonna get you sacked one of these days."

Jasper made no reply. Lewis deserved to give his opinion without challenge, especially after today. He hadn't suffered bloody gashes from the explosion at the factory as Jasper had, but he'd taken a wallop on the head from pieces of the falling ceiling. Such an injury could have been deadly.

Besides, Lewis wasn't entirely wrong about Leo. She

was untrained, intractable, and reckless. Yet, she had also been unquestionably integral to deciphering who had poisoned Gabriela Carter and why. Without her, Jasper might not have solved the Jane Doe case or discovered Andrea Geary's true identity.

"I owe you a pint at the Rising Sun," Jasper said to Lewis.

He laughed. "Make it two pints and another night, guv. The only place I'm for is home and to bed." Lewis started away. "And you should have your back looked at."

Jasper nodded, waving him on toward the department exit. The blood from the gash along his shoulder and back had dried, sealing his shirt to the wound. It pulled painfully, but there hadn't been time at the hospital to allow the nurse to finish tending to it. Certainly, Mrs. Zhao would be willing to help once he returned home. It was the least of his worries right then.

The other officers were beginning to file out of the Yard for the evening, none of them making eye contact with him as they went. He didn't mind. He'd never cared to be popular. But he did care to be respected, and there wasn't any question that today, there had been a setback in that area for him.

He was on his way to the lobby when a familiar officer emerged from a stairwell, coming into Jasper's path. It was the *Gazette* constable, Murray. The man saw Jasper and halted, standing to attention as he had outside Leo's home the other evening.

"Detective Inspector," he said.

"Constable," Jasper replied. He wasn't inclined to say anything more and merely wished to carry on and go home. But apparently, Murray didn't feel the same.

"I hope it wasn't out of line for me to walk Miss Spencer home the other evening," he said.

Jasper drew a long breath, his instant dislike for the man doubling. "Why would it have been, Constable?"

He floundered, color touching his lily-white skin. Did the man never step foot outside his office to see a blasted ray of sunlight?

"I know that you and she are close. Like family. Or at least, she and your father were close, and…" He floundered some more, and Jasper found he didn't mind seeing the constable discomfited. He merely arched an eyebrow, waiting for him to complete his thought. "And now from what I hear, she is assisting with some investigations, so—"

Jasper sharpened his stare. "Where did you hear that?"

He expected to hear that the article had given him the information. But it wasn't that.

"From Miss Spencer," he answered quickly. "We dined out a fortnight ago."

Two reactions gripped Jasper. The first, an unexpected streak of envy. The second, a flash of suspicion.

"You dined together two weeks ago?" he repeated. Constable Murray nodded.

"I asked her to a chophouse," he said with a faltering smile.

Jasper's mind clicked forward along that track of suspicion. "I imagine she told you about herself and her work at the morgue."

"Well, yes, she spoke highly of her work—"

"What about her family? Did she tell you what happened to them?"

A light of understanding flickered within the constable's irises, and Jasper knew he'd guessed correctly.

"No. I…already knew about that."

Jasper cocked his head. "Enough to write about it?"

Constable Murray licked his lips. "I don't…I don't take your meaning, Inspector."

"For sixteen years, not one story has been printed about the Spencer murders, and yet, less than two weeks after your dinner out with the one surviving member of that family, an article shows up."

Guilt was an interesting expression. It never failed to transform a face in the same ways. A softening of the brow, a tightening of the mouth. The flare of nostrils and the hard swallow of panic, or perhaps resignation.

Constable Murray's expression hit every tell appropriately.

"You fancy yourself a writer, do you?" Jasper asked now that he was certain. "Keeping your ears open for a good story to sell?"

The man didn't reply but at least had the good sense to appear mortified.

"Did you only approach Miss Spencer because you intended to write about her?"

He shook his head. "No, not at all. It wasn't my intention, but once she began to tell me about herself, I suppose…I was fascinated."

Jasper's temper spiked. "You betrayed her trust and exposed her in one of the city's largest newspapers because you were *fascinated*?"

"I thought it would be beneficial to show the world what a modern young woman is capable of," he said, stammering as he flushed more deeply.

At the lobby receiving desk, Constable Woodhouse pretended not to be looking on or listening, and a few passing officers also tried not to show their intrigue. Jasper lowered his voice.

"Bollocks. You wrote that article to benefit one person: yourself. And if I hadn't just had my own arse handed to me by my chief, warning me to be on my best behavior, you can trust that I'd be sending your teeth straight down your throat."

He stepped away from Jasper, who for several seconds considered making good on the threat anyway. The urge subsided, though only by a sliver.

"You owe Miss Spencer the truth. Am I understood, Constable?"

Constable Murray nodded tightly, shamefaced and unable to meet Jasper's fulminating stare. It was on the tip of his tongue to also order him to stay a far step away from Leo after he'd made his confession. But Jasper didn't want her to accuse him of interfering. Besides, there was no chance she would have anything to do with Murray after this.

Jasper turned and left the lobby, catching Constable Woodhouse's approving smirk as he went.

The kettle on the hob inside Mrs. Zhao's kitchen steamed. The housekeeper picked it up and sent Jasper a chiding frown.

"You should have stayed in hospital." It was at least the third time she'd said it in the half hour since he'd arrived home.

He sat at the table in the center of the kitchen, surrounded by bowls of peeled potatoes and carrots, a chopped leek, rising bread, and a crock of potted beef. She'd been preparing supper when he'd come in, his clothing bloodied and torn, and she'd dropped everything to tend to him. For Mrs. Zhao, that meant scolding him for his poor choices.

"I was occupied," he replied, also for the third time.

Jasper, straddling one of the cane chairs at the table, had removed his ruined shirt to give her access to his back. Mrs. Zhao poured the steaming water from the kettle into a bowl of vinegar and honey, then dipped a square of clean linen into the liquid.

"Hold still," she said. "This will hurt."

Hurt was an understatement. It felt as if the claws of several feral cats were attacking his shoulder and upper back as she dabbed the deep gash along the breadth of his shoulders. A piece of David Henderson's falling ceiling had inflicted the wound, and it had pained him then. But now, the agony of it was settling in. He leaned his forehead against his arms, which were crossed on the back of the cane chair, and endured it.

He was exhausted. His whole body hurt. And there was an unbearable kink in his stomach when he thought about Leo and that deceptive fool, Murray. Why would she have agreed to dine with him in the first place? The sodding constable didn't even walk a police beat or assist in the detective department. And now, the idiot might have reawakened interest in the Spencer murders and in the survivor the killers had not intended to leave alive.

At the front of the house, the brass knocker came

down twice in quick succession. Mrs. Zhao stopped dabbing Jasper's wound. "Are you expecting someone?"

"No. Send whoever it is away," he mumbled.

She left the kitchen, and as he waited, sleep pulled him closer. The bite of cold air against the throbbing of his back was all that kept him from dropping off.

The door to the kitchen swung open again.

"Who was it?" Jasper murmured, still resting his forehead against his crossed arms and speaking toward the floor.

"I thought you were going to come take my statement."

He straightened in the chair at Leo's voice but moved too quickly. Flaring pain rippled down his back, and he groaned in protest. She stood at the entrance to the kitchen, her coat and hat having been collected in the foyer. Belatedly, her attention shifted toward his exposed torso. Her lips parted, and she blinked rapidly as though dust had caught in her lashes.

Jasper took his shirt from where he'd tossed it onto the table and sought the sleeves. "Forgive me, I wasn't expecting company."

He hastily pulled on the shirt and buttoned it.

"Mrs. Zhao said your injury is quite serious." Leo had averted her eyes, but her cheeks were pink. The blush was rather fetching, he had to admit.

"I'll be fine." He finished with the buttons and tucked the hem into his trousers. "Mrs. Zhao, can you bring tea to the study?"

"I can't stay," Leo said firmly. "I just wanted to give you my statement."

Though he was now dressed, she still avoided looking him in the eye by opening the kiss lock on her handbag and taking out a sheet of paper. "I've already typed it for you."

She set the single sheet on the table. Jasper couldn't read the typed words from where he stood, but he did note that there weren't very many.

"That is your statement?" he asked. "It's two paragraphs, at the most." She couldn't possibly have described everything that occurred that day and why within two paragraphs.

Leo hitched her chin. "I kept it short, as I know my involvement in the case will only cause you more trouble with your superiors and the rest of the department."

He grimaced. He needed to tell her what Coughlan had demanded. "Leo—" Faltering, he stopped and turned to his housekeeper. "Mrs. Zhao, can you give us a few minutes alone?"

Her indefatigable raised brow expressed that she was not pleased one jot to be asked to leave her own kitchen. But she merely sighed. "Help yourself to some potted beef and bread." She then removed her apron and left through the door that led to her rooms.

Once they were alone, the tension spread quickly and grew thorns. Jasper picked up the typed statement. There was mention of Mrs. Nelson's confession letter, the bomb, the explosion, and Leo's coming upon David Henderson and Terrence Nelson at the hospital. The details were sparse, which must have pained her, and when she wrote about the exchange of prisoners, her account simply stated that Jasper had no choice but to relent or risk the life of an innocent woman.

He set the paper on the table. "Coughlan has given his

final warning. I am to cease associating with you, or I'm finished at the Met."

Silence followed. He waited a moment before looking up at her. Leo had her eyes pinned on the bowls of chopped vegetables, her teeth digging into her bottom lip. She lifted the cover on the crock of potted beef. Setting it aside, she started to fix herself a plate, as Mrs. Zhao had invited her to do. He watched her slice through the loaf of bread on the table, spread the potted beef on it, and then pull out a chair.

"Leo?" He released a pent-up breath. "Say something."

She took a bite and, only after a measured swallow, said, "Chief Coughlan is resting the blame on me."

Flipping his chair around, Jasper sat in it properly instead of straddling it. "It isn't your fault. If you hadn't been there for Carter to threaten, he would have found another way to get to Nelson."

"Perhaps. But you needed that arrest," Leo said.

"Yes. I did." He sighed, despising the feeling of futility. Everything in him fought against it. "But even without Nelson in hand, the murders are solved. Including one that I'd given up on."

"Regina Morris." At his nod, she added, "I'm glad you found answers for her. Her murder affected you. I could tell."

The question she wanted to ask was evident, even if she wasn't asking it outright. "You've wondered why."

Leo took another bite of bread, her gaze expectant. She waited for him to go on. He wasn't sure he wanted to, and yet he found himself speaking anyway.

"She reminded me of my mother."

Leo forgot the potted beef. She sat taller, her attention

riveted now. He thought he knew why. He'd never spoken of his mother to Leo except to say that she was dead.

"Did she...look like Regina Morris?" she asked.

"No. She died like her." Jasper cleared his throat, realizing he was being too vague. Leo wouldn't allow for that. "My mother was beaten to death, and at the time, she was carrying a child too."

"Oh, Jasper," she whispered, sorrow stealing over her expression. "I'm so sorry."

To his relief, it wasn't pity he saw as she searched his face, her lips parting with soft concern. It was her more typical curiosity.

"How old were you?"

Of all the questions she could have asked first, she had chosen one about him rather than the murder itself. He shifted in his seat. "Ten."

"Did they find the person who did it?" she asked next, and Jasper smiled. That was more like it.

However, telling her the truth—that the police had never investigated—would be a mistake. She would dwell on it. Question why not. And that was an answer he could never part with.

"Yes," he said. It wasn't a complete lie. People had known who'd done it. Hell, even Bridget O'Mara had known the truth.

After a moment, Leo picked up her bread and potted beef and took a small bite, looking pensive. "This is the first time you've ever said anything about your life...*before* the Inspector."

"I'm not going to make a habit of it," he said, maybe a little too brusquely. But she forgave him with a small grin. Then to his relief, she did not press him for more details.

Instead, she spun their conversation on its head, whirling back to that moment in the hospital alleyway.

"I can't help but wonder whether Mr. Carter was bluffing, and whether you might have been able to keep Mr. Nelson and avoid censure from your chief."

Jasper cringed, seeing again the point of the blade so close to the white of her eye. "Your safety is more important than anything having to do with my work."

Leo buried a smile with another nibble of bread and potted beef. He was becoming hungry, watching her eat.

"You put your life in danger today," he said. And she had done so *for him*.

"Your life was in danger too," she replied blithely.

"Danger is to be expected in my line of duty."

"That doesn't matter."

"It does. It's what I signed up for. It's what every police officer knows is possible. So, from now on, please, you must stay away from the Yard. Coughlan demands it. *I* demand it."

The warm tenderness she'd shown him iced over in a blink. "Very well. Then I make the same demand of you."

Rising from her chair, Leo took her plate and started toward the sink. Jasper got to his feet. "What demand is that, exactly?"

"To stay away," she said. "It's only fair we be equal in our neglect of each other."

She dropped her dish into a pail of soapy water. Next, she lifted a cloth as though intending to scrub with it.

"You should be aware that even if you wash your dishes, Mrs. Zhao will still wash them again."

She ignored him and set to her task.

"Would you please stop?" he said.

She kept her back to him and continued to wash her dish. Then, she set it on the rack to dry and reached for another one in the basin.

Provoked, Jasper went to her side and stilled her arm. "Stop being fractious and look at me." He peeled from her hands the cloth and the bowl she'd been pointlessly washing and moved her away from the sink.

"You're being a bully," she said. Sudsy dish water dripped onto his hands as he held her wrists up between them.

"You cannot come to Scotland Yard any longer, Leo, nor can you insert yourself into any of my investigations. But I will not stay away. And we don't need to cease speaking altogether."

She stared up at him, but the fire for an argument left her eyes.

Her wrists were still in his hands as he lowered their arms. She didn't move to pull free. Jasper slid his hold from her wrists to her hands. As one second fell into the next, he became less and less inclined to relinquish them.

He lost track of how long they stood there in suspended silence. Leo's gaze drifted from his eyes to his collar, then down to where their hands were joined. As though possessing a different mind than his own, his thumbs moved, circling the centers of her palms. Her skin was impossibly and stirringly soft—except for one spot on her right hand. His thumb met with the raised ridges of her scars. A memento of the night she lost every person she'd loved as a child. Feeling the scars now sent a jolt through him as effectively as an electrical charge.

He dropped her hands, and Leo caught her breath, her

cheeks beginning to glow pink again. Clenching her fists at her side, she retreated a few strides.

"Claude will be wondering where I am." She opened a space between them, and Jasper was, at once, grateful and bewildered. A hot coiling in his chest centered around his left pectoral muscle. Distractedly, he rubbed it through his shirt.

He shouldn't be feeling this.

He had no right to feel it.

"I'll summon a cab," he said. But she shook her head.

"No, I'm only walking to the morgue. Claude and I will go home together." She went to the swinging door and pushed it open, so disconcerted that she forgot to say anything more as she left.

Chapter Twenty

Nothing should have kept Leo awake that night. It had been a long, exhausting day, and when she'd at last settled into bed, she'd closed her eyes with the certainty that sleep would claim her.

Instead, her mind churned. The various outcomes of the investigation had been, for the most part, good. Three murders had been solved, including the Jane Doe that had been weighing on Jasper for the last month. And now, Leo understood why.

The mention of his mother had stunned her, but it was the circumstances of her death that continued to whip up Leo's curiosity. Beaten to death while carrying a child—Jasper's sibling. But who had killed her, and why? And had that been when Jasper went into the streets? Lobbing all her questions at him would have only made him regret saying anything at all, so she'd bitten her tongue. He didn't deserve an interrogation today, of all days.

There would be no avoiding a scandal in the newspapers the next day. Scotland Yard would handle the story of Mr. Nelson's disappearance the best it could. Leo presumed they would not reveal the truth—that their lead detective had relinquished the suspect to Andrew Carter willingly to save a woman from having her eye cut out. There would be some explanation…that Mr. Carter had battled the arresting officers, that Mr. Nelson had an accomplice waiting to ambush them, or whatever suited the Yard best.

But it would still be a disaster.

The papers would feature the explosion at Henderson & Son, along with the tragic story behind the reason for Mrs. Nelson's dynamite plot. Jack Henderson had bound the Nelsons by legal contract not to sell their story to the newspapers, but as they were now dead, that contract was effectively severed. Scotland Yard would have no qualms about explaining the Nelsons' motives, if only to focus the story on the manufacturing company's evil deeds and not their lead detective's shortcomings.

Once the factory was renovated, which the foreman said could take months, Mr. Henderson might suffer such backlash after the deaths of the Nelson children came to light that he'd have no choice but to change his pigments to a formula that was more modern and safer, just as Lawrence Wilkes had tried convincing him to do. So, even though Mrs. Nelson had not lived, her revenge had been realized. Leo found she could not be upset for it. Of course, she would have much rather not been inside the factory when the timed bomb had gone off. But, in the end, it had all been relatively bloodless. Just as Mrs. Nelson had designed.

Earlier at the morgue, as the evening ushered in and there was no sign of Jasper, Leo had begun to doubt he would be coming by after all. Instead, she'd typed her statement. It had taken several tries. She'd had so much to say, but every time she would start adding things, she would see Jasper's incandescent glare after being forced to relinquish Mr. Nelson to an East Rip thug. With it, came the inexplicable and most unwanted feeling of culpability.

She had nothing to feel guilty for, nothing at all. And yet, there had been a hollow pit in the very center of her chest when she thought of how much strife Jasper would suffer for the mess at the London Hospital. And worse, that he might blame her, at least partially. Alongside the image of Mr. Carter's blade glinting in her peripheral vision, now burned into her memory was Jasper's disappointed grimace when he realized he would need to give Mr. Nelson up in order to protect her.

So, she'd shortened her sentences to the barest essentials. No one at the Yard would probe too deeply into a woman's observations anyhow. She'd bottled that bitterness up and let it propel her to Charles Street, where she had planned to give Jasper the typed paper and then take her leave.

Things had gone awry the moment she stepped into that kitchen.

Leo sat up in bed, leaning back against her pillows. Around midnight, she'd tried to occupy her mind with another book, but the distraction hadn't been successful. Time and again, her thoughts returned to Jasper, spinning her away from the wash basin and standing so close that she could see his carotid artery beating in his throat. She'd noted the warmth of his body, the scent of something earthy and masculine. It was only when his thumbs began to massage the cups of her palms that she realized she'd stopped breathing.

Leo pushed off the blanket, no longer chilled despite the lack of heat in her room. The stoneware hot-water bottle under her bed coverings, which warmed her when first climbing under the covers each night, had long since gone cold. She pressed a hand to her forehead. She wasn't feverish. No, she was just being ridiculous with these thoughts of Jasper. It was all due to the tumultuous events of the day; she was certain of it. That, and having entered the kitchen at Charles Street to find him bare-chested—a second time in one day at that.

He'd hurried to put on his shirt, though doing so must have irritated the gash along his back and shoulder. However, Leo's memory would not allow her the grace to forget the image of him, even as briefly as she'd seen it. No, her cursed brain would store it forever with fastidious detail. Details she should not be cataloguing again and again in her mind, as if she were writing a damnable coroner's report. Specifically, Jasper's broad shoulders, the lines of definition along his abdomen and forearms, both of which were more muscular than she'd even thought to imagine, and a dusting of golden-brown hair just beneath his navel. A small, horizontal scar on his right shoulder from the shallow swipe of Sir Nathaniel's sword in January; three moles scattered like a constellation of stars on his left shoulder; and a larger scar in the shape of an arch over his left pectoral.

Leo closed her eyes. All night, she'd been restless, unable to stop raising the image of Jasper's bare torso. Both viewings of it had startled her to the point of distraction. Now, however, she had the time and privacy to study it for more minutiae.

Every additional exploration ended with that arched scar over his pectoral.

It intrigued her. The rough, warped crest of furrowed skin had clearly not been properly cared for. The Inspector and Mrs. Zhao wouldn't have allowed for such neglect, so the injury had to have been inflicted during Jasper's previous life, about which she knew so little, even after his unexpected confession regarding his mother.

The window of her room was brightening with the coming dawn. Leo rubbed the parallel scars on her right palm. Warmth swirled just under her skin at the phantom press of Jasper's thumb. Had it been her scars that had driven some awareness into him, causing him to release her? He'd done so with jarring swiftness.

Restless and muddled as she'd been all night, she now abandoned her bed with an objective in mind. The thin carpet on her floor pushed the early morning cold through the wool of her stockings as she crossed it toward her bureau. The piece of furniture was old and worn, the drawers stiff whenever she pulled them open or slid them shut, especially the bottommost one, which she rarely used. Recently, however, she'd opened it to store away the Inspector's file on the murders. It was a fitting place for it, as the drawer was also where she kept the few things held over from her childhood.

Almost everything from the Red Lion Street home had been sold off, Claude had once told her. She'd kept her brother's pocket watch, which Jacob had treasured for the short time he'd had it. Their father had gifted it to him at their last Christmas together, saying all young men should have one. Next to the pocket watch was the ragdoll Agnes had always held close like an extra appendage, with its yellow yarn hair, embroidered face, and calico dress. The indestructible ragdoll had been suitable for a four-year-old, but Leo had been five years older than Agnes, and so she'd had Miss Cynthia, a china doll, to cherish and care for. And she had, even after Jacob had thrown her to the floor and broken her leg. Leo had taken her doll to the attic, as much to sob about her broken leg as to try to figure out a way to piece Miss Cynthia back together.

The doll was now wrapped in several layers of tissue and tucked in the back of the bottom drawer. Such a childish thing, that doll. But if Jacob hadn't broken it, Leo would not have been in the attic when the intruders had come. She would have been with Agnes in their shared room. And now, Leo would be with her family in the ground at All Saints Cemetery.

Unwrapping the doll for the first time in several years, she was surprised to see the ivory lace at the dress's hem had faded to yellow. In the attic, Leo had removed Miss Cynthia's stockings to inspect the damage to her porcelain leg, and all the doll's accessories had been left behind. So had a few shards of her broken leg. One shard, however, Leo had kept. She'd clutched it in her hand for what felt like hours as she waited, hunched, cold and quivering in the pitch-black steamer trunk. The porcelain shard had been bloody when the Inspector had finally pried open her fingers and taken it from her. He could have thrown it away, but instead, he'd cleaned and returned it to her, telling her to be cautious of the sharp edges.

Leo picked up the shard, the largest of the broken leg

pieces. Each of Miss Cynthia's legs had been cast by the dollmaker using two hollow molds that, when glued together, left a seam down the front and back of her legs. When Jacob had thrown the doll to the floor, her leg had split apart at that seam. And later, when the attic door had opened and one of the intruders had climbed the steps, Leo had reached for the largest and longest shard. It was the whole of Miss Cynthia's thigh, the curved portion near her hip sharp as a spear.

She ran her fingertip along the edges now; they were still sharp, though not enough to travel more than an inch, at the most, below skin if pushed hard enough. Leo gripped the shard in her right hand the way she had that night. The edges of Miss Cynthia's broken thigh lined up perfectly with the dual scars on Leo's palm.

Looking again at the curved end that had once been her hip, Leo drew upon the image of Jasper rising from the hospital bed earlier that evening, his chest on full display. Then again in his kitchen. This time, she didn't meander through the various details that had made her breath hitch. This time, she went straight to the scar over his left pectoral. The length of it. The shape of it.

Leo dropped the doll and shard to the carpet as cold numbness stole over her. She got to her feet, but the floor seemed to tip sideways as she turned in a circle, her mind racing.

She was wrong. She had to be wrong.

Leo went still. Then, making a swift decision, she picked up the china shard, wrapped herself in her dressing gown, stepped into her boots next to the door, and left her room. The house was quiet. At just past five o'clock, Claude and Flora wouldn't be awake for another hour or more. If she made noise as she took her coat from the peg in the front hall, she wasn't aware of it. Nor did it matter. She wasn't trying to be silent. She wasn't thinking about anything at all other than that scar on Jasper's chest.

She put the shard into her handbag and hurried out. Duke Street was calm and slumberous as dawn encroached; a few lampposts were still lit from overnight. Her feet seemed to move of their own accord, her mind briefly touching on the good fortune that she'd plaited her hair into a single braid after her bath last night rather than twisting it into numerous curling papers like usual. She didn't know whether she would've had the patience to remove them all before dashing out. As it was, she'd forgotten her hat. It didn't bother her enough to turn around and go back though. Forward was her only option, down the Strand and toward Whitehall Place. The thrumming of her blood, her breathing loud in her ears, matched the cadence of her feet on the cobblestones.

You've never spoken of it, Jasper had said to her a few months back. *That night. You've never talked about what happened in that attic.*

He was right. She never had. Not even to the Inspector, who perhaps should have known about the shadowed figure in the attic.

Jasper had faulted his father for being obsessed with his persistent inquiry into the murders of her family, though Leo had never seen it that way. It hadn't governed the Inspector's life. No, it had just been there, lingering in the background, tempting him from time to time, when and if some new piece of the puzzle came into his field of vision.

At first, Leo tried to convince herself the boy in the

attic hadn't been real, that he'd been conjured by delirium and fear. Perhaps she had found her own way into the steamer trunk, and as the Inspector had assumed, sliced open her hand merely by gripping the doll's broken leg too tightly.

In the end, however, her rational mind could not dispute the truth. Leo could not lie to herself. But she found that she could indeed lie to others. There was nothing at all wrong or suspicious about a little girl hiding in the attic to escape murderers. To admit that one of them had chosen to let her, and her alone, live would have been a different story. She'd been too afraid to breathe a word about it. So, she'd kept it secret. What difference had it made anyhow? It had been so dark in the attic she hadn't even seen the boy's face. She wouldn't have been able to describe him or pick him out of a pool of suspects.

Her whole body had gone numb by the time she reached Charles Street. In a blink, she had walked the quarter hour there. She couldn't recall a single passing horse or carriage or person. It was as though she'd been moving through a thick brume, the rest of the world shrouded and muffled.

Her fingers shook as they reached into her handbag for the key the Inspector had given her several years ago. He'd said he couldn't stand the thought of his doors being locked to her, should no one be at home when she came calling. Only once had she used it, and that had been when Mrs. Zhao had been away, nursing her sister back to health for a week. Leo had stopped in during the day to surprise the Inspector with a mince pie she'd purchased at a bakery for his supper. Later, he'd confided that it was even better than Mrs. Zhao's, though she'd known that to be a lie.

Leo inserted the key and turned the lock. The door opened with a soft click, and she closed it again behind her. The house was still asleep. Though it had only been a handful of hours since she'd last been there, to Leo, everything had changed. She was an intruder in an unfamiliar house.

In her dreamlike state, she took the carpeted steps to the first floor, her hand sliding along the banister, and then she turned down the corridor. Jasper wouldn't have taken the Inspector's old bedroom. He would have kept his own, the one he'd chosen all those years ago. At the time, Leo had been staying two rooms down the hall in another guest room, and she'd been skeptical of the boy who would be joining her. He was so quiet, and his face was ugly, swollen, and discolored from a terrible beating. He wouldn't even tell them his name.

Her heart thrashing against her ribs, Leo came to a stop outside his door. She twisted the knob. It was too bold. Too improper. He'd be furious. And yet none of that would be enough to stop her from entering his room and getting her answer.

She wanted to be wrong. She *needed* to be wrong, and she would risk his censure for it.

The blue light of dawn reached inside his room, between window dressings that hadn't been drawn together. Leo's eyes went straight to the four-poster, where Jasper lay on his stomach, his bruised and gashed back bare. He was asleep, arms raised above his head on his pillow. The sight stripped away the dreamlike state she'd been existing in and planted her firmly in reality.

She had entered Jasper's home. His bedroom. With a prickling of intuition, as if her eyes alone had touched him, he awoke. Lifting onto his elbows and twisting his head toward the door, he saw her—and then he bolted up.

"Leo?" His voice was hoarse from sleep. "What in hell are you doing in here?"

He leapt from the bed, the linen sheet that was covering him slipping briefly before he caught it and held it higher. He wasn't dressed at all underneath, but Leo didn't startle at the sight of him as she had in the kitchen. She walked toward the bed, her attention solely on his chest.

"How did you... You can't be in here," he stammered while hurrying to wrap the sheet around his waist. "I'm not dressed, Leo, what the bloody hell are you doing?"

She couldn't think of what to say or how to explain that she'd needed to see that scar again. No words would come, so she didn't bother with them. She rounded the corner of the bed and stopped within an arm's length from him. Frozen to the spot, Jasper's alarm was complete.

"Leo," he said, quieter this time and without the same panic as before.

She stared at his scar. It was just as her memory had fixed it, right down to the jagged apex of the crescent. She opened the kiss lock on her handbag and reached inside for the shard of porcelain from Miss Cynthia's broken leg. Jasper stood stock-still as she lifted it and aligned its sharp, curved end against his scar. The end she had plunged into the shadowed figure in the attic sixteen years ago.

The shapes were one and the same.

Jasper's chest began to rise and fall on rapid breaths. He covered her hand, flattening it and the shard of porcelain against his chest. The pounding of his heart reverberated against her skin. Leo stopped breathing as finally, she looked up into his face. His constant expression of brooding indifference slipped. Dread fired through his eyes.

"Tell me I'm wrong," she whispered. "Tell me it wasn't you."

He kept her hand sealed against his chest as he took faster, shallower breaths. He didn't ask her to explain her meaning. Because he understood perfectly. Leo tore her hand out from under his, her fist closing around the shard again.

"You...*you* were the boy I stabbed." Tears stung her eyes. "*You* were the one who put me in that trunk."

Jasper's lips parted, but he said nothing. Leo backed away as the floor, the whole world, felt as though it was disappearing from underneath her. He reached for her, and she slapped his arm away.

"Don't touch me!"

Jasper held up his one hand that wasn't gripping the sheet in compliance.

"They sent me," he said, haltingly. "They sent me to the attic to look for you."

Leo's chest caved in.

He took a starting step forward, but she scuttled back, utterly repulsed, feeling as though she might be sick on the floor. He kept his arm raised in surrender.

"Who?" She shuddered. "Who sent you?"

He closed his eyes. "The people I was with. My family."

His *family*? She gaped at him.

"But I heard you crying in the dark, and I couldn't do it," he said. Her vision went watery and hot.

"What couldn't you do?" Though she asked, in her heart, she knew. And she was more afraid to hear him say it than she'd ever been of anything else in her life.

Jasper scrubbed his hand through his hair and down the back of his neck. He wouldn't look at her. "Kill you."

A whistling sound built in her ears. It scraped down her body, hollowing her out. A solid wall in her throat barricaded her lungs from gathering more air, and a poisonous thought sank through her.

Her voice broke. "Did you kill my family?"

Jasper's eyes flared. "No." He came forward, reaching for her and then blocking her battering arms as she tried to slap him away. "No, no, Leo, I didn't kill them. I didn't!"

She screamed, and he backed off.

"But you were there. You were with the people who did. Your...your *family*. My God, Jasper..." She stared at him, her heart breaking. This wasn't the Jasper she knew, the one the Inspector had known and loved.

He stalked around her toward a tall wooden wardrobe. As he pulled clothing from it, her tears dried in a snap. Leo wanted to hit him; she wanted to hit him *hard*. She wanted him to hurt like she was hurting.

"Why have you done this? Why have you been lying?" All this time, all these years, he'd lied. To her, to the Inspector, to *everyone*. "Who *are* you?"

Jasper held still, the clothing in his hand forgotten. When he turned toward her, Leo knew his face, yet somehow, she'd never seen him before.

"You know who I am, Leo," he whispered.

She shook her head. "I don't know you, and Reid isn't

your name. You never did say what it was, did you?" A thought tolled through her, flattening her pulse. "My God, is Jasper even your given name?"

He scrubbed his jaw and hesitated. He was *scared*. Even if he'd been fully clothed rather than draped with a bed linen, he would have still appeared exposed and vulnerable.

"You don't want to know what my name is."

She had to hold herself back from striking him this time. It was a physical urge that rushed into her arms and hands. She barely suppressed it. "Do not presume to know my mind better than I do. If I say I want to know your name, then by all that is holy, I want to know it!"

Slowly, he put on his shirt. But his hands fell away from the buttons, as if his arms were too heavy. "James."

She stared at his hands, uncertain if she could ever look him in the eye again. His name was *James*. Not Jasper. Leo began to shiver. She was afraid to ask her next question but couldn't leave until she did. Until she knew everything.

"And your surname. What is it really?"

He hung his head, his hands flexing in and out of fists. He strangled a word, barely able to get it out. Then tried again.

"Carter."

Leo stopped breathing. "What?"

No. This was wrong. It was all wrong.

"That is my name." He met her eyes. "It's James Carter."

The words shoved her squarely in the chest. Leo staggered backward, thinking she might fall. But she didn't. She stayed upright as she whirled toward the open bedroom door, or what she could see of it through hot tears.

"Wait, Leo. Wait, please. Let me explain." He followed her from his room, but she couldn't look at him. Couldn't breathe.

Carter. James Carter. An *East Rips* Carter? Bile filled her throat.

Finally, she reached the bottom of the stairs and flung open the front door. An inward gust of cold March air shuttled over her.

"Leonora, *please*. Stop."

The use of her full name bungled her legs. He hardly ever called her that.

He'd stopped moving in the center of the stairs. Any further down, and with the door wide open, as it was, early morning passersby might see him wrapped in a sheet. Her leaving like this, so early in the morning, would appear ruinous. And that was exactly what it was. Leo felt ruined, her heart shredded irreparably.

"Leave me alone, Jasper—James—whoever you are. I never want to see you again."

He took another step down. "You don't mean that."

"I do. Stay away from me." Leo stormed outside and slammed the door behind her, and as she went, everything she'd always known shattered.

Thank you for reading Method of Revenge, the second book in the Spencer & Reid Mysteries! Please leave a rating and review on Amazon to help other readers discover the series.

Turn the page for a sneak peek at Leo and Jasper's next investigation in Courier of Death.

Courier of Death

Chapter One

London
May 1884

Leonora Spencer hurried through the busy corridor at Scotland Yard, determined to be invisible. It was a risk for her to be within its walls and in the middle of the day, at that. But there had been no messenger boy hanging about, waiting to be hailed, near the Spring Street Morgue, and the deadline for unidentified corpse descriptions for *The Police Gazette* was noon sharp. As the top of the hour had neared and her agitation increased, Leo determined she would simply have to deliver the latest description to Constable Elias Murray at the news office herself.

It wasn't the constable whom she was attempting to avoid, even though a few months ago, he'd confessed to being the anonymous reporter who'd profiled her in *The*

Illustrated Police News. They'd dined out once, while he'd pretended to have a romantic interest in her, but he'd only been gathering information for his article. It had been disappointing to realize he'd had an ulterior motive, but she no longer carried a grudge against him. Elias Murray hadn't wounded her irrevocably.

Unlike someone else. A man she'd once trusted beyond measure.

However, discovering the identity of the Jane Doe lying in her uncle's morgue took precedence over her own discomfort, so Leo had gathered her mettle and set out for the Metropolitan Police headquarters herself.

At the front desk, Constable Woodhouse greeted her with some surprise before allowing her to pass through to whichever part of the building she intended to go. If the startled glances she received in the narrow corridor and stairwell were any evidence, her recent absence from the Yard had been noted.

Constable Murray shot to his feet when she knocked upon the open door to his cramped office. "Miss Spencer." His lips gaped. "I…I didn't expect to see you."

Leo overlooked his disconcerted state and handed him the typed description: a woman in her late sixties, found on the mudflats under Westminster Bridge. Her neatly trimmed nails, expensive silk petticoats, and her velvet dress from a high-end boutique on Oxford Street, had led Leo to believe that she was a woman whom someone, somewhere would be missing.

"There was no messenger boy today, or you wouldn't have seen me," she replied. It was honest, if somewhat rude. With Constable Murray, she no longer cared to be polite.

He took the typed description. "Thank you. You know, twelve bodies have been identified since we started running these descriptions in the *Gazette*."

"That's wonderful." The positive outcome was worth a bit of awkwardness, she supposed.

With a glance toward the wall clock, the sensation of ants crawling up her legs jolted her. Leo had been in the building for five whole minutes. Every additional minute she remained was another in which she might be seen by the one person she'd vowed never to see or speak to again. It was a vow she was determined to keep.

"Until the next John or Jane Doe then," Leo said before retreating into the corridor.

Unfortunately, Constable Murray followed. "Miss Spencer, I wanted to express to you, again, how sorry I am for my dishonesty. I think I convinced myself that ultimately the article would be of assistance to you, a way to shine some light on your stimulating work." He still gripped the typed description of the Jane Doe in his hand, but in his nervousness, he had crumpled it. "However, I've come to accept that I was merely doing a service for myself—and I genuinely regret it."

A few months ago, had she not been so disconcerted by Constable Murray's unexpected interest in her, she might have guessed at the truth. He'd expressed a far greater interest in newspaper reporting than in policing, which should have been a glaring clue. However, her resentment toward him had long since fizzled out. Even the handful of additional articles printed about her in various London newspapers, describing the role Leonora Spencer, *'the female morgue worker-turned-detective'* had played in solving a murder inquiry a few months ago—all of which Constable Murray swore he had no hand in writing—had failed to truly distress her.

"Thank you, Constable. Let's call a truce, shall we? Now, I really must go," she said and again turned to leave.

The longer she lingered, the greater the chance that she would cross paths with a certain detective inspector she'd been sidestepping since early March, when she'd learned he wasn't who he'd claimed to be for the sixteen years she'd known him.

Jasper Reid was not even his real name.

Because of her unusual memory, which captured images in minute detail and allowed her to return to them no matter how much time had passed, the sharp details never fading, Leo repeatedly had experienced the world-bending moment in which he'd confirmed her suspicion, the blade of his betrayal slipping between her ribs and into her heart again and again, taking her breath away each time.

His given name was James. James Carter. His family—his real family—ran the notorious organized crime syndicate known as the East Rips. And sixteen years ago, on the night Leo's family had been brutally murdered in their home on Red Lion Street, *he* had been the boy who'd come into the darkened attic looking for her. *Jasper* had been the shadowy figure she'd puzzled over ever since that night, half believing he was a figment of her imagination. Because instead of killing her, he'd hidden her in a steamer trunk to save her life.

"You seem particularly rushed today," Constable Murray observed.

Leo gritted her molars. He had followed her toward the stairs.

"Is it the date?" he asked.

The question was curious enough for her to stop and peer at him. "What is important about the thirtieth of May?"

"The way you're rushing to leave, I presumed you knew about the warning Clan na Gael sent back in the autumn. We're to be on alert today."

Leo didn't like the sound of that. Clan na Gael had come to power a few years ago when the Fenian Brotherhood, a militant political group seeking Irish independence from Britain, disbanded. The two groups were essentially the same, however, and had been waging a dynamite war on London for the last decade, attempting to instill terror among the British.

In the previous year alone, there had been explosions at *The Times*, at government offices at Whitehall, at Charing Cross railway station, and in a cloakroom at Victoria Station. A planned explosion on the London Bridge went awry when it detonated early, killing the bombers themselves. Had it gone according to plan, innocent people would have been killed.

"What warning was this?" Leo asked.

He gave a small shrug. "Nothing to take very seriously, I'm sure. They threaten to bomb the city all the time but hardly ever carry the blasts out. I won't trouble you further with it." He tipped the brim of his hat. "Good afternoon, Miss Spencer."

Unsatisfied with his response, Leo watched him return to his office. Men's voices echoed up the stairs and along the corridor, giving her what felt like a nudge in the back. She descended the stairs, her fingers clenched as she hoped to clear the building without seeing Jasper—or

James, if that was how she should be thinking of him now. That name felt entirely wrong though, as did the cinch of her stomach and the ache of her heart whenever she thought about him. Paired with the boiling of her blood, the mixed emotions never ceased to confuse her.

He had tried to speak to her several times since that morning two months ago, when Leo let herself into his home on Charles Street. She'd surreptitiously entered his bedroom to see the old scar on his chest, of which she'd caught a glimpse the night before, after Jasper had been injured in an explosion at a wallpaper factory. Only after a sleepless night had Leo realized why the scar bothered her so deeply. The shape of it perfectly matched the shape of the porcelain shard broken off from her old china doll's leg, the very shard a young Leo had used to stab the mysterious boy who'd found her in the attic the night of the murders. It was how she had received a pair of parallel scars on the palm of her right hand.

Jasper had followed her from his bedroom after she'd stormed out, a bedsheet clutched around his waist—the only thing concealing the rest of his naked body. But Leo had not paid any attention to his undressed state. It was a minor scandal compared to what he had just admitted to her.

"Wait, Leo. Wait, please, let me explain." He'd taken the stairs after her but abruptly stopped when she'd opened the front door. For her to be seen leaving his house just past dawn would have spurred rumors. For Jasper to potentially be seen in nothing but a bedsheet coming after her would cement Leo's ruin.

She had not allowed him to explain, as he'd begged,

and had slammed the door behind her. Predictably, he'd come to her home on Duke Street later that morning, but she'd instructed her Uncle Claude to send him away. The next day Jasper had shown up at the morgue. Leo told him that unless he left the premises right then, she'd upend a bucket collecting run-off from one of the autopsy tables all over his shoes.

When Jasper met her on the pavement outside her home the following day, he'd asked whether she would at least give him five minutes to hear him out. She'd held her temper and calmly stated, *"I cannot even look at you right now. Please, just give me space."* Reluctantly, he'd nodded and left.

She hadn't spoken to him since.

Not thinking about Jasper—or James— hadn't been as easy as avoiding him. Unless she occupied her time with other things, it was all she found herself doing: thinking of his lies and all the unanswered questions that cluttered her brain but were too unwieldy to unpack.

So, when her friend Nivedita Brooks invited her to a meeting of the Women's Equality Alliance, she had jumped at the chance. Not only did Leo believe in the cause, but focusing on the dearth of women's rights in England, especially the right to vote, gave her another injustice toward which to direct her anger. One that had nothing to do with Jasper Reid.

The women at the WEA meetings were forward-thinking and bright, and most had accepted Leo even after learning that she worked as an assistant in her uncle's city morgue. Some, of course, kept their distance, choosing another row in which to sit, but it hadn't offended her much, and it hadn't bothered Dita at all. Most of the WEA members, including their president, Mrs. Geraldine Stewart, were welcoming. In the past few months while she'd been attending meetings, her uncle had supportively pointed out that it was good for her to be a part of something that wasn't connected to either the morgue or the Metropolitan Police.

As she reached the doors to the entrance lobby , Leo turned her mind to the WEA meeting that she and Dita were to attend that week. But as one of the doors opened, her legs and heart came to an abrupt stop.

Detective Inspector Jasper Reid and Detective Sergeant Roy Lewis entered the lobby of Scotland Yard together. Jasper locked eyes with Leo, and whatever he was in the middle of saying to the detective sergeant fell off. He stopped moving, and Leo's throat cinched as she took in the sight of him. His hooded dark green eyes, his slightly rumpled clothing, and the dark blond stubble on his cheeks and chin. He'd either forgotten to shave that morning or he was beginning to grow a beard. A sense of helpless misery pierced her chest.

Sergeant Lewis tipped the brim of his hat to her before moving past them and further into the building. At the clearing of Constable Woodhouse's throat from where he stood behind the reception desk, Leo's sudden paralysis ended. Her heart thrashed against her ribs as she averted her welling eyes and stepped forward again.

"Leo, wait."

"I'm in a hurry, Inspector."

"I suspect you're only in a hurry to avoid me."

The accusatory tone brought her to a standstill. She

whipped around, the coals of her temper stoked to life. "Yes, I am, although it turns out that it's been a complete failure."

Jasper glanced toward Constable Woodhouse, who was openly listening to their exchange, then stepped toward Leo and lowered his voice. "It has been months, Leo. We need to talk."

Leo squared her shoulders as fury prickled under her skin. "I'm not ready to talk to you."

The muscles along Jasper's jaw tensed. "I didn't think it possible to underestimate your propensity to be mulish, but it seems I have."

Her lips parted on a gust of disbelief. "You have no right to be upset."

She barely suppressed kicking him in the shin before she turned for the doors again.

"Leo," Jasper pleaded. "I'm asking you to stop."

She didn't know why she complied. Maybe it was because, as furious as she was with him, as intent as she'd been to uphold her vow to never speak to him again…she missed him, which only made her more upset. Although this time, with *herself*.

He whisked off his bowler and, more quietly than before, said, "I think it is high time we spoke. Not here, of course—"

"No, not here." Leo struggled to keep her voice equally soft but managed to whisper, "If anyone here found out why I haven't spoken to you in two months, you'd be sacked, wouldn't you? You've lied to everyone, not just to me."

He pressed his lips thin, his expression injured and

subdued. Her eyes, already brimming with tears, began to sting. *Blast!* She needed to get out of there before they fell.

Leo rushed outside, into the courtyard behind the building. She filled her lungs with warm, late spring air and blinked back hot tears. What she'd said was true: Jasper hadn't just lied to her. He was related to one of the most powerful crime families in London, and surely, if anyone within the Met were to learn of it, he'd be released from duty at once.

How Jasper had managed to come face-to-face with Andrew Carter in March during the investigation into the murder of his wife, Gabriela, and not be recognized was beyond her comprehension. Had Andrew known who he was? Or had Jasper changed so drastically since he was thirteen years old that his own relative did not know him?

It was just one of the dozens of questions she'd been stewing over. Another was whether the late Chief Superintendent Gregory Reid had known the truth about him. The Inspector had rescued Leo from the attic and taken her in as a ward while searching for her aunt and uncle, Flora and Claude Feldman. At that time, Jasper had been a runaway from the East End, who'd been arrested for thievery. But after a show of heroics at Scotland Yard— stopping a drunkard from colliding with nine-year-old Leo—he piqued the Inspector's interest, and Gregory Reid had taken in Jasper as well.

He welcomed Jasper into his home, into his life, and loved him like a son. Leo couldn't bear the thought that Jasper might have lied to the Inspector too.

The courtyard buzzed with commotion. Officers, both in uniform and plain clothes, were arriving and departing, and hansom cabs were lined up, ready for hire. Scotland Yard was a hub of activity, and in the past, Leo had always felt a pinch more alive whenever she was there. Now, however, it was a place she only wished to evade. Jasper was the reason, and she bitterly held it against him. She increased her pace, eager to return to the morgue. There, the next postmortem report would distract her, and she could push Jasper and his lies from her mind. For a little while, at least.

Up ahead, a familiar constable crossed under the arch that led into the courtyard behind headquarters. For several months, Police Constable John Lloyd had been courting Dita, and Leo would often join them when they went across the river to Striker's Wharf, a nightclub and dance hall. John was an affable fellow and usually had a smile for Leo whenever he saw her. But now, as she walked toward him, tension creased his brow.

A fresh bruise discolored his swollen left eye, and gashes on his cheek and bottom lip were crusted with dried blood. Oddly enough, he wasn't wearing his policeman's uniform. His civilian clothes appeared rumpled, and in his left hand, he carried a brown leather valise. Leo slowed. It looked to be a lady's valise, adorned with floral embroidery. Only about ten or fifteen yards separated them, but Constable Lloyd had yet to see her. Leo lifted her arm to hail him, and his attention clapped onto her.

He stopped walking as abruptly as if he'd smacked into a wall. Then, he spun on his heel and started away in the direction from which he'd come.

"Constable Lloyd!" she called, worry mixing with curiosity. What on earth was he doing?

Beyond the archway that led into the yard, a man

wearing a brown wool cap pushed off from the iron hitching post he'd been leaning against and stood to attention. His scowl was fierce, Leo noticed, and he seemed to be directing it straight at Constable Lloyd. The man shook his head, as if to say, *"Don't."*

Before she could think twice about the man, a pulse of light blinded her. A violent, crushing blast lifted her feet from the ground. Heat raced over her skin and through her hair, and the brutal percussion of an explosion thudded through Leo's chest. The strike of it emptied her lungs even before she landed hard on her back, cracking her head against the ground.

The world went dark and still and silent.

She came to—how much later she was unable to tell—with a shrill chime filling her ears, followed by a burrowing pain. Slowly, Leo lifted her hand to her throbbing left ear. Acrid smoke filled her nose and throat, and she coughed as her eyes fluttered open. A river of smoke flowed over her, with pockets of blue sky cutting through it, then disappearing again as the black haze blotted them out.

Bomb.

It was a bomb.

Muted shouts filtered through the strident ringing in her ears. And then, Jasper was hovering over her. He was all she could see, his lips forming her name, his eyes filled with stark panic. She tried to sit up but found it impossible. In the next second, she was in the air again, this time, firmly locked in Jasper's arms. As he carried her back toward the building, her vision swam, and a surge of nausea gripped her. For over his shoulder, sprawled upon the ground, lay Police Constable John Lloyd.

Or what remained of him.

Courier of Death releases June 14, 2025 and is available for pre-order now.

Also by Cara Devlin

The Spencer & Reid Mysteries
SHADOW AT THE MORGUE
METHOD OF REVENGE
COURIER OF DEATH

The Bow Street Duchess Mysteries
MURDER AT THE SEVEN DIALS
DEATH AT FOURNIER DOWNS
SILENCE OF DECEIT
PENANCE FOR THE DEAD
FATAL BY DESIGN
NATURE OF THE CRIME
TAKEN TO THE GRAVE
THE LADY'S LAST MISTAKE (A Bow Street Duchess Romance)

The Sage Canyon Series
A HEART WORTH HEALING
A CURE IN THE WILD
A LAND OF FIERCE MERCY

THE TROUBLE WE KEEP

A Second Chance Western Romance

About the Author

Cara is the author of the bestselling Bow Street Duchess Mystery series. She loves to write romantic historical fiction and mystery, especially when the romance is a slow burn and the mystery is multi-layered and twisty. She lives in rural New England with her husband and their three daughters. Cara is currently at work on the rest of the Spencer & Reid Mysteries. The third book, COURIER OF DEATH, releases June 2025.

Printed in Great Britain
by Amazon